A Time of Love and Magick

by

Julie A. D'Arcy

Cover Art by *Lisa Dawn MacDonald*

The Wild Rose Press, Inc.
PO Box 708
Adams Basin, NY 14410-0708
Visit us at www.thewildrosepress.com

Publishing History
First Edition, 2026
Trade Paperback Print ISBN 978-1-5092-6402-5
Digital ISBN 978-1-5092-6403-2

Previously Published through I Heart Publishing
Published in the United States of America

Dedication

This book is dedicated with love to my mother, Dorothy (Dot) Brauman, and my father, James (Jim) Borserio, for your love and support in everything I did. I miss you unbearably.

Acknowledgments

I would like to acknowledge my two daughters, Errin and Tegan, for always being there when I need you.

And a special thank you to my test readers Susan Graham, Mary Brehe, Frank D'Arcy, and Steve Westcott whose observations and advice were invaluable.

I am also more than grateful to Sandra Allan, Anne Smith, and Ruth Ross for all those Saturday afternoons and to Heather Williams, Ian Deakin, and the rest of the NEWS writing group for being such hard taskmasters.

And last but not least, the Wild Rose staff and Josette Arthur my editor for your understanding and patience.

Prologue

First day of Imbolc,
600th Year of the Second Dawning.
In the realm of Rastehm

Aurelia, Queen of Rastehm, stood on a marble platform before a wall of flame. Her glance strayed to the man at her side. Mikkasah, her husband, the king, big boned, with iron-colored hair and the look of an eagle about him—astute, regal, and uncompromising. He wore black, with a single red dragon emblazoned on his tunic. Around his shoulders draped an ebony cloak trimmed with gold thread. His face was set in harsh lines as he met her gaze and gave her a gentle smile.

Aurelia had donned a simple gown of gray. A color of grieving, a color she would wear for many years to come. She clutched her small child to her breast with a resolve that burned fiercely within her soul. The child giggled and tugged at Aurelia's hair, oblivious to the tension that permeated the ancient stone walls and the unshed tears in her eyes.

Imbolc had come, snow fell from the sky, and the Goddess had returned from the Otherworld. Most of the Earth rejoiced. But some did not.

The Eternal Wall, a bastion of fire the width of the temple, leaped high and danced with menace. The Temple of the Goddess was deathly quiet as the nobles and commoners gathered to witness the banishment of their monarch's only child.

Aurelia stared down into her daughter's chubby face, determined to remember every curve. Her heart swelled with love. Silverdawn—so named for the brilliant new dawn that had appeared after the defeat of the *Evil*. How she wished they had never fought the demons! How she wished her husband had never summoned the Goddess. If only they had known the consequences—the price they would have to pay.

The Goddess Deharna approached. She was dressed in the austere robes of a temple priestess—black, trimmed with the color of blood, and a single adorning white rose above her heart. Black, red, and white—the colors representative of the three aspects of the Goddess—the Maiden, the Mother, and the Crone.

A minor priestess offered Deharna an ornate silver bowl filled with rich earth. To this the Goddess added water from a pitcher of red clay, then she held the bowl aloft, chanting the ritual of the four quarters in the ancient tongue of the gods.

Come to us from the Earth's four quarters,
Come Air, Earth, Fire, and Water,
Deliver your minions to this temple,
Undines, Sylphs, Salamanders, and Gnomes,
Ask your kings—Paralda, Nixsa, Ghob, and Djinn—
To bring them in.

The temple doors flew back on their hinges. A gust of wind blew a smattering of snow from the courtyard. The flames of the Eternal Wall leaped higher, and the assembly dropped to their knees in reverence to the Goddess, hugging their cloaks closer about their bodies. Deharna spoke again. The wind ceased, and the doors slammed shut.

Aurelia held her daughter as the Goddess dipped a finger into the silver bowl and anointed Mikkasah's brow and Silverdawn's with the sign of the full moon. Then the Goddess slipped a golden medallion the size of a hen's egg over the king's head. "To aid in your trip home," she said, looking knowingly into his eyes.

She turned to Aurelia and held her slender hands out for the child. " 'Tis time," she pronounced in a formal tone.

A roar went up from the crowd.

Aurelia shook her head and stumbled back a pace, clutching the child tightly to her breast. The king stayed her with a firm hand.

"No!" Aurelia cried. "You will not take my daughter."

****

Mikkasah gazed into his queen's frightened eyes and felt a weakening. He loved this woman with the whole of his soul. She was so beautiful, with her white-gold hair flowing to her waist, petal-white skin, and her begging, forest-green eyes. Had he been a common man, he could have taken up his sword to fight for the right to keep their child. As a king, he could not. He strengthened his resolve and bent his lips close to his wife's ear. "Aurelia, heart of my heart, you knew this day would come. It was only a matter of time before the council learned of the Magick she carried."

He reached out and cupped her cheek. "Can you not see that I am bound by chains of honor? Can you not see that my heart breaks? If there were any other course, I would take it, no matter the consequences. Do not forsake me now in my most desperate hour. I am forced

3

by law, the Goddess, and the people to do what no man should ever be asked to do. Banish my only child to an unknown future. A future where I cannot hold and protect her as I would wish." His voice took on a soft urgent note. "Do not add to my grief by denying me. This I beg, Aurelia."

She stood stony-faced, as if his heartfelt plea had never been uttered, and his hand fell to his side.

"If you are worried for Silverdawn's safety, do not. I have been through the curtain of flame. I have made provisions. The child will never go without."

Her head shook. "If you do this, do not come back. For as surely as you tear my babe from my arms, my love for you will be wrenched from my heart."

"You do not mean that."

Her expression remained stony. "Do I not?"

With downcast eyes, Mikkasah pried Aurelia's hands from their daughter and took the little girl into his arms. The baby held out her arms and screamed for her mother, but Mikkasah quickly turned and with three large steps entered the wall of fire and was instantly swallowed.

Aurelia's cries filled his ears as the cool fire surrounded him and the child.

He glanced back through the filter of flame and watched the Goddess and her priestess drag his queen, screaming and fighting, away from the fire. Only the anointed could enter the Eternal Wall. Any other would be burned to cinders.

In another time, thousands of years into the future, Mikkasah stepped from the fire into a strange, bright flower garden beneath a tree of white apple blossoms. A thin man with black-and-silver hair, gold-rimmed spectacles, and a suit of charcoal gray met him.

"Be good to my daughter," said the king, lowering the little girl to the soft springy grass. He knelt beside her, hugged her to his chest, then rose. "She is precious to me and her mother. Her name is Silverdawn. In our time it means *a new beginning*."

The man smiled kindly and nodded. Mikkasah knew he was a man of few words. He had known him before he was banished and remembered the man found it hard to express his feelings. He was one of the banished and expected nothing. With tears in his eyes, the man knelt to take the little girl's hand and tickle her beneath the chin. She laughed, forgetting her tears in the way a child would, and handed him a small crystal pyramid.

Mikkasah, seeing his daughter's acceptance of her new father, touched his hand to the golden medallion the Goddess had given him and spoke the incantation that would transport him home. He appeared on the platform where he had left his wife. The temple was devoid of life. Aurelia was gone.

The king tore the amulet from around his neck and cast it into the wall of fire, cursing himself for a fool. He dropped to his knees and wept for the love he had forfeited and the child he would never see again.

The price for saving his world had been too high.

Chapter One

London, Friday, Sept. 22nd
Present Day

Dr. Silverdawn Peterson typed in the final sentence on her computer, then read aloud what she had written.

Before the third dawning of time, after foul creatures had dragged themselves from the sea, grown two legs, and developed a mind; before a young man with broad shoulders and solemn face cast himself upon a cross to save humanity. There was an age in between, when silken strands of Magick wound themselves through all that had sprung from nature and some that had sprung from the loins of men. In a time when the names of the gods were whispered in awe, creatures of black fable crept across the Earth, bringing reality to nightmares. Sorcery was rife, and the helpless lived in fear of powerful warlords who grew fat on the toil of decent men.

In that time there existed a king of the Eastern Lay—a sorcerer and warlord who went by the name of Iraj of Istani. A grim shadow in black robes, who, it was told, floated more than strode across a room. And who—it was also whispered—traded souls and tortured flesh to the Hell Wraiths for his own immortality. He had an army of unholy creatures that would march across a continent for this sorcerer king, bringing slaughter and merciless death to any man, woman, or child who dared to stand in his path.

But there also lived one named Mikkasah, High King of Rastehm. A good man. He could see what was happening, how the kings of lesser and more fought among themselves. How their petty jealousies, selfishness, and vanities took toll upon the land, weakening its defenses. He watched Iraj's loathsome creatures sweeping across the landscape like an evil plague and knew that, should the slaughter and degradation persist, the time drew near when the world as he knew it would be no more. All that would survive the mass carnage of Iraj's militia to inhabit the second dawning would be Iraj and his hordes from hell.

Mikkasah formed his own army, but they were crushed by Iraj's cunning. Loath to lose more good men, in desperation the King of Rastehm fell to his knees and called upon Deharna, the one true Goddess, mother of mankind and beast, to show him a way to bring peace to his fallen land.

The Goddess opened her arms and her heart and gave unto Mikkasah a magickal device. A crystal pyramid, a third the size of a grown man. When activated, the pyramid would draw Iraj and his evil creatures to its heart, sealing them within itself, therefore cleansing Rastehm of their foulness. However, in exchange for the gift, Deharna exacted a brutal price. All that held the gift of Magick would be banished from the land or put to death. All teachings of the craft would cease. All script pertaining to the practice of the art would be burned, subduing the art of Magick to no more than a whisper spoken around a late campfire or, further over the mountains of time, a story in a child's bedtime book.

So true Magick would be forever lost from the minds of mankind.

Silverdawn shut down the program and turned off the computer. Carefully, she marked the place in the leather-bound tome beside her and closed the yellowed pages. She placed the tome in the center of her desk and breathed a heartfelt sigh. At any moment she had expected the wafer-thin parchment to dissolve to dust beneath her fingers.

A few glitches still remained in her deciphering, such as what the magical device given to King Mikkasah had actually been, but she was certain of her ability to uncover the answer.

She moved from her desk, pushed aside the heavy drapes, and stared down at London town. How much one could see from the third floor surprised her. Soft drizzle wreathed the treetops in the park opposite the museum and turned the road beside it to shining agate. People scuttled along footpaths gilded by the many streetlights. Workers headed for home at the dying of the day. Headlights turned to winking creatures, dodging in and around each other, constantly on the move.

The early darkness in the Northern Hemisphere never failed to amaze Silverdawn.

Barely four o'clock, and already daylight was fading. With longing she thought of Australia with its lazy, hot summers and long stretches of white, sandy, surf beaches.

In her early student years, most of her time had been taken up searching known inland prehistoric sites or, as she grew older, archaeological digs. But there had been a time when she'd spent the summer with her parents in

Maroochydore, Queensland. A familiar jab in her heart at the thought of her parents slammed the door shut on the images the memory evoked. Too painful. Too close. She would deal with them later. For now, they were somewhere warm, safe, and tightly locked.

Silverdawn removed her plain-glass spectacles and placed them on the desk. She didn't need glasses but had learned long ago that being attractive in the field didn't pay. Being noticed too much led to distractions and situations she neither needed nor wanted.

Years of study, hard work, and constant persistence had won her the position she now held in London, and she would allow no man to compromise her situation.

She leaned back against the windowsill and breathed in the smell of old books. She loved the scent. Sliding her gaze around the room to the overflowing bookshelves, high ceilings, elaborately sculptured fireplace, and deep ultramarine carpet, she had a feeling of coming home. Especially when she held an ancient manuscript or book of old-world legends in her hand, ready to decipher and translate onto a portable hard drive and memory stick. At twenty-six, she believed herself to be the youngest in her field and that she had achieved the goal she'd worked toward all of her life.

Graduating with honors in archaeology from the University of Melbourne, Australia, she had applied and been lucky enough to be accepted as junior assistant to Professor Peter Waymer at the London Museum of Rare Artifacts. In the last three years, many changes had occurred within the museum. Professor Waymer's senior assistant had left to join another museum, and his second assistant had foolishly become pregnant and left to raise her child. The professor, being so impressed with

Silverdawn's almost unnatural ability to decipher archaic writings, had appointed her second assistant and given her the job of transcribing onto computer the most ancient works recorded in the memory of man.

She didn't know why languages came so easily to her. It was as if she merely had to glimpse the words and their meaning immediately unraveled. Professor Waymer had once commented that she could read hieroglyphics with the same aplomb a great actor could read Shakespeare. And she thanked the heavens for old Professor Rouse, who had made her work immeasurably easier by coming in regularly to teach and guide her in the preparation of leather and papyrus scrolls.

The volume of ancient legends she had been documenting today was the most archaic she had been entrusted with thus far. In fact, it was so antiquated it had never been accurately dated. The forensic experts had been unable to agree on an origin. The text had been traced back to early Keltoi, a people mostly comprised of warriors and shepherds, but that was questionable. Nothing explained how such people had learned to read and write in this elaborate way.

Some believed the tome to be several thousands of years older than Christianity; others thought the site medieval. Silverdawn had her own ideas.

She'd studied languages and the decoding of old-world scripts as part of her training. The pigments in the illuminations, the spirals and trumpets in the writings, were unlike anything she had uncovered before. It was as if the book had slipped through the vaults of time.

But from where had it originated?

If the parchment was as old as forensics believed, why had it not crumbled to dust? Why had the ink not faded?

She reflected on the sections of book she had deciphered. There was a puzzle here. Were the contents of this tome merely works of fiction by an imaginative mind? Or could the *Legends of Rastehm* contain grains of truth? Special pains had been taken to preserve the work. A shiver, like that of a feather being drawn down her spine, ran the length of Silverdawn's body. But preserved by whom? And could it be that the creatures of dark depicted in the volume had really existed and that real Magick had thrived on this Earth? Had it been eradicated, as the words of the book led her to believe, by the hand of Deharna, Goddess of Rastehm?

A bodiless voice sounded on her intercom, calling Silverdawn from her musings. "A Mr. Haversham to see you, Dr. Peterson."

Silverdawn popped her glasses back onto her nose. "Send him in, Martha."

She moved to the specially humidified case across the room and replaced the leather-bound volume of Rastehm legends, locked the case, and then cast a glance over her shoulder at the stranger who stepped into her office. She raised a brow and appraised the young man before her. Medium height, medium build, sleek, brushed-back blond hair, designer slacks, silk shirt, narrow tie, Delti'er Cologne, and an engaging smile. Impressive, but she had seen a lot of smiles, brilliant to dazzling to toothy grins. None held the power to sway her, and this one was no different.

"Why a good-looking woman like you considers it necessary to hide behind those hideous glasses, I don't know. They told me you were attractive, but I'd say more like…stunning."

She gestured toward the papers he carried. "I neither care for your opinion, Mr. Haversham, nor ask for it. Now, if those are the notes on the French Armor Exhibition," she announced in the dry tone that she kept particularly for young executives or the boss's nephew, "put them in the basket on the desk and close the door on your way out. As you see, I am busy."

The smile dropped from the young man's face. "Now look here. I just wanted to be friends."

Silverdawn moved behind her desk, its massive structure giving her confidence, as did her thick-rimmed glasses. "I have no time for games." She picked up a small crystal pyramid from her desk, turning it this way and that, trying to catch the overhead light, then carefully placed it back down. The blue of the crystal was so dense it had the power to depress her every time she handled it. She stared down at the paperweight and frowned. The inanimate object seemed to have a life of its own. She didn't know why she kept the thing, except she had owned the pyramid since she was a small child.

The young man coughed, jarring her from her reverie.

Leaning forward, palms down on a pile of science journals, Silverdawn met his pale-blue gaze. "Is there a clause in your contract which says every new man under thirty who joins the Museum of Rare Artifacts must try to come on to me? Do you run bets on the lower floors to see who can date the dowdy doctor?" Heat rose to her face, and her hands began to sweat—a warning sign to her old malady. Her petit mal had been a constant part of her life since three years of age. "Keep calm," the doctors had told her. Yet sometimes it was not that easy. "I must tell you. I am not interested in men—period. And you can take that back to whomever sent you. Do I make myself—"

She never uttered the last word. She began to slip away, spinning out of reality. Brilliant light. Profound silence. When the spinning stopped, she opened her eyes, but she knew where she would be—in a world where she had no substance. Where only sight and hearing existed, and the sound of her voice held no sway...

It was night. Soft, silvery drizzle filtered down from the sky and surrounded the watchtowers of an unknown city, hissing in the torches of the broad gate and making the stones of the road leading to that gate appear like shiny ebony pearls. A lone rider approached the city, wrapped in a well-oiled traveler's cloak. The rider was a broad-shouldered man. His hair was blue-black to match the night, and his nose looked as if it had been broken in a tavern brawl. He rode effortlessly but with the watchfulness of a trained warrior. He sat a tall, black horse with a long nose, flowing mane, and wicked dark eyes.

The big horse shook the rain from its shaggy coat and approached the ironbound gates of the city. It stopped in the glowing circle cast by the torches attached above the gate.

A bearded guard in a leather breastplate, a dented helmet, and a patched blue cape that hung limply about his narrow shoulders staggered out of the gatehouse and stood wavering in the rider's path. "No one enters the city of Rastehm at night." His voice slurred with drink.

The traveler gave him a penetrating stare. He parted his cloak to show a heavy golden talisman hanging on a chain around his neck.

The drunken guard's eyes widened, and he stepped

back a pace. "My apologies, my lord. Proceed."

Another guardsman strode from the gatehouse. "Who is it, Kalab?"

"A Palladian Knight."

"What did he want?"

"As I said, he is a Palladian Knight."

The second guard grumbled and ducked back into the guardhouse, and the drunken man gave the knight a lopsided grin. "Some of these new recruits have no idea about the way of things." He winked at the knight in an exaggerated manner, and the dark traveler nodded.

"You'd best get in out the rain, Brother, or you will catch your death." He tossed the blue-caped guard a small coin and rode on into the city, treading the winding cobbled road with the big black's steel-shod hooves echoing back from the tightly packed buildings…

"Doctor? Dr. Peterson. Are you with me?"

Silverdawn was brought back to reality by the feel of a firm hand shaking her arm and a concerned voice. "What—what happened?"

The young man beside her frowned. "You were set on berating me when you blacked out. I took the liberty of easing you back into your chair and removing your glasses." He grinned.

"I'm sorry." She rubbed a hand over her eyes. "I must have frightened you, blanking out like that."

"Not at all. I had a sister who suffered from petit mal. She grew out of it at the age of nine."

She noted the sadness in his voice and the way his eyes dulled at the mention of his sister but refrained from commenting. There was a story there, but she did not want to impose.

She accepted the glass of water he pushed her way.

"I haven't had an attack in three years."

"I hope I had nothing to do with bringing this on."

She shook her head and took a gulp of water, letting it ease her parched throat. "I'm sure you didn't."

She felt as if she had run a marathon. Her heart pounded like a sledgehammer against her rib cage, and her head ached unbearably. She forced a bright smile, feeling foolish and ashamed of her earlier behavior. "Let me apologize for my harsh words. I'm not always such a b—" She ran a hand over the back of her neck. "I guess I'm just tired. Preparing for this exhibition has been trying. There never seems to be enough hours in the day."

"Perhaps I can help take the load off." The young man leaned back on the edge of the desk and offered his hand. "Haversham. Todd Haversham, the third," he announced in a James Bond voice. "The youngest son of Thomas Haversham, of Haversham and Haversham."

She gave a small chuckle at his impersonation. "The hotel chain?"

He threw up both hands. "Guilty—but also new personal secretary to Professor Waymer. It was the professor who sent me to pass along the notes on the French Armor Exhibition. He said to remind you that the exhibition would be arriving in the morning." Brilliant white teeth flashed in a smile. "Along with the armor's very own chaperone."

"What happened to Perry, his other secretary?"

"Quit. I don't know the story."

She pushed a strand of hair from her eyes, leaned forward, and took his hand in a brief handshake, partly to stop her own hand from trembling and partly because she liked him. "Sorry, I didn't know. I get so caught up with my work." She laughed nervously. Todd's hand was firm, warm, and dry. "You have an impressive name, Mr. Haversham. I'm afraid mine isn't half as grand. Silverdawn. It was written on an old necklace my mother once found."

She winced inwardly at the lie. How could she share with a stranger that the same necklace had been around her neck on the day her adoptive parents found her abandoned in the gazebo at their summerhouse in the south of France? The necklace hadn't said her name at all. She had never been able to decipher the word printed on the necklace, but she was certain one day she would. And on that day, perhaps the truth of her birth would be revealed.

Her abandonment was still hard to comprehend. Along with the knowledge that her adoptive parents had been murdered the same day they informed her she had been illegally adopted. Both facts were too fragile—they were stowed away for sorting through later. When she could deal with them. When she felt stronger.

"I detect an accent." Todd filled the awkward silence that invaded the room.

"Australian." Silverdawn frowned. "Is it so obvious? I've lived in London for three years now."

"I flew back from a conference in Melbourne last Tuesday. Otherwise, I would have taken you for a 'dinky-di' Englishwoman."

She laughed softly at his attempt at Australian slang and leaned over to gently lay a hand on his arm. "I'll be fine. Thank you—"

The young man smiled and held up a hand to cut her off. "I feel a dismissal coming on, so I'll make it easy." He stepped away from the desk. "I'm going back to my office to collect a few papers, then I'm out of here. You sure there is nothing else I can do to help? A ride home, perhaps?" He raised a brow. "Dinner at an expensive restaurant?"

She shook her head. "My apartment is across the park. I enjoy the walk."

"A storm is brewing."

"No. But thanks for the offer."

He gave a short laugh. "Then I better get along before my mother rings Scotland Yard to send out a search party. The chief there is an old chum of my father's."

She raised a brow. "Mother?"

Todd shrugged and ambled toward the door. "At least someone cares," he tossed over his shoulder in a mournful tone.

She smiled and rested back into her chair. He really was quite sweet. But as the door closed with a soft click and his footsteps receded down the hallway, her thoughts were already drifting toward a man with short, ebony hair who rode a black, shaggy warhorse, and the name of the city the guard had uttered—Rastehm. The same name mentioned in the book of legends she'd been studying.

How uncanny.

Chapter Two

London, Sept. 23rd
Present Day

"High in the Jura Mountains, the sky darkened, thunder boomed, and rain pelted. The wind dropped, the earth trembled, and the ground split. A gaping crevice tore down the mountainside toward the French border town of Montbéliard.

"Shock waves continued to ripple two hundred kilometers from the site. The quake was picked up on seismographs several thousand miles across the seas.

"Tremors raced through villages and cities. Fierce storms lashed the coasts of Europe, England, and France. Sheep and cows aborted, and giant stones from ancient burial sites toppled..."

Iraj of Istani settled back into the overstuffed chair in his lounge room and listened to the female broadcaster drone on. The woman stood in a field at the bottom of Mount Jura. Large gray menhirs of all shapes and sizes lay strewn in the field behind her.

Just meters beneath one such stone, Iraj knew, lay an ancient artifact from another time. An artifact from a mystical age that had long ago slipped from the memories of man. A crystal pyramid no larger than a child of three summers, yet it contained all the evils of hell—*his* dark minions.

The pyramid was now cracked.

The crystal pyramid had caused the land upheaval. Such was the case every time it shifted course. Iraj had already discovered the pyramid's location. Unfortunately, he also sensed that it was damaged. Being several meters beneath the Earth's surface, below a huge standing stone that had toppled as the result of the quake, its removal would mean extensive excavating, drawing a lot of unwelcome attention. Iraj rose and glided across the room to the hearth, staring down into the flames.

He decided the pyramid would be safe as it was for the time being, though he must hurry. His fist pounded the wooden mantel. Was there no escape from this husk he now inhabited? The body of Professor Waymer was naught but a worthless vessel. Unless he could find the key to the pyramid and unlock his demons to release him from the human shape he now possessed, he would be trapped until his powers dwindled to nil or he wasted away and died.

In all his thousands of years of life, he had never felt so helpless. The key would release his army of darkness, then his Magick would be restored to its full capacity, for his power grew from tortured souls. His army would sweep across this world of puny humans, as it had Rastehm, destroying every living creature in its path. Nothing could stand in his way. For who could slay that which was already dead? Or had no real substance.

He laughed out loud, and it echoed down the empty corridors of Waymer's house.

****

The Palladian Knight stopped at a crossroad where ramshackle two-story houses appeared to topple forward and a torch burned fitfully on one corner of the street.

Beneath the pale light crouched an ancient white-haired man, wrapped against the rain in a threadbare maroon pelerine.

"Alms, sire," he croaked, his eyes wide and fearful, his face lean and hungry. He was so thin he seemed emaciated.

Faren leaned down from his black stallion and pressed a token into the man's skeletal hand. "Go to the hospice," he told him. "Ask for a man named Barageld and say these words. 'Faren reminds him of the code of benevolence.' "

The frail beggar hugged the token to his chest and turned away.

Faren took to the night and blended back into the shadows, his thoughts lost, to the last nine seasons spent in Asspehn—mountains of hard rock, plains of burning sand, a sun that beat down without mercy day upon day, turning sweat to salty rivers that coursed down face, legs, and arms. Then to top this, his army had to battle weremons—creatures half human, half beast, conjured by King Nordal's court necromancer, Amras, to protect the king's heir from banishment.

The weremons had elongated snouts, slavering gums peeled back from poniard-like teeth, wolf-like ears, and long, taloned fingers, coupled with prodigious strength, which could rip into a man and tear an arm from the socket. They also had the speed and proficiency with a short sword to match his best knight. He'd lost two hundred and twenty men to the weremons on the first day. They had been ambushed and his men dragged from their horses. Their heavy armor had made it nigh on impossible to rise before the beasts set upon them. The blood, the screams, and the stench of the beasts would live in his memory until his last breath. He'd barely escaped with his life and still bored scars on his chest where four razor-sharp talons ripped through his plate armor.

It had taken nine seasons to defeat Nordal and his enchanter.

Faren had sent across the Magiane Mountains for two thousand Forgian archers.

Longbows could shoot up to three times the distance of a short bow. They could fire arrowheads that could cut through steel, and for every arrow loosed by a crossbow, a longbowman could fire two. Archers did not just kill; they stopped charges, broke defenses, and won wars. Faren knew the times of living in the glorious past were over—times when knights in shining armor fought other knights in shining armor, and the common foot soldier in the field or archer stringing a bow in a dirt trench was not worth swinging a sword at. War was no longer a nobleman's affair. Nordal had not played by the rules, so neither had Faren.

He ordered the knights under his command to discard their heavy armor for a breastplate made from toughened leather, enabling them to maneuver faster. They exchanged their long swords for short swords more suitable for close-quarter fighting.

Nordal's weremons had fallen. The prince apprehended and the wizard killed by one of his own creatures. King Nordal had died by his own hand.

Faren often questioned himself if the stamping out of Magick was worth such senseless loss of life. In the beginning he'd believed, as all the others believed, that it was for the continuation of his world. Sometimes he wondered. Yet he could not allow himself to doubt, for in doing so he would have to question the blood that stained his hands, the way he lived his life, and his belief in the ways of the Mother Goddess.

Baltimore Castle rose up before him. It appeared, in every sense of the word, grim, with high walls surmounted by battlements, limp bedraggled pennants, and bleak towers at each corner. However, outward appearances were deceiving. Within the high walls, the palace could be called no less than grandiose, its furnishings having been rifled from deserted castles laid to waste twenty-eight years before, in the time of the warlord Iraj of Istani.

The studded iron gates of the palace were broad and brightly lit by several torches hung on each side of the gray stone walls. The gates were guarded by a half-dozen men draped in royal-blue capes, which denoted them as part of the regular palace garrison.

"Halt!" one barked, stepping in front of Faren with his pike slightly advanced.

Faren gave no indication that he had heard. He urged his stallion on toward the gate.

"I said halt, Sir Knight!"

Faren's horse bored down on the guard until a second guardsman jumped forward, seized the soldier's arm, and dragged him out of the black's path.

"That's Faren of Malaan, First Knight to the King," said the second man. "No man stands before *him*."

Faren reached the central courtyard.

An apprentice knight who had not yet been invested with his ceremonial armor and medallion rushed forward to take Nagor's reins. He held his lantern high to capture Faren's features. "Welcome home, Sir Knight. Much time has passed."

"It is good to be home, Brother." Faren hooked his shield into his saddlebow and swung down from the stallion's back. "Where can I find the king?"

"I believe His Royal Highness is in his chamber, my lord. Shall I see to your mount?"

He nodded to the lad. "And you." He laid a hand on his stallion's nose. "Behave and don't kick."

The novice took a step backward, still holding the reins firmly in his fist.

The black flicked his ears and stared at his master with malicious, flat-black eyes.

"It was only fair I should warn him, Nagor," Faren chided as he moved away across the courtyard.

He started up the stairway leading into the centuries-old palace and heard the stallion whinny as he was led toward the shadow-clustered stables. Faren smiled. Nagor was a brute, but his great heart more than made up for what he lacked in demeanor. Faren would rather have none other beneath him in the midst of battle.

The halls of the palace were narrow and dim, with high ceilings and little warmth. What servants he encountered scuttled away at the jingle of his spurs and the sight of his set countenance. Not until he scaled the steps and reached the west wing was he challenged.

Two young Palladian Knights, standing at attention on each side of the heavy double doors leading into the king's chambers, stepped in to block his passage with crossed pikes. One had the short fair hair of the people of Rastehm, the other the dark coloring of the Western Lay.

Faren hid a smile. The king was nothing if not democratic, even though democracy in the true sense would not be practiced in their world for at least another six thousand years.

He was refused entry.

"Move." He sighed heavily. "I am tired, wet, and hungry, and the king has summoned me. I have no time for ceremony. If the king denies me, then you can *try* to throw me out." He smiled coldly.

One of the guards made to step forward, but the other stopped him and rapped on the door with his pike. He gingerly eased it open, while the other man held Faren at bay. "What name did you say?" questioned the dark-haired soldier.

Faren pushed aside his black cloak to display the golden amulet swinging from the chain around his neck. "Faren of Malaan…" He paused a heartbeat to attain the reaction of the two guardsmen. "First Knight to the King."

The first Palladian announced him instantly, while the second took a hasty step back, almost tripping over his feet.

"Show him in at once. I have been expecting him." The king's voice echoed through the open door.

The king sat in a padded chair beside a marble hearth of blazing logs. Several silver candelabras stood on oak sideboards against the silk-covered stone walls of the tower room, giving the room a sense of artificial warmth. Thick red drapes hung before tall, stained-glass windows, and large gilt-edged paintings of ancestral importance stared down at Faren as he crossed the deep blue Angarian carpet. Faren dropped to one knee before his monarch and bowed his head.

The king motioned to the guards. "Leave us."

Faren heard the doors close.

The king leaned forward and rested a broad hand on

Faren's shoulder. "Arise, Sir Knight, and welcome home."

He pushed to his feet, unclipped his oilskin cloak, and draped it over the high back of a nearby chair. Then he stretched out his hands to the brilliant heat of the flames.

"I swear you are fully soaked to the bone. Why did you not return to the Temple-House for dry attire before you sought me out?"

"Your message seemed urgent, sire."

"So it is, but you are no use to me dead."

He grinned. "I have just returned from a battle with Nordal's weremons. I think it would take more than a fever to lay me under my cairn."

The king smiled and relaxed back into his chair. "Sit, Faren. You are as a son to me, and within this room there is no need to stand on ceremony. Now, how goes the battle?"

Faren settled himself before the fire in a chair the twin to the king's. "Over. We lost around ten and a half thousand, to their seventeen thousand. Nordal and Amras are dead, the weremons destroyed, and what men Nordal still had have sworn fealty to you and the crown. I had to bring in Forgian archers, purchase leather breastplates, short swords, and scabbards before I could bring about a swing in the battle. My intuition paid off."

"Leather, you say, and short swords?"

"The leather to enable the men to move faster. Short swords for close-quarter fighting. The strategies of battle are changing, my lord."

Mikkasah moved his wide shoulders and sighed. "It appears so."

Faren met the king's gaze. "You owe the Forgian

king five thousand ruples in gold."

Mikkasah nodded. " 'Twas well spent."

"Was it?" Faren's voice held an edge.

"Don't question it, lad. I found long ago that questions only bring heartache. 'Tis the will of the Mother Goddess; therefore, we obey." He shifted his gaze from Faren's. "There can be no other way." The king paused. "Nordal...how did he die?"

"By his own dagger, rather than face the banishment of his only heir."

The king nodded and ran a hand over his eyes. "He was once a good friend. Why do these men struggle so when they know the outcome is inevitable? Surely, life in the distant future cannot be so bad. You have been there, Faren. Tell me of it."

He shrugged his shoulders. "What can I say? All things move fast. People are forever in a hurry. There are great bird-like machines, which carry people through the air and across the water."

"They fly?"

Faren nodded. "There are boxes that can capture your voice and send it back to you, other boxes that can capture your image for an eternity with the flick of a tiny knob. And more boxes still, known as televisions, which carry moving, talking, colored images within."

"It is a land of boxes, then?"

Faren gave a half laugh. "No, not exactly. However, a great deal of their technology does come in the shape of boxes. There is technology there, sire, that here would be deemed witchcraft, yet people accept it as a way of life. There are also weapons which shoot flames and thunder."

"It seems from your enthusiasm that you are quite

fond of this future, Sir Knight."

"Not all is good, my lord." Faren's tone turned grave. "They do not believe in the Mother Goddess. They have no care for the Earth. They strip it of its riches and return nothing. They clog the waterways with refuse and foul their air and then complain there is no clean water to drink and their lungs are diseased."

The king held up his hand. "No more." He rose, agitated. "And to this place I have sent my only child?"

"Forgive me, sire. Perhaps I go too far. In fact, on my last mission, I noted there were those more enlightened who unwittingly fight on the side of the Mother Goddess."

King Mikkasah threw the knight a look of suspicion. "And who are these enlightened ones?"

Faren slid one hand behind his back and crossed two fingers. "The Knights of Greenpeace, my lord. I believe they are made up by a certain number of the banished."

Mikkasah settled his bulk back into his chair. The hair that had changed to iron gray on the day he turned twenty hung to his shoulders and matched his beard. In his early days, he'd been known as the *Iron Eagle*. His shrewdness in battle had been next to none. But now the vigor of youth was gone. Stripped from him by years of sorrow over the loss of his only child and an unforgiving wife whom he still loved.

"Perhaps there is hope for that world yet," the king said at last.

Faren released a hefty sigh and leaned forward, clasping his two hands between his knees. "Perhaps." He hated speaking of the Third Dawning. He preferred not to think of it.

The last time he had been sent to track down a rebel,

it was in the early 1930s, during the American Prohibition. Even now he could picture the mutilated body of the child—slashed from throat to navel, ribs splayed out, the heart still beating. The suffering in the child's eyes begging for release...

"What's wrong, lad? Are you ill?"

He found the king's hand resting on his arm and pulled back. He ran his fingers over his eyes, partly to wipe away the vision and partly to clear his mind. "No."

He did not elaborate. He had not told the king of the incident. It was something he never spoke of and tried not to remember. Mikkasah rose and strode to the sideboard to fill two pewter goblets with *aris*.

"You have servants for that."

"I know, but I would prefer our conversation stayed within these walls and not be bandied about the servants' quarters."

He nodded and rose to meet the king at the center of the room. He took the goblet offered by his monarch and returned to stand by the fire. "So what is it that could not wait, that you should summon me from a battle? Albeit the end of a battle."

The king's expression remained grave. "There are two matters at hand. The first dealing with Iraj."

Faren took a swallow of his *aris*. It burned all the way down and left a mellow glow that warmed his innards. "You have located him?"

"No, although we believe he is residing in the last year of the Third Dawning. But that is not the importance of the matter. For many years, the astrologers have searched the skies for some way of locating the Pyramid of Rastehm. Using the calculations of the lunar and solar motions, they have finally pinpointed the exact position of the pyramid."

"You wish me to fetch it back?"

Mikkasah nodded. "Sir Kalden volunteered for the task…"

"And?" He paused for a moment, noting Mikkasah's bleak expression. "When is the beginning of the Summer Solstice?" he asked hesitantly. "I lost track of the days. All feel the same when you are fighting such a long, drawn-out battle."

"Summer Solstice and Midsummer's Day have come and gone. Kalden did not return."

He stood silent, watching the flames swirl and dance within the grate. "No." He shook his head in dismissal. "Kalden." He ran a hand over his eyes. "Not Kalden. I will not believe it."

"I am sorry, lad. If I could save you the pain, I would."

Faren thumped his fist onto the marble mantel. "By the Goddess! If this was Iraj's doing—"

"We suspect Kalden has body-crashed and cannot remember his identity."

Faren swirled the deep-red *aris* in his goblet and closed his eyes against the memories flowing to the fore. Boyhood memories. Adulthood memories. Bittersweet.

Next to him, Kalden was considered the best knight in the Palladian Order. He was also Faren's adopted brother and dearest friend. They had realized their mind powers together and apprenticed themselves to the Order of Palladia on the same day.

Faren wondered what it would be like to body-crash and dwell within another's body, having no idea of his real identity. Living a lifeless existence, unless by some freak chance he remembered his name. For only with that memory could he be set free. He shuddered. It was the risk all Palladians took when they transported themselves into time. A risk they all accepted with their oath to become a Knight of the Goddess.

"I am going after him." Faren's voice broke the hard silence that had descended on the room.

"No. This may sound heartless, but Kalden must wait. I need you to restore the pyramid. We believe it to be damaged. You must bring it back. I do not even wish to contemplate what would happen should Iraj get to the device first. He could unleash his demons on the unsuspecting world in which he now resides."

"You think he knows the pyramid's position?"

" 'Tis too much of a coincidence that he has chosen to surface in the same vicinity and period of time."

"He is no fool; I know that. His cunning is unmatched." Faren upended his chalice and finished his *aris* in one swallow. "So where is the pyramid?"

The king explained the locale of the elusive icon.

"And if I should happen on Kalden while searching?"

"You know 'tis a fool's quest. You will never recognize him."

He pushed up the loose-fitting sleeve of his tunic. A red fire-breathing dragon lay tattooed in its entire splendor along the length of his left arm. "These are never lost."

"Even so, should you come across him, you cannot simply announce who he is. You are aware of what happened to Evain?"

Faren compressed his lips and allowed his sleeve to fall back into place. "It caused him to go insane."

"Two beings cannot occupy a single body at the

same time. He must remember who he is by himself. It is most important you do not speak his name in his presence."

"I will remember. Now, the key to the pyramid. Your daughter still holds it?"

"I can only presume." King Mikkasah slumped back into his chair, appearing to age before his eyes. "I have had no contact with her since I transported her to the Third Dawning. You have no idea how hard it was for me to abandon my daughter to the arms of strangers, even though I knew she would be well cared for. Queen Aurelia has never forgiven me. She thought I should have fought harder for our daughter's right to stay."

Faren knew part of the story but not all. He sank into the chair opposite the king. "Forgive me, my lord. I spoke without thought. So that is why the queen spends her days in Malaan?"

The king nodded. "You were not to know. It is something I rarely speak about. Faren?"

"My lord?"

"I fear Silverdawn may be in danger. Iraj will stop at nothing to gain the key to the pyramid."

"I shall protect her with my life, sire."

"Yes, but you will do more." The king ran a hand over the back of his neck and looked Faren in the eye. "When you have used the key to heal the pyramid, you will bring my daughter home."

His breath caught. "My lord, no one has ever returned from banishment. What about the Goddess? Her wrath may be great."

The king's eyes darkened. "Let that be of no concern to you. I will deal with the Goddess when the time comes."

Chapter Three

September 29th
Present Day

Silverdawn wished the elderly watchman good night and stepped through the double glass doors of the museum into the night. Silvery rain sifted from the sky.

A moonless night, ebony dark with a wind that chilled her to her soul, the sort of night in which evil lurked. She turned up the collar of her woolen coat against the blowing rain and proceeded down the white marble stairs of the museum, guided only by the patches of pale light cast from the streetlights. The night had an eerie mien about it, almost silent, almost still. Not another soul marked the street.

Usually, a pair of stone statues—a lion and a griffin—guarded the steps. Tonight, she noted their absence. *What had happened to them?* Perhaps the committee had elected to have them replaced. She was not privy to all of their decisions.

She stepped onto a road devoid of traffic. Lightning flashed above the treetops ahead, and thunder echoed close by, heralding that the steady rain was becoming a serious storm. A sudden gust of wind tugged at the edges of her overcoat and blew a deluge of heavier raindrops into her face.

She hadn't meant to stay so late at the office but had

become immersed in an article in the *Archaeological Gazette*. An old friend of hers from university, who worked at the Paris branch of her museum, had on a field trip unearthed a burial cairn in the South of France, complete with the skeletal remains of a warrior and his mount. The skeleton was miraculously intact. She'd been so fascinated by the article that she called Emile and spent another hour questioning him on his find.

She stubbed her toe in her absentmindedness and tripped on the gutter, breaking from her reverie as she regained her footing. She stepped through the park's arched gateway, and several dark shadows rose before her—tall, long, and grotesquely misshapen. Her heart slammed into her ribs, and her breath lodged in her throat. She stilled momentarily, then moved closer. Trees. She gave a self-conscious laugh and hurried up the path she had taken for the past three years. The gravel crunched beneath her feet, the sound comforting, the noise real and familiar.

The rain came down in a deluge, plastering her hair to her head, making a mockery of her severe hairstyle. She removed her dark-rimmed glasses and pushed them into her tapestry satchel. She didn't know why she still wore them. Habit, she guessed.

Ducking her head against the force of the rain, she cursed herself for not remembering an umbrella.

Then it came.

An eerie cry from within the trees. Once more she stopped to peer around. Thunder grumbled overhead. Lightning lit up the tops of the trees not fifty feet away, and above the din of the storm came another sound—the soft growl of a large cat before it pounced.

Silverdawn didn't hesitate. She had no idea what

kind of beast lurked in the shadows, but she was not about to stay and find out. She raced for the nearest lamppost, risking a glance back to see what stalked her— a lion, all snarl and teeth. She fled up the path, and another creature swept in from the side. A misshapen monster was poised above her, and she screamed. The creature's head was that of an eagle, its body that of a lion. Massive wings were attached to its back, and long sharp talons protruded from the beast's outstretch feet.

A griffin!

Impossible. They were creatures of myth. However, it didn't look too mythical as it bored down on her. A hideous screech issued from its wicked beak, and she screamed and ducked, the wind from the beast's wings wafting over her, missing her head by a hair's breadth. The griffin rose, wheeled in the sky, and dropped again, and the lion crept closer.

Lightning tore the blanket of darkness, and in that instant a man appeared. Dressed in the garb of a warrior—medieval black leather pants and a chain-mail vest that glinted beneath an ebony cloak, which swirled around him like a giant bat's wing. From beneath the cloak, he drew a long sword, and reflected lightning danced along its deadly blade.

The griffin swooped low. The warrior thrust Silverdawn to the side, then swung his sword in a broad arc, opening up the beast's belly. Blood sprayed from the fatal wound as the griffin rose screeching into the air, then crashed to the ground, landing not twenty feet away. Ever so slowly, the creature, as if programmed to attack even near death, began to drag itself toward them.

The warrior turned, sword in readiness, as the lion growled low in its throat. The large cat crouched some thirty paces away on the opposite side of the path. The cat's tail slashed from side to side in the mud, and its ears lay flat atop its head.

"Run!" the man shouted.

Silverdawn glanced from the lion to the knight, decided she had no choice, and bolted.

The lion made to follow, but the man shouted again, and the feline changed direction. As the lion sprang, he dropped to one knee and held his sword in readiness in a double-handed grip. Unable to stop its momentum, the animal impaled itself upon his blade. He rolled and came to his feet as the lion, with the sword still buried deep in its chest, flew over him and fell heavily to the ground. He scrambled to withdraw the blade from the dying beast, then turned to face the griffin.

****

Iraj hunched in a padded chair on the first floor of the Museum of Rare Artifacts and watched as the museum griffin, in the throes of death, reverted to stone.

"Hell spawn!" He leaped to his feet, glided across the room, and cast the contents of the bowl into the fire. As the water from his conjuration hit the flames, the fire hissed. *Damn!* It had been such a good plan. Simple—kill the girl, have the creatures retrieve her satchel, and if the key was not within it, ransack her apartment and rifle through her office. Whatever it took to find the pyramid's key. With the girl out of the way, everything would be so much easier, and he would also have his revenge on Mikkasah. Two birds with one stone. Some of these human sayings were quite apt.

He had been so close. Blast Mikkasah for sending another knight. Or was it the same one?

He had not seen the warrior's face, but there had

been a certain something about his bearing—a confidence and deadly grace. The last time a Palladian came after him, he'd barely escaped with his life. If not for the knight's misguided compassion for a boy within minutes of death, he would surely have been trapped.

He thumped his fist into the wall beside the hearth. "No, no, and no!" He would not think of that. He had to have the *key*. It was the answer to all that plagued him. He knew the location of the pyramid, he had tracked it as it slipped through the centuries, but he had only recently found the girl.

Mikkasah's daughter—the answer to his problems. She was easy to recognize with the aura encasing her body. Iridescent yellow, like the precious jewel she was. And with hair and eyes the exact replica of her mother's, how could he not know her? How good it would feel to rip open her body and offer her heart up to the Goddess of Hell.

Surely Samioa would reward him, perhaps even restore his Magick to its full potential.

A light knock sounded on the door, and a young woman poked her head around the edge. "Oh, so you are here, Peter. When you didn't ring or come home, I thought I would come to you. I know how you get so tied up in your work."

She rushed into the office, shrugged off her heavy coat and sodden woolen scarf, and pushed aside the papers on his desk. Then she proceeded to pull several lidded containers and a bottle of wine from a hamper. "Surprise! I thought you might be hungry. I brought all your favorites. Sweet and sour chicken, Peking duck, Singapore noodles, a bottle of aged Cabernet Sauvignon from the cellar…"

That childlike voice—how it grated on his nerves. How had the late professor tolerated such noise?

"Enough! Who gave you the right to come here, Serena? I did not summon you."

"Summon, Peter? Whenever have you had to summon me?" Her large, pale-blue eyes glistened with tears. "I only wanted to be with you. We are just married, yet we hardly spend any time together, and you know what the doctor said about working too hard."

"That charlatan! Since they laid me in that infernal radiation machine and fired my body with that strange power—"

Iraj picked up the bottled wine and hurled it into the fire. The glass shattered into a thousand shards, and the flames leaped higher in the grate.

Serena came around the desk and hesitantly held out a small hand, like a young child touching something she was afraid might bite. "I'm sorry, Peter, I didn't mean to make you angry. You get upset so easily these days. I only wanted to have dinner here in the privacy of your office, by the fire, like we used to when we were courting. Then I thought we could go home together and snuggle up on the fur before the fire and make love." She smiled sadly. "Perhaps tonight, God willing, I might conceive."

Fornication! Iraj shuddered at the prospect of such intimate contact. *Is that all the women of this modern world are capable of thinking about?* She was not the first woman that had wanted to fornicate with him. There had been that woman in the 1930s…

A soft sob escaped Serena's lips, stirring Iraj from his musing. "Don't send me away. I get so lonely in that big, old house."

He weakened and lifted his hands to her mahogany hair, and it flowed through his fingers like silk, glistening the orange-red of blood in the firelight. Warm, beautiful, he could almost imagine the salty taste of the blood on his tongue.

He placed his thumbs at the base of Serena's throat and pressed them against her rapidly beating pulse. Her bones were so fine. It would be so easy to snuff out her life.

She obviously mistook his touch as a yes and pulled his shirt from his slacks, pushing her long, delicate fingers up over the planes of his chest and back, wrapping herself around his body like a vine around a tree.

Her touch came as a shock. He had taken special pains to refrain from contact with her. Staying at the office too late, not going to bed until he was sure she was asleep. Now he knew why.

Iraj felt his body respond to her touch and was powerless to stop it. Desire mixed with his anger. He lowered his head and felt Serena's tongue curl into his mouth.

Her hands cupped and caressed. Her neck went back, and her chest arched up. And all the while, she urged him on, whispering encouragement in her little-girl voice. When she finally drew him down onto the pile rug before the fire—her skirt up around her waist, her tongue darting over his nipples—he was caught between wanting to crush the life from her body and demanding she never stop tormenting him.

But one day soon it would be his turn to do the torturing. He would splay her ribs and hold her softly beating heart in his hand as it died. Even as the thought crossed his mind, blood rushed to his groin and his body hardened. He shifted his mouth to her breast, and she gasped as his teeth grazed her nipple. But he would bide his time with his revenge, for his position as Waymer was too precious to the deadly game he played to be given away lightly on a moment of pleasure and the sweet elixir of blood.

Chapter Four

Silverdawn awoke to the harsh sound of a police siren ringing in her ears. She blinked against the bright light streaming through the lounge window into her eyes. London was awake. She was in the lounge on the couch. What had possessed her to sleep on the couch?

She shivered, her gaze straying to the clock across the room—*9:30*. She forced up a hand to push her hair from her face. Her head pounded like a bass drum. She could swear she had a hangover. Except she'd stopped drinking after she'd become a commode-hugging drunk at a college party when she was eighteen. She never wanted to feel that sick again.

Teeth chattering, she rose and stumbled to the kitchen. Cold, so very cold. She must be getting the flu. Why hadn't she switched on the heat? With trembling hands, she fumbled with the thermostat on the kitchen wall, then turned to the medicine drawer to rummage for headache tablets. She pushed two capsules from the protective foil pack, picked up a glass off the sink, and reached for the tap.

Her hand stilled as it all came flooding back—the eerie feeling on leaving the museum; the missing statues; the creatures in the park who had tried to kill her; and the man who had appeared in a flash of lightning dressed as a medieval knight.

Who was he? What were those creatures? Why had

they seemed so intent on pursuing her? She sagged onto a wooden kitchen chair and ran a hand over her eyes. Had the whole episode been another vision?

The visions were becoming so closely entwined with her real life that it was often difficult to distinguish between illusion and reality. Like the names Mikkasah and Rastehm. Both names were mentioned in the ancient tome of legends. And the dark knight who came to her rescue had seemed so like the man she had envisioned in her office. Her petit mal was occurring more often, so much so she was certain she should see a doctor. Yet she was reluctant to do so. Memories of bright lights, wires clamped to her ears, and doubting, drawn-faced specialists flickered before her eyes.

Needing to escape the memories, she rose, filled her glass, then swallowed the tablets. Since the death of her parents, all had become so complicated. In fact, that had been when all this craziness began.

But she wouldn't think about that now. She had to get to work. She was already an hour late.

Half an hour later, Silverdawn purchased the *Morning Tribune* from the tiny newsstand across the road from her apartment building, like she did every day. She smiled at Mr. Kawinski, paid her three shillings, unfolded her newspaper, and was slammed between the eyes by a headline that read—*Museum Statues Stolen and Vandalized in Kennedy Park.*

Suddenly, the events of the night before became clear. There were no such creatures as those that attacked her. Well, perhaps the lion, but definitely not the griffin. She must have come across the vandals, and the shock had sent her into a trance.

Her mood much lighter now she had fit together the

pieces, she hurried through the park toward work. However, she could not refrain from casting furtive glances over her shoulder into the high bushes lining the path.

Two police cars were parked in front of the museum. Silverdawn climbed the building's white steps and pushed through the double doors. All seemed as it should be until she reached the third floor. Martha met her as she stepped from the elevator and fell into step beside her.

"What's happening here?" she asked the elderly woman with the blue-rinse hair and gold-rimmed spectacles.

"I think you should see your office."

She rounded the corner and halted in front of a burly uniformed policeman blocking her office door.

"Sorry, miss, you can't go in there. The place is being dusted for prints." Over the outstretched arm, she could see Professor Waymer deep in conversation with a man in a charcoal suit.

Her office appeared as if it had been struck by a tornado. Desk drawers had been wrenched free. Their contents strewn across the floor. The papers and paraphernalia from her desk had joined the debris on the carpet. Thankfully, her computer still stood in one piece.

Professor Waymer glanced up from his conversation and smiled briefly as a look of relief flitted across his face. "You can let her pass. It's Dr. Peterson. She works here. This is her office."

The detective with Dr. Waymer dismissed the two men in dustcoats and nodded to the officer at the door.

Silverdawn entered the room in a daze. Her precious memory sticks had been upended from their case and scattered across the carpet. She dropped to her knees to gather them up. "Who did this?"

"We thought *you* might know." The detective held out his hand to help her stand. "Inspector Rhys-Jones of Scotland Yard," he announced.

"Me? You think *I* did this? I've put two years of my life into this work."

"No, of course not. Do not distress yourself, Doctor. I thought you might have noticed something out of the ordinary. I understand you worked late last night."

She shook her head. It began to pound. "Nothing to do with this, but I did notice the statues in front of the museum were missing." She glanced at the professor and could have sworn something furtive flickered in his eyes before he shifted his gaze across the room, but it could have been a change in the light.

"What time was this?" Detective Rhys-Jones took a notepad from his pocket and began to jot down notes.

"I left my office at ten thirty p.m. I remember glancing at my watch, thinking how late it was."

The detective nodded and scribbled in his notebook. "Now think, Doctor. Did you see anyone lurking about?"

She frowned, recalling the warrior in the park, and looked away from the detective's knowing gaze. Bending to retrieve a stack of papers strewn at her feet, she took a moment to still her shaking hands and remembered she had decided to classify the stranger as a vision.

Taking a deep breath, she stood. "No, no one, and there is nothing I can tell you. But perhaps you can explain what the statues have to do with my office?"

The detective tucked his notebook into his coat pocket and ran a hand over his jaw. "I'm afraid I have no idea. In fact, it is yet to be determined whether the two crimes are related. Your secretary noted your door ajar and found this mess. As I was already in the lobby investigating the case of the vandalized statues, I was assigned to this case as well."

She cast him a small smile. "Is there anything else, Detective? I would like to see to the cleaning of this mess." She crossed to the bookcase on the far side of the room and bent to retrieve the books from the floor. She straightened out the pages and smoothed a hand lovingly over each cover, then returned the books to their rightful places on the shelves.

"Make a list of anything missing and give it to Constable Ford at the door. He will pass it on."

She nodded.

"I'll send Martha in to help you clean up," the professor said, patting her arm.

Silverdawn noticed the chill of his hand even through her shirtsleeve. "I'd appreciate that." She watched him stroll to the door with the detective. Then she slid her gaze to the destruction around her and let out a loud groan. The glass on the special cabinet where she had placed the tome of Rastehm legends was shattered, and the book was gone.

She hurried forward and checked the floor around the case. The tome was definitely not among the scattered books. "Wait!" she called to the detective. "There was a book I had been working on. A rare book of legends."

The professor's face paled. His words came in a harshly coiled whisper. "The Rastehm legends?"

She nodded.

"That book was priceless. There is not another like

it in this world."

The inspector noted the book's description and details. "I'll contact you should any new information come to light. But I have a hunch this was the work of juveniles. The book's probably already been dumped." He bade her good day and disappeared through the door.

Professor Waymer made to follow when a stranger spoke from the doorway.

"It would appear that I have arrived at a most inopportune time."

She turned toward the sound of the voice. The magazine she'd been retrieving slipped from her hand. She could tell at a glance this man was her savior from the night before—the man from her dreams—although he was not dressed as a warrior and carried no sword. He wore a black, high-neck sweater and black jeans, yet she knew him—her black knight. And he had a decidedly impatient look on his face.

"Dr. Peterson?" he asked.

Professor Waymer cast Silverdawn a penetrating look, then spoke from beside her. "I am Dr. Waymer, the curator of this museum. May I help?"

"I am here to see Dr. Peterson." The man peered over Constable Ford's outstretched arm.

She wasn't familiar with his thick accent. His deep voice rumbled along her nerve endings and filled her body with delicious dread. What was he doing here? What did he want with her? "I am Dr. Peterson," she announced, finding her voice. She moved toward the door and nodded to Ford to allow the stranger to pass.

"And you are?" the professor asked, stepping forward to meet him.

"Forgive me." The man moved farther into the room

and stretched out his hand. "Faren Malaan, manager of the French Armor Exhibition. I was to meet with Dr. Peterson on arrival to pick up the paperwork."

Dr. Waymer ignored the hand, and Silverdawn stepped into the breach and took it. His grip was firm, his skin warm and dry. "Ah yes, Mr. Malaan. So sorry you find us in such a state. As you can see, my office has been ransacked."

****

Faren met the other man's gaze. He had the distinct feeling the curator did not like him and wondered why. "I hope nothing of significance was taken."

"Did we mention anything was taken?" the other man remarked dryly. "But as a matter of fact, it was a rare book of legends. The police are working on the situation. I'm sure they will soon find our culprit."

Faren nodded, still not dropping his gaze from the curator's. "I am certain they will."

The men remained staring at each other for a moment longer, then the curator relented, turning to Silverdawn. "I will see you in my office at noon with a report on the breakages and any other known thefts. I am sure you will help Mr. Malaan in any way possible. This exhibition is quite a prize from what I hear. Oh, and get in touch with Stilwell in security and have him hire whatever extra guards are needed. We cannot be too careful with this business." He gestured with his arm around her office and strode for the door.

The police officer stepped aside, and the curator disappeared, his footsteps surprisingly soft on the hallway's polished boards.

The doctor bent to retrieve a stack of magazines from the floor beneath her desk. Faren crouched to help, his hand going to the small glass pyramid beside the papers. Their hands touched as they both reached for the pyramid, and their gazes locked.

"May I?" he asked, the timbre of his voice soft yet persuasive.

She nodded and handed him the paperweight.

He closed his eyes, feeling the weight of the cold object in his palm. He had known what it was the moment he saw it. Even as he cradled it in his hand, he could sense the evil within. Minute vibrations radiated to the fleshy tips of his fingers and up his arm, leaving him in no doubt. Only one of his order could have detected the Magick.

Reluctantly, he placed the piece onto the young woman's outstretched hand. "Lovely," he said, rising. "It appears to be very old. May I inquire as to its origin?"

She came to her feet in a rush and stumbled. He reached out and caught her arm before she fell, their eyes locking and holding momentarily. He thought he detected recognition and a spark...of desire, then she pushed away.

"I'm...I'm sorry," she murmured, her cheeks reddening. "I'm not...usually so clumsy."

His lips twitched. "The shock of the burglary, I dare say."

She nodded, her eyes solemn. "Yes, the burglary. I must admit the discovery was quite unnerving. Now what were you asking? Ah yes. The origin of the paperweight? I wish I knew myself. It seems—" She shrugged. "I've had the pyramid since I was a baby. I don't know where it came from. I assume my father acquired it in his travels. He was in the import business, importing bric-a-brac and furniture from all over the

Julie A. D'Arcy

world."

"He is retired now, of course."

"No, he's dead."

Faren frowned. "I am sorry to hear that."

She did not elaborate. She sat in the chair behind her desk and hunted among her papers in silence. She retrieved the paperwork for the exhibition, signed the form, and handed it to Faren. "I believe this is what you came for, Mr. Malaan."

He accepted the form and pushed it into his pocket. Not taking his gaze from her face, he leaned forward and laid his hand over hers. "Where is it you live?"

She straightened defensively. "That, Mr. Malaan, is none of your concern. Across the park," she said and then frowned.

"I will walk you home."

"I don't walk with strangers."

"But you will walk with me," he said, giving her hand a gentle squeeze.

"I will?"

He smiled. "You will."

Chapter Five

The wind blew cold, and the rain pelted against the stained-glass window. The old St. Agnes estate squatted on five acres of land on the edge of London. For four hundred years, the building had stood the test of time. It had once been a monastery, but all records had long ago been destroyed by fire. To Iraj, the dampness and chill of the place suited him fine, reminding him of his castle in Istani and all he had lost and left behind. He snapped shut the ancient tome on his desk and hurled it brutally at the fire burning in the grate.

"Damn Mikkasah to the deepest, darkest hell pit!" The last page of the book of legends was missing. The page had to contain a clue to the description of the key. Without that clue, he was helpless. The creature he conjured from the grave had failed in his attempt to uncover the key in Silverdawn's office. If only he knew what it looked like. The task was the equivalent of searching for an unknown coin in a wishing well.

He turned back to watch the tome burn, cursed long and loud, and hurried around the edge of his desk to the fireplace. He poked at the book of legends with a fire iron. Blue-gold flames reared and curled back from the ancient yellow pages. Mikkasah, that son of a cur, must have had the tome protected by glamors—no doubt the Magick of Mikkasah's court magician, Pendragon— before the magician's banishment. Without the full extent of his powers, Iraj would be helpless to undo the spell. Yet how had the page been removed if the book was ensorcelled? Only one with the Magick could have achieved that feat.

Or was it because the page was not really destroyed but merely removed? Perhaps there was a chance yet of its recovery. But who was responsible? Surely not Silverdawn, who had no knowledge of her heritage or the significance of the page.

Concentrating, Iraj stared into the flames. A swarthy figure swam at him through the haze—azure eyes, short dark hair, and a familiar bearing. Of course! He should have known—the minder of the armor exhibition—a Palladian Knight, all in one.

He would have to tread very carefully. His one advantage was that the knight did not know his identity. He must have as little contact with the man as possible. The game would be difficult, but Iraj thrived on difficulty. Had he not escaped Mikkasah's pyramid?

He grinned, then drew a ragged breath and grimaced as biting pain stabbed into his thigh. He rubbed at the ache unconsciously. If not for Peter Waymer's accursed, diseased body, he would have held the page and the key in his hand already.

Iraj expelled a heavy breath and made his way to his desk. He reached for his cell phone.

The time had come to call into play his alternate plan.

****

Silverdawn peered into the street below. The asphalt absorbed the dim glow the streetlamps threw onto the road, barely allowing enough light to see the shadowy outline of the tree-lined path.

The air was damp and thick with moisture. Ponderous black clouds had menaced the sky for most of the afternoon but refused to give up their burden. The night and weather seemed to conspire against her yet again. She peered hesitantly toward the park. Would the griffin and lion be there tonight? Had they been real? And if not, why did Faren Malaan seem so familiar? The events of last night still haunted her, and she found it hard to get a grip on reality.

She poured a glass of water from the jug, slipped two headache capsules from the foil wrapper, popped them into her mouth, and swallowed.

The afternoon had been spent picking up and rearranging after the burglary.

Apparently, the only item stolen was the book. She was saddened by the theft and had been unable to think of anything else for most of the day.

For two years she had worked on the translation of that book. Now, because of some thoughtless thief, she would never know the knowledge contained on the last page. What was the conclusion? Were the legends merely tales, or was there truth to the words? Had there been a massive cover-up to deny true Magick?

She put a hand to her throbbing temples. Would these questions never cease?

She reached for the tiny pyramid on her desk. It felt so cold in her hand, even more so than usual. She held the ornament to the glow of her desk lamp and peered at its glossy surface. Why had Faren Malaan shown so much interest in the piece? It was a mere trinket, nothing of consequence. If it were anything special, she was certain her father would have told her. He knew antiques, and from him, her own love of them had stemmed.

She had studied different cultures and periods of history since she was a young girl, but never had she seen a piece like her pyramid. She shook the small crystal pyramid and held it closer to the light.

No. It was merely a child's toy—a legacy of her lost past. However, as she watched, tiny specs of white and silver seemed to manifest within a spectrum of blues. It was almost as if minuscule creatures clawed at the inside, trying to escape. She backed away from the light, dropped the trinket into her satchel, and scraped her hands down the sides of her skirt, trying to rub away the uneasy feeling the pyramid had evoked.

She gave a mental shrug. No matter the strange sensations the piece induced, tonight she was unwilling to leave the pyramid on her desk. Perhaps the break-in had unnerved her, but the pyramid was one of the only two links she held to her real parents—the other her necklace.

Donning her coat, she left her office and made her way to the foyer. Bidding good night to the doorman, she stepped into the night.

He was waiting. Leaning against the outside wall by the door, he loomed large, dark, and dangerous. Still dressed in black, he had added a leather coat in the same shade that belted at the waist and fell below his knees to meet his ebony boots. All this Silverdawn noted at a glance before she passed him by. It was late. She had not really expected him to be there. In fact, she had deliberately stayed late in order to avoid him. He straightened and fell into step beside her.

She had not shared company with a male since high school. Those embarrassing attempts at fumbled passion by the captain of the hockey team, and his rumor spreading the next day, had been enough to cure her of men for a very long time. She felt uncomfortable in their presence.

"You don't have to do this," she said, descending the marble stairs.

"But I do," he returned, his voice like the rumble of distant thunder.

"It's cold, it's late, and I wouldn't think any less of you if you were to leave now."

"But *I* would."

They crossed the road toward the darkened park in silence. Chills feathered up Silverdawn's spine and prickled her scalp, but her gaze never left the darkness beyond the gates. The grounds seemed even blacker than the night before—more intimidating, as though whispering her name. She stepped up onto the curb and hesitated.

"Is there a problem?"

She flinched at Faren's words and paused in thought. When had she begun thinking of him as Faren? She shook her head and sighed. Too many strange things had happened lately, and Faren Malaan was one of them. Despite the cold, perspiration beaded her forehead. Small rivulets of sweat ran between her breasts. "No. No, of course not."

He knew she was afraid, and he knew she knew. She could sense it. She didn't understand what game he played, but it could not be all bad, since he had rescued her the night before. Hadn't he?

She raised her chin, stepped through the gate, turned left as always, and screamed as something leaped at her from the bushes. A second piercing scream ripped from her throat as she fought off her attacker. Then she was in

Faren's arms, and he was laughing.

His chest rumbled against her cheek, and the warm deep sound sprinkled the night. With as much dignity as she could muster, she pushed away from his arms. Heat radiated from her face.

In the light of the streetlamp, she could see he held a trembling ball of fluff. A kitten—frightened and shivering. She closed her eyes, breathed deeply to control her shaking, then smiled up at him hesitantly. "May I?"

Faren nodded and placed the tiny animal into her hands.

She stroked its small damp head with one finger. The kitten was shaking nearly as much as she was. Murmuring soft words of comfort, she attempted to tuck the kitten down the neck of her coat, but her hands were cold and stiff, and the kitten refused to cooperate.

Faren moved to help.

She glanced up, and their gazes met in the dim light. The clouds parted, and the moon shone down, revealing his solemn, handsome face. Their bodies were but a whisper apart. He lowered his head. His eyes sparkled bright in the moonlight. His aura wrapped itself around her body and cocooned her in the knowledge that this man was safe, dependable.

The warmth of his breath on her lips gave the distinct impression he was going to kiss her, and her stomach gave a little twist. *Strange.* She had known him for no more than a day, yet she wanted his kiss more than she had wanted anything in a long time. She closed her eyes and waited. She yearned to lean into him, wrap herself around him, and just for a moment allow herself this one small measure of comfort. His hands closed over hers, and her eyes sprang open.

"The kitten, *ma belle*. It is cold and frightened. Perhaps we should see to its comfort." He guided the kitten into the lapel of her jacket. His large, warm hands closed over hers for a fraction more than necessary. Then he released her and stepped away.

She felt bereft and more chilled than snow in winter. Shaking herself, she asked quietly, "What was that you called me?"

"Nothing of consequence, *mademoiselle*. I spoke out of turn. I apologize. It is just that—" He shrugged.

"Just what?"

"You are much lovelier than I expected. Though I should have realized…"

Silverdawn let his statement go unfinished. With heated cheeks she refused to meet his gaze. Compliments did not sit well with her. She was so conscious of this dark, good-looking man at her side it was almost palpable. She felt awkward and downright frumpy. She could not remember the last time she'd combed her hair. Yet she was certain he had called her beautiful. And although she couldn't detect the dialect, she remembered hearing the accent somewhere in her past.

Faren waited in silence for her to move.

She smiled briefly. "Very well, as you say." She stroked the kitten under the chin and heard him purr. "Poor little fellow is cold and hungry. I'd best get him home."

"How do you know it's a male?"

"I don't, but it seems somehow nicer than calling the little bundle of fur *it*." She smiled up at him shyly.

He nodded and took her arm, and they moved through the night in silence. At the end of the park, they crossed the road and stopped at the bottom of the five steps leading up to the door of Silverdawn's apartment building.

She pulled back as he made to climb them with her. "I will be fine from here."

"I will take you to your door."

"I have walked home alone for three years. I know the way to my apartment, I assure you."

Faren reached out and ran a knuckle lightly down her cheek.

A warm tingling spread along her jawbone and up into her hairline. Her resolve weakened, and she felt helpless to resist the compulsion. "If you wish," she replied softly, uttering the words before she could think.

"I wish."

He removed his hand.

How did he do that?

****

The second floor was dim and narrow, with one bare globe burning fitfully halfway down the hallway. Faren watched Silverdawn fish her key from the small satchel she carried and fit it into the faded, bottle-green door's tarnished lock. She paused, a frown marring her brow.

"Something wrong?" he asked.

"The door is open. I could have sworn I locked it."

He shifted her aside, deftly loosened the belt on his coat, and drew the dagger strapped to his side.

"What the—" she began.

"Hush!" He silenced her with a frown and reached behind to stay her with his hand, and she stepped back.

Faren pushed the door open cautiously and peered around the edge into the darkness. Not a sound emanated from the blackness within. Yet the distinctly pungent odor of freshly dug earth hung thick in the air, imprinting itself on his senses.

He pulled back. "The light switch," he murmured. "Where is it?"

"Around the corner, halfway up."

"Wait here."

He flicked on the light and stepped into the room, holding his dagger and body in readiness. Nothing stirred. He moved farther into the apartment to explore the tiny kitchen and study and then beckoned her to enter.

Hesitantly, she peered around the door, then stepped more boldly into the room. The kitten made a tiny hissing sound, leaped from her jacket, and scuttled down the hall of her apartment.

"Now see what you have done!"

Faren raised a dark brow.

"Look, I don't know what is going on here, but it appears there's no one here but you and me. Therefore, I would like you to take that *thing*"—Silverdawn emphasized her words by pointing to the ten-inch, black-hilted dagger in his hand—"and disappear."

"Sorry, Doctor, I cannot do that," he answered, his voice even. "Now, could you see if any of your possessions are missing?"

She frowned and remained unmoving. "What is this about?"

Faren tucked the dagger into its scabbard and folded his arms across his chest. "Humor me."

****

She glared at him for a moment longer, then stalked into the kitchen and glanced around. As she thought—everything perfect.

After taking her headache tablet that morning, she had disposed of the empty packet, rinsed her glass, and wiped the sink. She was about to turn away when she noticed the drawer. Had she shut that drawer? She rubbed absently at the pain in the back of her neck.

Sometimes she found it so hard to think, and the man standing behind her, watching her, wasn't helping. The drawer was shut now, but she distinctly remembered glancing back as she hastened from the room in an effort not to be late for work. She was certain the drawer had been open. Or perhaps that had been yesterday.

She shrugged, crossed the hallway into the study, and moved around the room, examining her books and family photographs. Tears came unbidden to her eyes at the sight of her parents' smiling faces. Quickly, she turned away. How she missed them. Her mother's gentle, consoling words when Silverdawn's world was not going as planned, and the way her father had of parting with just the right words of advice at a time it was needed most.

She moved to her desk and slouched into her office chair. Seeing Faren watching her from the doorway, she straightened. Her papers were all in order. Her pens were all in their holder. *Pens in their...holder?*

She frowned and took her favorite pen from the terra-cotta jar, noting as she did so a faint smear of brown across her blotting mat. She rubbed at the stain absently with her finger.

"Something wrong?"

Silverdawn jumped at Faren's words. He had moved across the room to stand behind her without her knowledge. "This mark. I don't remember it being here. And this pen. I always leave it on my desk."

****

Faren did not have to look closer to know the origin of the stain. He had seen the signs many times. The small traces of dirt and the telltale stink of a freshly dug grave. This was Iraj's work. "Get your things. We are leaving."

"Don't be ridiculous. I'll call the police." Silverdawn reached for her satchel, searched around, and drew out a business card.

Looking over her shoulder, Faren noted it held the name of a police inspector. "*Your* police cannot help you in *this* matter."

"What matter? As far as I can see, nothing has been taken, nothing has been trashed, and I am still in one piece," she said, spreading her arms wide.

"This is not debatable. I said get your things."

"Look, I don't know who you are, but this isn't funny anymore."

"I am not trying to be funny. Please, you must trust me. Time is of the essence. I only wish to help you. You must understand that." He hated using his powers on her, but he had no choice. He had promised her father to keep her safe. He reached out and touched her arm.

She nodded and pulled away. Without a word, she moved from the study and crossed the hall into her bedroom. He followed. The smell of wet earth was even more pungent than before, and he watched her wrinkle her nose as she pulled a suitcase from beneath her bed.

"The kitten is under the bed," she murmured, standing. "I'll see to him when I finish packing."

He nodded in response.

"I suppose I'll have to spend the night at some dreary motel." She groaned, looking around her room. "I'm already homesick." She gave a small smile. "This is the only room in the apartment that I allowed my imagination free rein."

He took his gaze from her and glanced around. A large four-poster bed hung with ultramarine satin dominated the center of the floor. It seemed she had a passion for heavy antique furniture. It cluttered the room, and tapestries lined the walls.

He froze.

She swung around as he crossed the carpeted floor to inspect her work. "What is it?"

He pointed to one of the hangings. "Where did you get these tapestries?"

She frowned. "I made them. Why?"

"And…this place. Where is it? It appears…familiar."

Familiar! Faren's mind fairly screamed. He had left the location only yesterday.

Here was Baltimore Castle depicted in all its glory, including its bedraggled pennants. Another tapestry showed a black knight—*him*—with a cape tossed around his shoulders, visor down, and a golden medallion hanging casually from his neck. The knight was mounted on a big black warhorse. She had even captured the wicked twinkle in Nagor's eye.

Faren tightened his lips as he stared at her other works—Deharna's Temple, the castle in Malaan where Silverdawn's mother resided, rivers, bridges, mountains, all surrounding Rastehm. The queen would be proud. The princess sewed a fine tapestry indeed. But his mind spun with unanswered questions. How could she have known of these places? How could she have remembered such fine details? She had only been a babe when she had been banished and brought forward to the Third

Dawning. Something was horribly wrong here.

"You never answered my question," he said, swinging to pin her with his gaze. "Where is this place? And," he asked with a short mirthless laugh, "who is your black knight?"

She studied his countenance. Her eyes were such a brilliant piercing green in her pale, beautiful face. A tingle of fear played down his back. It was as if, for that fleeting moment, she peered into the far reaches of his soul. As if she had the power of coercion herself.

"I thought, Mr. Malaan," she answered coolly with a raised brow, "you might be able to tell *me* that."

He returned her stare, keeping his expression neutral. How much did she know? Had she recognized him from last night, or was she guessing? "I do not know what you mean, Doctor. But I do believe you were packing."

****

Silverdawn noted that dark brow of his come into play. He had just the right way of looking at her and speaking to her that made her feel like a thirteen-year-old schoolgirl. She stood staring into his deep, fathomless eyes, then nodded. "The kitten. Perhaps you could fetch the poor wee thing a bowl of milk from the kitchen while I crawl under the bed and gather him up?"

"The kitten can look after itself. We need to go."

"No. I didn't rescue him from the park only to abandon him to starve."

"You are a stubborn woman, Silverdawn."

"I can be."

"If I get the food, you will pack, right?"

She gave a mock salute. "Right."

He released a ragged sigh and headed for the door.

She waited until she heard him pottering in the kitchen before scooting under the bed for the kitten. Grasping the bundle of fur, she noted a small pile of dirt and a faint trail leading from the far side of the bed into the bathroom. Extracting herself and her burden from beneath the four-poster, she decided to investigate. The bathroom was dark, with only a dim light showing from the bedroom. The stink of rotting vegetation and dirt struck her as she entered the room. She flicked on the exhaust fan and light switch, and bright light flooded the bathroom.

It took only a few steps to find the source of the stench. Bile rose in her throat and coated her tongue. She sank stiffly onto the edge of the bathtub, her gaze remaining riveted in fascinated horror on the freshly dug earth and fat squirming maggots filling her washbasin. The kitten mewed and squirmed in her hands. Her fingers wouldn't function to release it from her grasp. She tried to call Faren, but a petrified squeak had replaced her voice.

He found her there when he entered the room, cursed, and threw back the shower curtain that hung behind her in the bathtub. She flinched and turned, only to be confronted by more horror. Thousands of maggots inhabited the bottom of the bath, squirming and gyrating in a mass of off-white foulness. She swung away and hunched over, hiding her face in the kitten's fur.

Faren shook her gently. "You have to move."

Move? She couldn't move. She wouldn't. Her whole world was crumbling!

He peeled back one rigid finger at a time and released the squirming kitten from her steely grip. Then he knelt before her. "We must leave here. This place is no longer safe."

Not safe? This had been her only haven after her parents' death. Filled with the beautiful furniture her father had bought her and her tapestries, this was her only joy.

She nodded absently and rose.

"Don't look," Faren told her, taking her shoulders and turning her away from the bathtub.

He slid the heavy gold medallion from around his neck and held it out toward the filth in the sink and then the bath, a beam of pure-white light radiating from the golden disk. The maggots turned to white flame and then disintegrated, leaving nothing but a pile of gray ash, which he flushed down the drains. He took her arm, turned off the light, and led her from the room, closing the door behind them.

Silverdawn sat on the side of her bed. At least she could think rationally again, even if her hands did tremble like leaves in the wind. Who would dump maggots in her bathtub and sink? She peered up at Faren.

"Do not ask," he said. "It would be better if you did not know."

"Don't you think I have a right?"

"Later."

He was right. She really didn't want to know. She nodded. *When did I become such a coward?* "Fine, I'll throw a few things in the case, and we'll be off. You can drop me at a hotel." She realized how little she knew about the man standing by her bed. "You do have a car, don't you?"

He gave her another one of those raised-brow looks.

She sighed. "We'll grab a taxi."

She hurried to her great-oak wardrobe, flung open

the door, and leaped back in horror, the scream dying in her throat. A creature of death lunged toward her. Skin like sun-dried tomatoes, milky eyes, and hair that hung in gray straggles filled her vision before Faren knocked her to the side, and she landed haphazardly sprawled across the bed.

Faren's coat flared wide. His dagger flashed into his hand. With a stabbing motion, he pinned the creature's decomposing hand to the wardrobe door. A hiss emanated from slack jaws and stumps of rotted teeth. The creature from the grave wrenched free, leaving its hand pegged to the door still flaying. Maggots dripped from the remaining stump and pooled at its feet. Faren tore his knife clear of the wood and stabbed again. With speed belying the creature's appearance, it veered, ducked, and lurched toward Silverdawn. She scrambled off the edge of her bed, wrenched a gilt-backed hand mirror from her dresser, and waited in readiness.

Faren leaped and kicked, intercepting the living corpse, knocking it from its feet. He then plunged his dagger into the creature's parchment-like throat. The stink emanating from its rotting flesh was close to unbearable. Silverdawn gagged as bile rose in her throat.

Black blood and yellow pus oozed from the monster's ravaged neck. A rattle emanated from between its emaciated jaws and blackened teeth. As it thrashed its legs in the last throes of death's agonizing embrace, its eyes rolled back in its head. Finally, it lay still.

She sagged onto the side of the bed as Faren loosened his knife and wiped it clean on the creature's rotted cloak, then he rose to meet Silverdawn's gaze across the room. Concern showing clearly in his eyes.

She felt drained.

"How are you feeling?" he asked, closing the gap between them.

She could only shake her head. "What was that?" Her tone held an edge. "Who are you? Right now—tell me who you are."

"You know who I am."

"No. I don't."

"Who do you think I am?"

"I know you are not who you say you are."

"Look, this is getting us nowhere." He grasped her arm. "Come. We are leaving."

She made to pull free, but his hand locked tight around her arm. "I'm not going anywhere with you until I know who you are."

He released his grip, and she staggered back a pace.

"Very well, if that is the way of it. If you would prefer to stay here with that!" He pointed to the rapidly decomposing body on the floor as he strode toward the door.

"Wait!"

"You called?" he answered dryly as he turned.

She crossed the room. "What about my clothes?"

"I will fetch them later."

"And that...that thing. Shouldn't we call the police?"

"I will take care of it."

"I'm not leaving without my cat."

Faren expelled a heavy sigh. "I'll get the cat. You meet me at the door."

She nodded and scuttled down the hall.

Chapter Six

Todd Haversham stood, uncertain of what to do. The grandfather clock chimed midnight in the corner of Professor Waymer's study. The man had bid him enter the study, then had gone on putting the finishing touches to a paper on his desk, totally ignoring him.

Todd had an uneasy alliance with his employer. In fact, he did not really like the chap at all; however, he did owe Waymer a certain amount of respect as his employee. He wondered what was so urgent that he'd been called to the curator's home at such a late hour. He cleared his throat. "You wished to see me, Professor?"

Waymer glanced up. No emotion marred his pale face. "It is time we talked," he drawled.

Todd pushed a slender hand through his sleek fair hair. "I don't understand. Couldn't this have waited till morning?"

The professor slid open the top drawer of his desk and withdrew a large manila envelope, which he threw down in front of him.

Todd took it up and slipped five large photographs from the envelope. At first, he couldn't believe what he held in his hand. The images swimming before his eyes blurred as heat flushed his face. Anger replaced shock, and his hands closed over the photos, one by one, crushing them into balls and dropping them back onto the desk. He strode to the faded red leather couch several feet away, started to sit, then straightened and approached the desk again.

Slashing his hand across the desk, he knocked the ruined photos to the floor. "What is this filth? Some sick joke?"

The other man's eyes gleamed. "No, Haversham, I assure you this is no joking matter. They are a very good likeness, don't you think?"

"No. It may look like me, but you know as well as I that it isn't me," said Todd, each word ground out harshly. "Where did you get these? Who made them, and what do you want?"

Iraj held up his hand. "Please, one thing at a time. I would ask you to keep your voice down. My wife is a light sleeper. And I assure you they are very much you." He gave a short, mirthless laugh. "Or should I say, very much of you. Remember the New Year's Eve party held in this very house?"

"I told you when you asked me last week. I remember nothing of that night. I woke up in one of your top bedrooms with a head that felt like it was filled with lead. You drugged me!" He leaned over the desk, and his fist crashed down in front of Waymer, scattering the papers before him. "I am not gay and never have been gay! In fact, I will listen to no more of this. I am not interested in anything you say." He turned, strode for the door, and turned the handle.

"No, but your father might be interested in what I have to say."

Todd stilled and turned. "What has this to do with my father?"

"Is it not true that he has been displeased with you for some time? That you attended a drug rehabilitation center in Australia? That you were caught taking money from your father's coffers to feed your addiction?"

"That was four years ago. I was a kid. I'm clean and haven't touched that stuff since."

"Would your father believe that? Did he not threaten to disinherit you if there should be further trouble? What would he say if it were known that his son enjoyed the company of young men instead of women?"

Todd's face heated. "I am not gay! Never have been. Never will be. Not that I have anything against them, but I like women."

"You are a healthy young man, but to my knowledge, you have not kept company with a woman in the three months you have worked for me. And you must admit the photographs are convincing."

"You have been spying on me?"

Iraj gave a sly smile. "You could say that."

****

Serena stood rigid outside the doorway. She had heard voices raised in anger and come to investigate. Now she was in a quandary as to what to do. She knew by the voices Todd Haversham was in the study with her husband, but she could not comprehend what she had just overheard. Todd, a homosexual and an embezzler? Never! And what was this about photographs? What photographs? She pressed her ear to the door to gain better access to their words. The deep timbre of Todd's voice sounded from the other side. A tingling ran down her spine that she always associated with the velvet timbre of Todd's voice. But this time he was angry.

"You drugged me. You must have—and those photos have been computer enhanced. Even drugged I would not have committed *that* depravity."

"You will never prove it. My people are good. Very good."

Serena gasped, then covered her mouth, afraid she might have been heard. She straightened away from the door. She had heard enough to know that Peter was threatening Todd with blackmail. But why? It was so unlike her husband. Or was it? Did she really know Peter all that well? She had met him only four months before they had wed. And since Peter had become ill, he had grown so moody and unpredictable. It was as if he were an altogether different person than the man she married.

Lately there had been days when her husband was quite uncomfortable to be around, and she knew within herself that stress was causing her self-doubt. Even now, she hesitated to enter the study. But she knew she had to do something. In the short time since she had met him, Todd had treated her with nothing but kindness and respect. She had never met a *less* gay man in her life, and she would not allow her husband to mistreat him.

She reined in her thoughts, wondering if she were being unfaithful to Peter in her mind. However, she could not stand by and do nothing when she knew something wrong was taking place and that an innocent man would be hurt.

Also, if she were confident of anything, it was the fact that Todd Haversham was innocent. She was convinced this was not Peter's normal behavior. She was certain the pain from the cancer must be making him aggressive. How unbearable must it be to live with such agony every day?

She drew a deep breath to give her confidence, wrapped her plush, pink robe more tightly around her body, and stepped quietly into the study.

****

Iraj glanced up and ceased speaking. "Serena. What are you doing here?"

"Darling, you should have told me we had a guest. You should've had Mary awaken me."

Iraj noticed Todd's gaze softened as it rested on his wife's face. The fact could be useful. "Mr. Haversham was just leaving," he stated with a touch of impatience.

Serena pushed her unruly hair back from her eyes. "Don't be silly. I will call the maid, and she'll fetch a pot of tea."

"No. There is no need, Serena—I mean, Mrs. Waymer. As the professor said, I am leaving."

She drifted toward Todd. "I will not hear of it. On a cold night like this?" She laid a hand on his arm. "Just as I thought, you are chilled to the bone. It's ice cold outside and not much better in here."

"Serena! I said go back to bed."

She flinched, and her eyes widened at her husband's harsh tone, but when she spoke, her voice was soft, gentle. "Now, Peter—"

Iraj glided around the desk and grasped a fistful of her dark-red hair.

Todd flushed. "Let her be!"

Iraj ignored him and stared intently into his wife's face. "I said...leave...this room. Do you not understand?"

Todd took a purposeful step forward, his eyes as cold as chipped ice, his face set.

"I would not if I were you, Haversham." Iraj's gaze did not stray from Serena's frightened green eyes as his fingers tightened in her hair.

She whimpered.

"Do you understand, Serena?" His tone was icy. "You are to do as you are told."

She tried to nod and whimpered again as her hair pulled harder still.

Iraj released her and pushed her aside. "Go!"

She stumbled, and Todd caught her arm and helped her regain her balance.

"Are you all right?" Concern laced his tone.

She nodded but kept her eyes lowered.

"How touching," Iraj mocked. "Now get out, woman, before I forget we have a visitor…" He left the threat hanging.

Serena pulled silently from Todd and made for the door.

The portal closed quietly behind her with a flick of Iraj's fingers.

****

Todd stood staring at the door for a moment before speaking. "Was that totally necessary?"

Waymer's lips thinned. "The woman must learn who is master."

"I thought she was your wife."

"Enough! It is none of your affair."

"You're right. You can play your sick games with someone else. You will have my resignation in the morning." Todd turned.

"I do not think so."

He stilled. "And why is that?"

"You are quite taken with my wife." Waymer paused to gauge Todd's reaction as he swung back, but Todd grasped his shirtfront and heaved him to his tiptoes.

"You touch her—"

"Yes? And what will you do? She is my wife to do

with as I will." An evil smile lit his eyes.

Todd gave a ragged sigh and backed down. "What is it you want?" He stalked across the room and flopped onto the couch, running his fingers through his hair. "Surely, your spies have reported that my father has frozen my trust fund until I turn thirty. I have no money of my own other than what I earn at the museum."

"I do not want your money but your services."

He leaped to his feet. His fists worked at his sides. "I told you. I am not one of *those*."

"Do not be ridiculous, boy. Not that sort of services."

"Then what?"

"You do what I tell you, without question."

He folded his arms across his chest. "As easy as that? What is it you want, Professor, that it would push you to such lengths?"

"I want you to watch Dr. Peterson."

"Silverdawn?" He frowned. "Why?"

"I want to know her every movement. Whom she phones. Whom she sees. Whom she eats with, and if necessary, whom she sleeps with. She has something I want."

"Why should I do anything you ask?" He scooped the photographs from the floor, took two steps, and flung them into the fire. "There, now you have no proof," he said with satisfaction. He was about to leave when something caught his attention.

He watched the paper crinkle, turn black, burst into a blue flame, then ash. Acrid smoke poured into his eyes, and he backed up. When his vision cleared, he spied an open book beneath the ash from the photographs. By the laws of nature, the book should have burned beyond recognition; in reality, not a page was blackened.

"That is the *Legends of Rastehm*. What the hell is *that* doing here? I thought it was— You…you stole the book? But why? And why burn it? And why—"

"It will do you no good burning the photos." The professor cut in, ignoring him. "I have the negatives."

Todd grasped the fire iron and attempted to drag the book clear of the grate.

"Leave it! It is of no consequence."

"No consequence." His fist tightened on the fire iron. "It is books like this that we put years of research into finding. How can you do this?" He dropped the poker and strode to the desk, pointing. "You—"

Iraj nodded. "Yes, I stole the book."

"But why destroy it? It's priceless."

"The only page of worth is missing."

He glanced again at the flames and the way they reared back from the tome. It was the strangest thing he had ever seen, and for a moment the phenomenon took his mind from his problem. "You must allow me to save the book. There has to be something remarkable about the tome if it won't burn."

Iraj raised a hand and pointed. "Enough!"

Todd was hurtled, spread-eagled, to the ceiling. His breath knocked from his body. His arms and legs worked as if, in trying to grasp the plaster, he could hold back the power of gravity.

"You will leave the book!"

Todd closed his eyes. This had to be a dream, a nightmare. Things like this did not happen in real life. He opened his eyes again. He was still pinned to the ceiling. Peter Waymer stood below. "What sort of creature are you? Release me!"

"You are in no position to make demands, boy." With a flick of Waymer's wrist, Todd was released.

He thudded to the carpet. The air expelled in a gush from his lungs. For several minutes he lay panting, gaining his breath, then he dragged himself to his feet and lunged at Iraj across the mahogany desk. "You bastard!"

Waymer pointed, and Todd hurled across the room to slam into a walnut bookcase. As he slid to the floor, a tumbling book caught him painfully on the temple. Fire flared up from the floor, forcing him back against the bookcase.

The fire left him untouched, although he could feel the heat emanating from the flames. Sweat slicked the sides of his face.

"This is only a sample of my power, boy. I could disintegrate you where you sit, and none would find your ashes. Now, shall we do business?"

"Yes...yes! What do you want?"

Waymer leaned back into his chair, made a gesture with his head, and spat out a jumble of words. The fire died, leaving no mark. "An ancient key. Have Dr. Peterson's office bugged. I know she has it."

Todd came gingerly to his feet. "Do I get the negatives?"

"When the key is in my hand."

He dragged a cotton handkerchief from his pants pocket and mopped his brow.

"Sit." The other man motioned to an overstuffed chair by the fire.

"I would prefer to stand."

Waymer's eyes darkened.

"I can't promise I'll be successful, what with the

small amount of information you have given me."

"Then you will try harder."

He scowled, grunted, and made for the door.

"Did I say you could leave?"

He expelled a sigh and turned. "Now what?"

Iraj formed a claw shape with his hand.

Pain, powerful and excruciating, gripped Todd's insides, then ran down his legs and swept up into his chest. He dropped to the carpet with a cry, clutching at his heart. "Let me go, you bastard. I'll...do...what you want."

"I will have respect. Understand? That means you leave when I say you leave."

"Okay." Todd gasped.

Iraj lowered his hand to his lap. "Now get up and get out. I will have your report in two days."

He climbed to his feet, but as he reached the door, he threw one more glance at the fire.

"Forget the book. For you, it does not exist."

He nodded and strode from the room, leaving the door open in a final act of defiance.

****

Iraj curled a finger, and the heavy oak door slammed behind his assistant.

He smiled. All in all, his meeting with Haversham had gone well. The boy had been harder to convince than he had first anticipated, but he did not foresee further resistance. After all, he had Serena as an extra morsel of insurance.

He rose from his desk and moved across the room to pour a glass of ruby wine from the cut-glass decanter, then sipped slowly. The wine soothed a mellow path to his stomach, and warmth enveloped his body as he settled on the couch. He rested his head back and closed his eyes, smiling inwardly.

Whoever would have thought the worldly Todd Haversham would have an infatuation for the innocent, carping wife of Peter Waymer? What would the long-deceased curator have said about that? Or what would Haversham have done had he known the man he worked for had been responsible for the disappearance of his sister? He could still hear the music of the girl's screams and the resurgence of his power as his teeth had closed over her still warm heart—as his teeth would close over Serena's when the game reached its final conclusion and the key to the pyramid rested in his hand.

Chapter Seven

The narrow, serpentine lane wound and twisted between a conglomeration of ancient buildings and modern, towering monstrosities. With no moon, all appeared gloomy and shadow filled.

As if she had not experienced enough traumas for one night, Silverdawn now found herself being dragged—soaked and exhausted—into a part of London time appeared to have forgotten. She never knew places like this still existed. The stench of rotting vegetation rose from dark corners to attack her senses, and furtive noises of nocturnal creatures haunted her at every turn. On entering the alley, she made sure to keep one hand hooked firmly around Faren's arm.

Stumbling in the darkness, she cried out as her foot slipped into fast-flowing rainwater running down the center of the blue-stone pathway.

Faren steadied her with a firm hand. "Are you all right?" His voice came cool and low in the darkness.

She lifted her waterlogged foot from the inches-deep drain and emptied the water from her shoe. How did he see in this gloom? Was he part cat?

"Sure. Just fine," she answered dryly, slipping her shoe back on and following after him. How much farther? She would not ask again. She had already done so twice. Each time Faren's answer had been a low grunt, accompanied by a "not far." The last response had been over two hours ago.

She had been furious when he rejected her offer to hail a taxi. She refused to speak to him for at least the first fifteen minutes of their walk. She was certain that he found the whole situation amusing. As if he killed monsters every day. Did nothing faze him? She had even glimpsed him smiling after her first refusal to engage in conversation—the clouds had cleared for an instant, and she had caught the glint of his teeth in the moonlight.

Then she suggested she register at a motel they passed. Another argument ensued. He said he was taking her to stay with a friend of his. He wanted to make sure she was safe. She pointed out that she wore no coat, and it was raining. He simply removed his own coat and draped it around her shoulders.

She questioned him again on the events of that evening, but he refused to be drawn into conversation. So they'd proceeded in silence.

Now here she was in a strange part of London, at what must be two in the morning, with a man she had never met before today. What was happening to her normal, ordinary world? She sighed heavily and pressed on, trying to keep pace with Faren's long strides. All the trouble had started the day she found her parents in the garden.

She groaned and pushed a hand through her bedraggled hair, trying to block the pain and the images from tumbling through her mind and screaming for freedom. She couldn't release them. To do so she must relive those moments. And she was not prepared for that. Not yet. Would she ever be?

"This is it." Faren's low-spoken words rumbled in the darkness.

He stopped suddenly before her, and she thudded into his back.

"You could have warned me," she said, stepping around him and rubbing her nose. "How can you be certain this is the door? They all look the same in this darkness."

He grinned. "I have my ways. And I have been here many times." He gave the door three hard thumps, followed by two lighter taps.

The door swung open. In the glow of a dim light stood a wrinkled old man. He beckoned them in. His floor-length robe was of royal blue, with a tiny red dragon embroidered over the heart. A cowl was pulled forward around his weathered face, in which eyes burned as bright as polished topaz. Perhaps it was a trick of light, perhaps not. All she knew was that he wouldn't have been out of place in the days of Arthur and Merlin.

Faren followed the old man down a darkened passageway. She trailed behind them into a small room, which appeared to be a study.

The room was lined with chunky antique furniture and bookcases. She was drawn to a huge cherrywood cabinet, which—when she bent to discreetly check the tradesman's mark—dated back to the early thirteenth century. She gazed around the room in open curiosity. Two ancient sideboards held several thick white candles, whose flames danced brightly, casting ghostly shadows upon the oak-paneled walls and high-beamed ceiling.

"You must think me quite eccentric." The stranger smiled, beckoning her farther into the room. He cleared a pile of books from an overstuffed chair by the fire and offered Silverdawn the seat. "Please make yourself comfortable. Let me assure you I do have electricity, but to me candles lack the sterility of modern-day living. I enjoy the comfort of their mellow glow. It reminds me of the home from which I once hailed."

A heavy silence filled the air. Hailed? Candles? She puzzled over his words with a frown. He did appear quite elderly. She'd hazard a guess between seventy-five and eighty. Perhaps that explained his peculiar clothes and words. She supposed, once one reached a certain age, one was entitled to do as one pleased.

She removed Faren's coat and held the garment out toward him as he strode across the room to join them.

He took it from her and draped it over his arm. "Pendragon is an antiques dealer," he said, as if offering an explanation.

She lifted a brow and met his gaze. "I see," she responded, not really seeing at all. Something in this little ancient study was not quite right, but what? Who was this strange old man beside her?

"Sorry, let me introduce myself," Pendragon said, casting Faren a disapproving look. "I have often commented on Faren's lack of manners. Though I cannot fathom that lack, considering his upbringing."

Faren threw Pendragon a warning glare. "I hardly think Silverdawn would care to be bored by such tales, Pendragon."

Pendragon cleared his throat. "No, of course not." He gave a deep bow. "May I have the honor of welcoming you to the humble abode of Archimedes Pendragon, Your High—"

"Silverdawn!" Faren cut in loudly, covering the old man's words.

"You don't have to shout, lad."

"What's wrong with you, Faren?" Silverdawn

pursed her lips, glaring at him. "Goodness, you have already told Mr. Pendragon my name. I am certain he is not deaf." She gave the older man a brilliant smile. "Pendragon is an ancient and distinguished name. Have you tried to trace your origins?"

The old man's eyes twinkled with a strange light. "No, but perhaps one day."

Faren raised his gaze heavenward and released a ragged breath. "I am sure Silverdawn is tired, Pendragon. Perhaps you could see to her room?"

"Yes, yes, of course, but which room?" the old man asked, flustered. "I only have the two."

****

Faren ran a hand through his still damp hair. "Give her mine. I can sleep down here on the couch." He watched Silverdawn's gaze go to the large, overstuffed couch in the corner, the only piece not an antique.

"The elderly must have some comforts," offered Pendragon. "The furniture of the past can be most beautiful, but alas, not all was built for comfort."

She laughed shortly and agreed. "And I am tired." She squeezed a lock of fair hair between finger and thumb, and water dripped down her silken blouse onto her breast pocket.

Faren was riveted to the damp patch just above her left nipple. Desire knifed through him, and his flesh hardened, pushing painfully against the constraints of his black jeans. He hurriedly glanced away, not remembering hardening so easily or painfully with a maiden since he was fifteen. And certainly not with one who was the king's daughter. He thanked the gods for the wet coat he still held on his knee.

She had obviously noted the angle of his gaze, and

a scowl marred her face as she met his eyes when he glanced back. She folded her arms across her chest. "You were talking about bed."

His eyes locked on hers in surprise. "Bed?" he repeated.

Her brow rose. "You know? Sleep?"

He shook his head to clear his mind. How could he be so foolish? What was it about this woman that attracted him so? The soft beauty of her face? No. He'd had his fill of beautiful women. The color and texture of her hair, the way she pinned it atop her head, and the way it always seemed on the verge of toppling. What would it be like to remove the pins and spread the white gold about her alabaster shoulders? In his mind he could picture those same shoulders bared to his view, pale as porcelain, like the fine, soft texture of her cheeks. And her breasts would be of the same hue with nipples rosebud pink…

"Perhaps I can help?" Pendragon interjected.

He blinked and stared at Pendragon as if he were demented. "Help?"

"For goodness sakes, lad, keep your mind on the conversation. 'Tis not like you to be fluttering off with the faeries. Now, if the young lady would care to follow me, I will show her to her room and perhaps see to a bath. I have no maid, of course."

Silverdawn stared at Faren, who had settled comfortably into a chair by the fire, his legs thrown out before him. "A maid?"

Faren met her gaze. "He can be a bit eccentric. But he has a good heart."

She nodded. "What about work in the morning?"

"It is Saturday," he pointed out. "I will go in for a

short time and arrange for someone to take over for me. You are not expected, are you?"

"No, but I really should be there, considering the burglary and all, but I don't feel up to it. I'll ring Todd in the morning and ask if he can help Martha finish cleaning up. I can trust him to see matters attended to properly."

"Todd?"

"A friend."

He raised a brow. "What sort of friend?"

"The right sort," she countered over her shoulder, slipping from the room.

His voice followed her. "At the top of the stairs, first door to the right."

****

Silverdawn stood at the center of the bedroom. She had found the room on her own, guided by Faren's hasty directions. Of Pendragon, no sign, but she could see where he had been. The coverlet on the four-poster was turned back, and the mountain of pillows plumped. Just like the man who apparently slept in it, the bed was huge and dominated the room. Although not much in the way of personal belongings, Faren's presence screamed out from every corner.

Tranquil scenes of luscious countryside counterpointed with torturous battles were depicted in tapestries hung about the walls. On the wall opposite the bed, a wall hanging of a shaggy black warhorse with mischievous eyes covered ceiling to floor. She had seen that horse before in her own visions. But even more unsettling was the suit of armor laid out on a table in the corner, partially covered by an ebony cloak. It very much resembled the armor the warrior in the park had worn when protecting her from the lion and the griffin.

However, as tempted as she was to make a closer inspection of the armor, she turned away. This was not her house, and the less she knew about its strange occupants the better. Tomorrow she would go back to her own apartment and hopefully would only have to see Mr. Malaan at work.

Purposefully, she strode over to the dark wooden dresser, removed the pins from her bedraggled hairstyle, and shook her head gingerly, allowing her damp hair to tumble down around her shoulders. Her head pounded like an ancient drum. Pressure built in her skull that needed to be released.

Where was this whole sorry mess leading—her parents' deaths, the attack in the park, Faren's appearance, the break-in, and the creature in her apartment?

She had always been fond of history, but tonight she seemed to be living it. Between Pendragon's candles and this room with its ancient aura—nothing was as it should be.

Noting an open door across the room, she entered to find a scented bubble bath, still steaming. Even the bathtub was antique, except for the modification of hot and cold fixtures.

She didn't know how Pendragon had achieved the feat of the bath so quickly, but she was grateful. A hurried crossing of London in the dead of night—on foot and in the rain—had a way of revealing those not-so-used muscles. She slipped her shoes from her feet and loosened the top button of her blouse, then another. A knock sounded at the bedroom door.

She grasped the gaping edges of her blouse together with one hand and hastened to open the door.

Faren filled the doorway, dark and brooding. Not an emotion flickered across his swarthy face. A fleeting thought that he would be a great asset to Hollywood gave Silverdawn an inward smile. He could certainly fill the role of the dark, smoldering hero Heathcliff to perfection.

"Yes?" The word came from her throat in a croak. She coughed to cover her embarrassment.

His gaze was deep and probing. It was as if he were stripping away every layer within her mind. He tucked something white into the waistband of his jeans and reached for her shoulders. He slipped his hands beneath her hair and drew her toward him.

"What?" she asked quietly.

"Hush." He put a finger to her lips, then moved his hand back to her shoulder. She was afraid yet accepting and closed her eyes to his touch, breathing deeply to cover her nervousness.

Slowly, his hands worked her flesh, soothing the tired, aching muscles of her shoulders and neck. The tension in her skull drained away, the rhythm of his hands releasing the pain with his firm but gentle touch.

The scent of his body cushioned her in a warm sensation of citrus, sunny skies, and renewed hope of happy days. She opened her eyes, and he was still watching her. A heavy languor like nothing she had felt before traveled through her body, and a tingling sensation started at the tips of her breasts and flowed down to the junction of her thighs, then out to the ends of her toes.

She felt drawn to this strange beautiful man and willed herself not to submit to his unfathomable, hypnotic allure. She straightened and pulled away.

"Thank you. How did you know?"

"It was in your eyes—the pain."

She smiled weakly. "I thank you again—my headache is gone. But you came here for a reason. You wanted something?"

****

Faren restrained himself from laughing out loud. Oh yes, he wanted something all right. He wanted to appease the ache in his loins. He wanted to sweep her into his arms, toss her onto his bed, and cover her body in one easy movement. He wanted his heat against her heat. His flesh buried within her flesh. His lips sliding over her skin, driving her insane with longing only for him.

But he knew it could not be. She was the king's only child, and although he was the king's First Knight, he would not disgrace a princess of Rastehm and the daughter of the man who had been the closest he'd had to a father for the past fifteen years.

His gaze feasted on her. She was so much like her mother—same white-gold hair, startling green eyes, tip-tilted nose, and full lips. He had caught only two glimpses of the queen in his lifetime, but what he saw left a lasting impression. No wonder the king had never put her aside and still lived in hope of reconciliation.

Silverdawn laid a hand on Faren's arm. The touch broke him from his reverie. He drew a ragged breath and straightened, pulling a bundle of white cloth from the waistband of his jeans. "Pendragon sent this. He thought you might like it." He shook out what appeared to be a nightgown. "Sorry. It is a bit creased."

Her eyes widened. "It is beautiful." The nightgown was of linen inlaid with lace. "This seems very old and delicate. It's exquisite. I am almost too afraid to wear it, but I will." She smiled. "Can you tell Pendragon thank you? I will return it in the morning."

"He wishes you to keep it."

"But I couldn't..."

He gave a brief smile and touched a finger to the tip of her nose. "Yes, you could, Princess. It would please him a great deal. He has no family in this country and has never had a daughter. It would wound him deeply should you return his gift."

She nodded. "Tell him I am most grateful."

"I shall, and I bid you good night," said Faren, but he made no move to leave. Instead, his gaze strayed to the four-poster in the center of the room. A slight smile played on his lips. "And if you should be too lonely in that big bed..."

"I know where to find you," she finished dryly. "Good night, Mr. Malaan." She closed the door slowly in his face, and he heard her curse softly as he laughed.

****

A woman sat at an oakwood dresser, brushing white-gold hair that reached to the middle of her back. The room was lit by a single candle that cast dancing shadows into every corner and made it impossible for Silverdawn to pick out the woman's reflection in the mirror. Though she wore a voluminous linen nightgown buttoned to the throat, Silverdawn could see she was slim. Her hands seemed almost too delicate to hold the gold-backed brush she dragged methodically through her hair.

She was humming a song that sounded sad yet vaguely familiar.

A knock sounded, and an elderly woman entered the room. She wore a staid, bottle-green gown and carried a bunch of keys, scissors, and a small coin pouch on a girdle at her waist. Her face was chubby, and although her hair was dragged back in a severe chignon, she had a kind twinkle in her brown eyes.

"Here, my lady, allow me. I can do the chore more quickly. Your husband, the king, just rode in. He demands to see you." The elderly woman took the brush gently from the younger woman's hand. "Will you not see him, just for a moment?"

The woman at the dresser shook her head and slowly turned. If Silverdawn could have cried out, she would have. The face held a likeness to her own. The woman's skin appeared translucent and would have been perfect, except for the tiny lines spidering from the corners of her forest-green eyes, belying the first impression of youthfulness and putting her age in her early forties.

"He knows my answer," said the queen. "Why does he come?"

"For the same reason he has come here every other month for the last twenty-four years. Because he loves you and hopes you will forgive him."

The queen came to her feet. "Never will I forgive that man. He stole my only child from me and gave her to strangers to raise."

"He did it for the good of Rastehm. He could not let it be said that he treated his child any differently than the children of the people. I also lost a son to the banishment."

The queen touched her hand to the woman's arm. "Please, Antoinet, forgive me. I forget myself in my anger. I know you, too, were hurt."

The lady-in-waiting took the queen gently by the arm and led her back to her stool where she continued to brush her hair. *"Hush, my lady, of course you are forgiven. My Marcas was old enough to look after himself anyways, being a lad of seventeen summers. I am sure he now enjoys a fine living in the future world. Perhaps he even has his own cottage or a farm. He always said he would like a small farm one day. But what I do not understand, if I may be so bold, is why you never bore another child."*

The queen stared into the mirror straight ahead, unshed tears glistening in her eyes. "Two children were born to me that night, Antoinet. One dead. One, the daughter of my heart. What if I had borne another child and that child too was born to the Magick? Would Mikkasah also have snatched that child from my breast to appease his Goddess? It was a risk I would not take, for two children sacrificed to the gods is more than any being should have to bear."

Antoinet placed the brush on the oak dresser and laid her hands on the queen's shoulders. "That it is, my lady, and I understand. But what shall I tell His Majesty?"

"Tell Mikkasah," she answered, tears trickling down her cheeks, "that the day my child stands before me once more is the day his sin shall be wiped from my mind."

The lady-in-waiting took a lace handkerchief from the girdle at her waist and dabbed at her lady's tears. "He thought that would be your answer. That is why he told me to tell you that Sir Faren has gone on a quest to bring your daughter home."

****

She awoke with a start. Faren! Her mind screamed the name. Faren—*her* Faren. Her black knight! It had to be. What was this madness? A dream? A premonition? Who was this woman with white-gold hair who wept for a lost child? And who was this daughter Faren was fetching home?

A scratching noise sounded at her door. Silverdawn glanced around. Her kitten! She crawled groggily from her bed and retrieved the small smoky-gray ball of fluff. A sand box had been placed by the bathroom door. She deposited the kitten into the box and left him happily digging.

On the end of her bed, she noted another surprise—a quilted robe. She belted the ruby dressing gown at the waist and moved to the window. She drew back a heavy brocade curtain of royal blue and blinked as early morning sunlight splashed into her eyes. Leaning over, she noted the window faced onto a narrow alley. The same alley she had traveled in the dead of night with Faren Malaan. Funny, the lane did not seem half so frightening in the morning light.

She stooped to retrieve the kitten as it brushed around her ankle. "Who brought you here, little fellow? Was it Faren? Did he go back to the apartment?" She remembered how Faren had gone in search of the kitten last evening and been unable to find him.

The kitten mewed and reached up to nuzzle her chin. She laughed. "I suppose you're right. I should ask the questions of the man himself. I need some answers, and I think it's about time he gave them. Not just about your traveling habits, but about the identity of the woman with the face like mine. And who is Mikkasah, other than the King of Rastehm?"

The kitten mewed again and reached to paw playfully at the necklace hanging about her neck.

She moved to the bed, settled the kitten in the center of the counterpane, then reached for the necklace. Unclipping the chain, she studied the piece more carefully than she had for some time. A small, silver pendant shaped like a rose. A single word inscribed at its heart. A word she had never been able to decipher.

There was something vaguely familiar about the lettering, but her tongue would not wrap around the word. The embossed rose on the pendant seemed so similar to the design on the back of the brush the woman in her dream had used to comb her hair. Silverdawn frowned and strengthened her resolve to question Faren. She closed the bedroom door behind her so that the cat did not escape, hurried down the hall and staircase, and entered the study where she'd left Faren the night before. The room stood empty, but the distinct sound of male voices floated in from a room on the left.

Silverdawn crossed the study and was about to enter what she thought must be the kitchen, when instinct told her to wait.

"There you are, lad. Ham and eggs just as you like them, crisp and soft. Didn't think I would remember, did you? Eight years is a long time."

"I see your powers are as strong as ever," Faren returned flatly.

"Oh, I know I am not supposed to use the Magick. But what harm can it do when no one is about? I am getting old, and the elderly must have some comforts. They are only minor spells after all," Pendragon defended.

"You, old?" Faren scoffed. "You will never be old. What are you now, six—seven thousand? To one such as you, that is but a drop in the ocean, to quote a modern phrase."

Silverdawn stifled a gasp. Six or seven thousand what? Years? How could that be? But her question was soon answered.

"Even Druid sleep cannot hold back the ravages of certain ailments on the body," Pendragon commented from the other side of the door. "My arthritis has been excruciating of late."

"I thought you had a potion for that."

"I have tried bogbean, as well as ginger and wintergreen, but neither seem to eliminate the pain completely."

"Perhaps one of the modern remedies."

"What, and poison my body with their chemicals? No, thank you. I'd rather suffer than fill my body with those unnatural substances."

Silverdawn straightened, yet still she didn't enter. She knew she should announce herself; however, the conversation was far too interesting. She leaned in again.

"Have you told her yet?" Pendragon asked.

"No." Faren seemed to hesitate. "Do you think it could be possible that she has some recollection of her early life? It is the strangest thing. The bedroom of her apartment is filled with tapestries."

" 'Tis not unusual for a young woman to enjoy sewing, Faren."

"No, but all of the tapestries were of Rastehm. The scenery, the castle, a knight on a black horse."

"You?"

She didn't have to see to know that Faren nodded. Her intuition had told her the warrior in the park was her black knight, complete with shining sword and golden medallion. He had been no vision. He was real!

She could hold back no longer. She pushed the door wide and stepped into the kitchen. "All right. Just who *are* you two?"

The old man glanced around, and the two eggs that had been sailing through the air toward his plate dropped with a splat to the floor. "Oh."

"Oh? Is that all you can say?" She glared at the two men in turn, her hands on her hips.

Faren, who was about to fill his mouth with ham and eggs, lowered his fork and pushed aside his plate. "How much did you hear?"

"Enough to know that you are not who you say you are."

"If you wanted to join the conversation, perhaps you should have announced yourself."

"Don't make me out to be the bad guy here, Mr. Malaan."

Faren grinned. "So, I am back to being Mr. Malaan, am I?"

She threw herself down onto a kitchen chair across from Faren. "This is no laughing matter. I've been attacked by monsters, dragged across London in the dead of night through the pouring rain, lied to, and goodness knows what else. So don't you dare make me out to be the one in the wrong. I want some answers, and I want them now. Who are you? Where do you come from? And why do I see you in my visions?"

His eyes widened. "You have visions?"

"Well, sort of visions." She frowned. "More like trances, where I see strange places and people."

Faren considered her words. "The same places and people you stitch in your tapestries?"

"Yes."

Faren frowned. "Could this be possible?"

The old man shrugged. "She did have Magick as a child. After all, that is why she is here. It could have transformed into these visions when she came through the fire. Many do change after passing through the Eternal Wall."

She glanced from one man to the other, trying to grasp what they were saying. "Fire? Eternal wall? I think you've lost me."

"What do you think, Pendragon?"

"I think the child should be told."

"I am no child," she countered.

"No," Faren said, staring down at her, his eyes darkening. "You certainly are not."

Silverdawn flushed and turned away from the look in his eyes, remembering their closeness the night before—and how close she had been to succumbing to his charm.

He stared at Silverdawn as if gauging what reaction his next words might bring. Then spoke quietly. "I am a Palladian Knight. I have come to take you home."

Silverdawn drew back. She stared into eyes the color of a winter's sea. "I beg your pardon?" Faren's accent was thicker than usual this morning, but she was sure she had heard him right. *I have come to take you home.*

Faren pushed a hand through his short, black hair. "Perhaps I should start at the beginning."

She sighed and leaned back into her chair. "Perhaps you should."

"I am Faren of Malaan, Palladian Knight, in service to Mikkasah, King of Rastehm, and the Mother Goddess, Deharna."

"I think I need coffee," she said, glancing at

Pendragon for permission.

He nodded, but instead of moving away to brew the pot, he snapped his ancient fingers, and a mug of steaming coffee appeared before her on the table.

She stared down at the mug, momentarily shocked, then drawing a deep breath, took the mug between both hands, and turned back to Faren, her voice wavering. "I have traveled and studied most of the world, and I don't recall your country's location."

"No. You would not. My homeland is not known in your Third Dawning."

"Third Dawning?"

"This time in which you live."

"So, you are saying you travel through time?" Silverdawn lowered her cup to the tabletop to stop it from shaking. "Look, I don't know who put you up to this, but I think this lark has gone far enough. The thing with the maggots was disgusting, and I don't know how you did the trick with the monster in the cupboard, but…but I could tell it was fake."

"Maggots? Monsters?" Pendragon frowned at Faren. "You told me nothing of this."

"Iraj's doing. It was naught to be alarmed about. I took care of it."

Silverdawn came to her feet. "You still persist with this farce? Look, I will pretend we never met. That will be best." She strode toward the door. It slammed in her face. She rounded to see a determined look in Pendragon's eyes.

"Sorry, lass, but I cannot let you go before you listen to Faren." The old magician turned to the bench. A plate of warm blueberry muffins appeared in his hand. He placed them in the center of the table.

"Now sit," said Faren, "and this time listen with your heart, not your head."

Silverdawn crossed her arms over her chest and flopped back down at the table, leaving the muffins untouched, although their aroma tempted her. "How do I know you two aren't criminals and this is some elaborate kidnap plan? That you don't plan to slit my throat and dump my body?"

"Who would pay your ransom? As far as I know, you have no living family left in this world."

She winced, a lump akin to a boulder catching in her throat. She picked up her coffee and sipped, eyeing Faren nervously over the rim.

****

"And if I were going to ravish you or murder you, I could have done so any time last night, as well as slit your skinny throat."

Faren watched Silverdawn's throat as she worked to swallow her coffee. His nose wrinkled in dislike. Coffee—a foul-tasting beverage he had first sampled when he visited this world in the sixteenth century on an assignment. He still could not palate the brew. "Now will you listen?"

She nodded and lowered her cup, and he relaxed back into his chair.

"I am here for three reasons. To save your world, to find my brother, Kalden, and to take you back to Rastehm. And to tell you the truth, it is nothing to me if I fail in the third task."

She cringed at his harsh tone. "I see."

"I ask you to forget everything you have been taught about Magick and open your mind to the truth."

"I will do my best." She sighed.

He nodded and folded his arms across his chest. "That is all I ask."

He told her how Iraj had attempted to conquer his world. How Mikkasah had bargained with Deharna, and how the king had defeated Iraj's minions with the crystal pyramid.

"Iraj escaped by harnessing the power of the crystal before it swept him to its heart and was cast thousands of years into the future. It is feared he tracks the pyramid, trying to regain his army of darkness." Faren ran a hand through his hair. "Iraj's interference produced an imbalance in the pyramid, which caused it to become unstable, fluttering in and out of different time frames, but never returning to its own. Our oracle has pinpointed the crystal to this year of the Third Dawning. However, that is not all. The pyramid is cracked, and something in this world has caused the rift."

"Do you know where the pyramid lies?"

"In the country we call Rastehm—*your* France."

Silverdawn's eyes widened, and she leaned forward on her elbow. "Rastehm was in France?"

"Rastehm *is* France."

"Then why are there no records?"

"We dwell in what you would call a different dimension, or the Otherworld. The veil between the Otherworld and your world is gossamer thin, and at times it is possible for some to travel between these worlds, but we have been careful never to allow our history to cross into yours."

She thought of the book but allowed the question to rest. Perhaps Faren was not aware of the book's existence. "There was an earthquake in France about a month ago. Perhaps the quake caused the crack. Tremors were felt for hundreds of miles."

"You may be right. It is said that when the pyramid shifts course through history, land upheavals and tidal waves are known to happen, along with other strange occurrences—animals aborting, frightening winds, ice caps melting, seas rising, electrical storms, erupting volcanoes, and more."

"I remember hearing news of strange events the day of the quake."

"That confirms it, then. The pyramid is where our oracle has foreseen."

Silverdawn glanced at Pendragon, who was leaning against the kitchen bench. "Didn't you hear of the quake?"

"I try not to get too caught up in the events of this world," the old man said. "I have enough with my little business to keep me busy. For that reason, I keep no television or radio."

Faren grimaced. "I admit to being as guilty. I have no interest in this world. It is not to my liking. It is far too fast and far too noisy. As I stated, I am on a mission entrusted to me by my king. Clearly and plainly."

"I'm sorry, but you will have to change your plans relating to me. I am not going anywhere. I have worked too long and hard to get to the position I now hold at the museum. Do you think I would throw that away on people I don't even know and a story I only half believe?"

He sighed, dug his hand into the back pocket of his black jeans, and removed a crumpled page of parchment. He smoothed out the paper and placed it on the table in front of Silverdawn. "Read this."

Her expression darkened. "I could have you arrested

for this. Do you know the penalty for stealing from a museum? This page is from the Rastehm legends."

"It was not necessary to steal the book to remove one page. Nor did I ransack your office, if that is your next question. But I believe the person responsible was after this page. It contains knowledge that could be dangerous in the wrong hands."

****

She stared at him for a moment longer, then fixed her gaze on the parchment. The words took her a few moments to translate in her mind, then slowly she began to read aloud.

Mikkasah had a daughter who, by an act of fate or the playful gods, had been born to the Magick. With a heavy heart, the King of Rastehm was forced through his promise to the Goddess to send her from his side. Henceforth, he took her to a place where he thought she would be safe and well-loved.

With the help of the Goddess, his daughter was transported two thousand years into the Third Dawning. The only reminders of the past to go with her—a silver, flower-shaped necklace from her mother and the key to the Crystal Pyramid of Rastehm.

Mikkasah sent the key to a place where he thought there would be none who could unlock its power.

Silverdawn finished reading and lowered the parchment. She reached for her necklace for the second time that morning, but this time with a sense of ownership she had never experienced before. This time she knew it belonged. "So it is true? The visions were real. The places. The people. Mikkasah is really my father?"

He acknowledged her words with a nod.

"I see now why you didn't want to tell me. Why my parents kept it from me—I should say my adoptive parents. I knew I was illegally adopted…but from a time that people don't remember? A time never mentioned in the history books?"

"You are the Princess of Rastehm, daughter to Mikkasah and Aurelia."

"Aurelia," she whispered, testing the word on her tongue. "My mother's name. It is lovely."

"As is the woman herself."

"The fairest maiden in all of Rastehm she was when the king won her heart," ventured Pendragon, stopping his tidying of the table to study her. "So much like yourself, I could be looking at her twin."

"I've had visions since I was young. I would go into trances. I would see things. Castles, people, a world different from mine—strangely enchanting. There was a man with steel-gray hair. In the beginning he was young; then the years passed. The last time I saw him was two years ago—he had a thick beard. You think he was my father?"

Faren nodded. "He now sports a beard, yes."

"Doctors conducted all sorts of tests with wires and screens. Finally, they told my parents I had a form of epilepsy. However, they couldn't explain away the visions—the things I would see. In the end the doctors decided I was making up stories to fill the void of being an only child. I tried to tell them I had no void, I was happy, but adults have a way of not listening when they don't want to hear what a child would say. I realized the visions were best kept to myself. My parents seemed stressed whenever I spoke of them, but for a long time there was something in my mother's eyes. It was almost as if she were afraid I would start up again." She paused for a moment, staring into her empty coffee cup. "My real mother, she has hair the same as mine, doesn't she? And green eyes."

Faren rose and stood behind her. He lifted a lock of hair from her shoulder and allowed its silken threads to glide through his fingers. "White gold," he murmured.

Silverdawn drew back from his touch.

****

He gave an inner smile. He was not offended. He knew she had much on her mind. Suddenly, the silver chain of her necklace caught his attention. He lifted the chain from the back of her neck and ran his hand around to the front to view the locket.

She attempted to pull away, but he restrained her.

"No, wait, be still." He leaned forward so that his cheek brushed hers. "Silverdawn?"

"That is my name." Her words came on a breath.

"That is also the inscription on your locket."

"You mean—" She spun to face him. "My adopted parents must have known what the inscription read all along. That was why they called me Silverdawn. I can't believe they lied to me. They told me they didn't recognize the language."

Faren straightened. "To protect you, yes. And to protect themselves. What do you think people would have said had you started bandying about tales of another dimension, a hidden place in time? They would have thought you mad."

"And as I grew older, and years passed?"

"They probably found it easier not to tell you."

Silverdawn remained silent. When she spoke again, her words were slow and evenly spaced. "I think they

101

were going to tell me that day…the day… Do you think my visions are a result of the Magick I carried? Why I was banished?"

Faren shook his head. "No. As Pendragon explained, the Magick can transform or dilute. Some lose the power altogether when they step through the Eternal Wall. Not so Pendragon, I am afraid." He raised a brow and glanced to the old man, wrist deep in a sink full of dishes. Pendragon cast him a guilty look.

"The Eternal Wall?" asked Silverdawn. "You mentioned that earlier."

"A wall of cleansing fire through which the banished must walk into another time."

"A time portal?"

Faren shrugged. "If you like."

"And these banished. Who are they, and why were they exiled?"

"They possess the Magick. It is forbidden."

The crash of porcelain hitting tiles resounded around the kitchen. Silverdawn looked around. Pendragon bent over the pitcher that had held the juice. Tiny pieces of porcelain littered the ground at his feet.

He smiled weakly and shrugged. "I beg your forgiveness, my lady."

"You don't need to call me that, Pendragon."

"Oh, but I do. You are the princess."

Silverdawn rose to help the old man with the task of cleaning up. "Then let the title only be in private."

"If you wish, my lady, and I would not have you help me. 'Tis unfitting. Go on with your conversation. I will see to this mess."

"If you're sure."

"I am sure. And please call me Pen. Faren does."

****

Silverdawn sank back into her chair and helped herself to one of Pen's blueberry muffins. The cakes had been sitting on the table for some time; nevertheless, they were still warm. She wondered fleetingly how this could be, then let the thought filter away. "You were telling me of the banishment, Faren."

He met her gaze. "You have read our history. *Legends of Rastehm.* You know our world was almost destroyed by Magick. 'Tis not our way to question the ways of the Goddess. She did what she had to do to save the people and keep us safe."

"I see." She frowned. "But I have another question. How could a book from your world come to be here in *my* time?"

"Guilty." Pendragon approached the table and took a seat. He reached for a muffin and bit into it, smacked his lips appreciatively, then went on. "As others did, I brought with me possessions from my home in Rastehm. I had written the book; I saw no harm in taking a reminder of my former life."

"You wrote the book?"

He nodded and grinned. "Quite brilliant, is it not?"

She smiled. "Quite. But how did it come to be in the museum's possession?"

Pendragon contemplated his next words. " 'Twas the twenty-sixth anniversary of my banishment. Did you know I was banished the day you were born?"

She shook her head. "No. Then how did you know to write the last page?"

"I had been in my shop three years when your foster father came to see me and told me of your arrival and the events leading up to it. But that is another story.

"I was feeling especially maudlin that day. The same day the book disappeared. I was careless; I left the tome sitting on the counter in the shop. I had been reading it when five youths entered. They distracted me by calling me to the back of the store to ask about two swords. I realized later it was merely a ploy. While I was speaking, three of the boys began to wander toward the front counter. For a moment only, I looked away. The boys left, and when I returned to the counter, I found my book missing, along with two bejeweled knives that had been on display in the front window. I hastened to follow, but they were fast and had long vanished around the corner."

She patted the old man's hand. "You called the police?"

Pendragon shook his head. "I thought it was best to let the situation be rather than have the police ask a lot of awkward questions. That was the last time I saw the book."

She ran a distracted hand through her hair. "I'm sorry, Pen. If the book was still in my possession, I would see it returned."

"No matter," Pendragon replied quietly. "But how did you come by it in any case?"

"It was left to the museum in an old man's will. That's all I know."

Pen smiled sadly and climbed to his feet to resume his cleaning. As she followed his movements, she noted a jug—the exact replica of the one that had been on the floor broken—sitting on the sideboard.

Faren followed her gaze and glared at Pendragon. "It might be best if we continued this conversation in the study." He rose, took her arm, and led the way into the adjoining room. He waited for her to settle into an armchair before the fire. "Any more questions?"

She stretched out her toes to the warmth of the flames. "Quite a few actually."

He grinned. "As I would expect." He settled into an armchair opposite her. "Therefore, I am at your disposal, my lady."

"For a start you can stop calling me my lady. Silverdawn will do nicely." She smiled shyly.

He nodded. "As you wish."

She frowned, wondering if he were teasing. However, there was no glint in his eye to suggest he was anything but serious. "This goddess," she asked, "does she really exist in person?"

"The Goddess Deharna returns to our world on the first day of Imbolc every year and brings with her the new snow."

"Imbolc? On the Christian calendar, that means Candlemas, the Purification of the Blessed Virgin. Is she the same goddess mentioned in Celtic mythology? The Maiden, the Mother, and the Crone."

Faren shrugged. "I believe so. Many of the banished traveled to that period in your history. Perhaps they carried with them their belief in the Goddess."

"Weren't they bitter for being banished?"

Faren leaned forward, folding his hands before him. "Banishment is not a punishment, but a precaution should the evil manifest itself from the Magick and be reborn. Those banished can take with them what wealth they accumulated in our world. They do not go empty-handed. That is the reason why Pen opened his store. To help those coming through to find a market for their goods."

"Hence all his antiques," Silverdawn remarked.

"How sad it must be to leave all you know and love and travel into a strange world. Then have to sell most of what you still own in order to start a new life."

"I agree it must be frightening. There are those who, even after all these years, still fight against the banishment of their loved ones. And those who, when sent to the future, use their power too obviously and must be cautioned. Like some of the magicians you see on stage and on your television."

"You mean some of those guys are real? They aren't just using fancy illusions?"

Faren nodded gravely. "Consequently, the knights of the Goddess."

"The Palladians? So you are a type of police force, come to put people in their place?"

Faren rose and folded his arms across his chest. His back was to the fire. "*You* might see it like that," he answered stiffly, looking down at her.

She stood, measuring to his chin in her bare feet, and laid her hand on his arm. His flesh was strong and unyielding beneath her touch. "You think I am criticizing you? Never think that. I admire you; I have never met anyone quite like you. I was just trying to put matters into perspective."

Faren looked down at her for a moment more in silence, then took her hands in his own larger ones. "Of course. I am sorry I was offended so easily. Your head must be swimming with all this talk of Magick and kings and banishments. But one more thing—do you have the key? The small crystal pyramid you had in your office?"

"You mean *that* is the key? I have had it all these years and didn't know what I held?" She released a heavy breath. "I could have lost it or thrown it away."

"Not so," countered Pendragon, stepping into the room. "Your father had me place a protective glamor on the pyramid key before I was banished. The key would have always found its way back to you had it been discarded, stolen, or lost. For it is more than a key to mending the pyramid. If the creatures within should find a way to escape, it might be the end of the world as you know it. Not even your nuclear bombs can kill an unending army of the dead, wraiths, and demons who rejoice in slicing your still beating heart from your tortured body and eating it while your flesh grows cold."

The icy hand of fear prickled Silverdawn's nape. "So what do we do now?"

"We find the pyramid," Faren and Pendragon said in unison.

Chapter Eight

Todd raised his hands as he stepped into Iraj's office. "Before you say anything, I know I haven't made a report, but I don't know where she is. She called me three days ago and asked if I would finish cleaning up the mess in her office. She said she was ill and was staying with a friend. That is all I know."

Iraj leaned back into his office chair and regarded the young man before him. He decided to be lenient. Everything was going as planned. "I know. She called me." He pointed to a chair by the hearth. "Sit."

Todd took a seat on the edge of a padded chair. "You know where she is?"

"No. But she asked for a leave of absence to join a dig in France. She said a friend of hers—a Dr. Emile Rousseau of our Paris branch—has unearthed an ancient Celtic warrior. The full skeletal remains of man and horse."

"I remember reading about it in last month's journal. But how on earth am I going to keep tabs on her now?"

Iraj rose and hobbled to the window to stare out onto the street. He rubbed absently at his aching thigh as he spoke. "I suggested she allow the museum to pay for her expenses, and that she speak to her friend about the museum acquiring the spoils of the dig. I told her I would be sending you along to photograph any worthwhile artifacts. I read in your file that you are quite an accomplished photographer."

Todd's face darkened. "As are you, Professor."

"If everything works out as planned, you shall soon have your negatives. Do not go sour on me now, boy."

"As long as you keep your bargain. How is Serena? I mean Mrs. Waymer."

"My wife is none of your concern."

Todd came to his feet. "She *will* be my concern if you harm her. She is a lovely woman. I won't see her hurt."

"Nothing nasty will befall Serena as long as you keep your part of the bargain. And I do not like threats, Haversham. You wish for a repeat of our last meeting?"

The young man took a step backward and turned to stare into the fire, his fists clenched within his pockets.

"No. I did not think so." Iraj limped back to his desk to retrieve a handful of papers. "You are to leave for France tomorrow morning. I told Dr. Peterson I would book the accommodation. Here, take these." He held out his hand.

Todd accepted the tickets and papers and pushed them into the pocket of his gray suit pants.

"You are to take the channel tunnel train; you can be there in three hours. Go to the Paris office and pick up a four-wheel drive. Drive to Besancon at the foot of the Jura Mountains where I have booked a room in a small hotel in your name. Ring me at ten tomorrow night with a report."

Todd nodded and, without another word, left the room. The butler saw to his exit and closed the door quietly behind him.

Chapter Nine

When Faren announced they were going after the crystal pyramid, Silverdawn had protested loud and long. She didn't care if they found the artifact or not. She had worked hard all her life to gain the respected position she now held at the museum. She was not afraid, but she did not need the danger. Life was fragile enough. The death of her parents had taught her that lesson.

But the vision of the fair-haired woman sitting at the dresser brushing her hair beckoned—the mother she had never known.

She longed to hear her mother speak to her personally, and she had convinced herself that she would be doing a good deed for mankind. Also spending more time with the enigmatic man who had rescued her twice in three days was a bonus.

If what Pendragon and Faren told her was true, Iraj would not stop until he conquered the entire world with his army of undead. She could do nothing more than go along to help.

So she had put her kitten into a cat kennel and agreed, and here she was, opening her car door and crawling from the driver's seat in central France.

At last. She drew a deep breath and stretched her legs. "We must have driven the best part of four hours."

"Five," Faren corrected from the rear of the vehicle. She joined him as he lifted the hatch.

Todd slung his backpack and camera case over his shoulder and climbed out of the car. "I'll see to our accommodation." He raised a hand and loped away toward the main entrance of the L'barrsola Hotel.

Pendragon stretched, then bent to retie his shoelace. "Good choice of town, a nice-sized place to get lost in should the need arise."

She hid a smile. She could not get used to Pen—she had decided to call him Pen as he suggested—in his baggy denim jeans, flannel shirt, short-sleeved padded vest, and hiking boots. He had worn his long robes the night she met him and continued to do so even in his shop. He'd said it helped create the atmosphere, and his customers had come to expect from him a certain amount of eccentricity.

"It was Professor Waymer who booked the accommodation, Pen, because of the darkroom it provides for its guests. Do you think Iraj will follow us?" Silverdawn asked, glancing around the small car park.

Faren dragged one of her suitcases from the back of the rover and slung his own canvas backpack, which she'd insisted he buy, over his shoulder. "I would say there was a good chance of either he or one of his spies showing up, once he finds you have left London."

"How could he know?"

Pen came up alongside them. "You forget we are dealing with a master necromancer."

"As you have told me, but what exactly does a master necromancer do?"

Faren gave Pendragon a warning look and shook his head. He finished unloading the hand luggage and locked the hatch. "That, Princess, is something I hope you never find out." He took her arm and led her up the cobblestone path toward an attractive old building surrounded by a country garden of roses, hollyhocks, and a variety of tiny daisies.

****

Silverdawn stood in the center of her room and kicked off her shoes. Wriggling her toes into the deep carpet pile, she cast a glance around her room at the heavy dark wardrobe, a Louis XV dresser, a king-sized bed, and a low, cherrywood table set between two padded chairs by the gas fireplace. A small bathroom branched to the side, and large sliding-glass doors led onto a balcony that gave a panoramic view of the waterfront.

After checking in, she had eaten with the others in the hotel's stately, wood-paneled dining room. The manager of the hotel had insisted they try the house specials, which consisted of *bouillabaisse*, a rich fish soup, followed by *cassoulet*, a stew of white beans, tomatoes, sausage, and duck. She excused herself after the meal, pleading tiredness and explaining she must prepare for her meeting with Emile Rousseau the next morning.

Todd offered to see her to her room, and they climbed the stairs to the first floor together. He had taken the room next to hers. Faren and Pendragon were sharing the suite across the hall. Todd bid her good night, and she opened her door and stepped into her room. As she did so, she remembered the conversation she'd had with Todd the night before leaving England. He'd seemed upset about the inclusion of the other two men in their traveling plans. But after she explained that Faren asked to join their excursion, as he had a special interest in ancient armor, and that Pendragon was an antique appraiser and dealer who was taking advantage of the trip to snoop out bargains for his shop, Todd had relented. He now appeared to enjoy their company as much as she did.

She picked up her suitcase, tossed it onto the bed, unlatched it, and began hanging her clothes when a knock sounded at the door. Thinking that it was Todd, who had forgotten to tell her something, she crossed the room and opened the door.

Faren was leaning against the wall with a bottle of vintage Chablis in his hand. He held up the bottle for inspection. "I thought we would go through tomorrow's details over a glass of wine."

She moved aside, noting he'd shaved. It was the first time she'd seen him without the five-o'clock shadow he habitually wore. If not for the nose that had obviously been broken at some stage, she would have thought of him as classically handsome.

She had forgotten his words already, as she was drowning in the deep-blue depths of his eyes and the perfect smile he was bestowing upon her. Had she actually seen this man smile before? Or had they always been caught up in some life-threatening situation? She had neglected to notice the whiteness of his teeth and the tiny lines at the corners of his eyes when he laughed. She smiled inwardly. Or how he made her insides feel like they were melting.

Faren frowned and touched her arm. "Are you all right?"

"I don't drink," she said, breaking from her reverie and swinging back into the room with a touch of embarrassment.

He followed, grasped her arm, and turned her to face

him. He ran a gentle knuckle down her cheek. "Just a little, perhaps? It is not good for a man to drink alone."

She offered him the semblance of a smile, settled into a chair by the fire, and popped her clear eyeglasses onto her nose. She had set them on the table between the two chairs after returning from dinner. "Just a taste, then."

He took two long-stemmed glasses from the pockets of his denim jacket and placed them on the coffee table. Slinging his jacket over the back of a chair, he then pulled the loosened cork from the bottle. He poured the wine, handed her a glass, and sank into the chair opposite, then, as if changing his mind, he leaned over and lifted her glasses gently from her nose. "I think you can discard these. I know you don't really need them."

Silverdawn looked down at her wine. "I suppose I did give myself away by walking to Pendragon's the other night without them." She glanced across at him. "I've been hiding behind them for so long it's hard to come out." She gave him a small smile. "I feel…well, exposed, I guess. Even a little frightened." She took a dainty sip and set her wineglass down.

"You are among friends. Do not forget that." He leaned over and touched her hand. "Pendragon and I will protect you with our lives."

She looked away, uncomfortable. Not knowing what to say. She was still quite intimidated by this large handsome man yet, despite herself, strangely drawn. She took a breath and faced him. "What did you wish to talk about? I have already explained we are to meet Emile at the site at six in the morning."

He leaned back into his chair. "Can a man not make an excuse to see a beautiful woman?"

She gave a small laugh. "Not you."

He laughed with her and met her gaze. "Already you know me too well. You are right. I do have an ulterior motive." He ran a hand through his short dark hair. "Has this Emile told you what to expect tomorrow?"

"I've read several articles on his find and conversed with him at length. I've viewed a replay of a television report made after the earthquake. I believe I'm up-to-date with all information concerning the site." She raised a fine brow. "Are you?"

"I have been there, yes."

She leaned forward in her chair. "Been there? How could that be? You haven't had time."

"With Pendragon's help," he replied simply.

"Pen? I don't understand."

"He is extremely old and has many powers. I thought you realized that. He was a great sorcerer in your father's court."

She released a heavy sigh. "Still, you will persist with this Magick business?"

"And still you will not believe, after all you have seen."

"What? I saw a couple of eggs fly across a room, a cup of coffee and a plate of muffins appear, nothing a sleight-of-hand magician could not do."

"And the pitcher?"

"The pitcher?" She frowned. "You mean the jug Pen broke?"

Faren nodded.

"Don't tell me he put the pitcher back together? I thought he had a duplicate," she murmured softly.

"And what of the maggots and the decomposing creature that attacked us in your apartment?"

She shrugged. "A bit harder to explain, but no trick a master of illusions could not achieve." She frowned. "Pendragon didn't conjure that thing in my room, did he?"

"No, that was the work of one of Iraj's raisings."

"Raisings?"

"He has the power to bring inanimate objects to life and raise the dead."

A shiver slid down her spine, and she sagged back into her chair. "I see."

"If you do not believe in the Magick, then how do you explain Pendragon and me?" He frowned. "And why are you here?"

She laughed shortly. "I wanted to prove to myself it *was* true. I wanted to see this crystal pyramid of yours for myself."

He leaned forward and took her hand. "And see it you will, I promise. But first we must find it."

She smiled wryly and pulled from his grasp. "How do you propose to do that? You said the pyramid was buried under several meters of earth, beneath a large standing stone. You've been to the site. You know how many different kinds of menhirs—standing stones—are in that field? They're calling the occurrence a phenomenon. Standing stones toppled, yes, but there were never that many to begin with. They seemed to have multiplied by the hundreds."

"Iraj," Faren stated dryly.

"He made the rocks appear. He can do that?"

"And more. He has brewed this Magick to buy time to search for the key."

"How could he know where the pyramid is?"

"He body hops. He has done so throughout the ages,

slipping into some unsuspecting soul's body and possessing him."

She rose, rubbing her hands together, too anxious to remain seated. Turning her back to the fire, she stared down at Faren. "What happens to the person whose body he inhabits?"

"I would say they die, but I am not certain. I am no man of medicine."

"And how do we know whose body he inhabits?"

"We don't unless he shows us through his actions. He often leaves a trail of bodies behind him. We believe he draws a portion of his power from feasting on the hearts of the innocent."

Silverdawn felt the blood drain from her face and swallowed hard as bile rose into her throat. She leaned forward and retrieved her glass with a shaking hand and took a hefty swallow. The wine warmed her all the way to her toes and helped settle her nerves. "How does Iraj know in which time to find the pyramid?"

"Our oracle has a theory that the creatures locked away in the pyramid act as a homing beacon of sorts." He shrugged. "When the pyramid changes course, Iraj knows and follows accordingly."

"What if the pyramid disappears before you find it?"

"It is due to shift again with the new dawning. By your time, one and a half months from now."

She frowned. "The end of the century and the beginning of the second millennium. New Year's Eve."

He nodded. "As to how I will find it…" He placed his empty glass on the table beside hers and pulled from beneath his shirt a chain bearing a flat golden medallion about the size of a hen's egg.

She leaned across the table to inspect the piece more

Julie A. D'Arcy

closely. "I saw this medallion in my visions. It was raining, and you flashed it at a guard at a gate. You were riding a black horse."

He paused for a moment, then nodded.

"If what you say is true, and this sorcerer knows where the pyramid is, why hasn't he claimed it?"

"He is searching for the key."

"Then why haven't I seen him?"

"Because he has never known where the key was before."

She shivered as the hair on the back of her neck stood on edge. "And he knows now."

He slumped back into his chair and gave her a bitter smile. "I believe so."

"Then why haven't you caught him and stopped him?"

"To coin one of your modern clichés, he is a man of a thousand faces. I have already told you he body hops. He could be anyone, even someone you know."

"Have you never been close?"

"There was once, in the 1930s."

"You lived in the thirties?" Her tone was incredulous. She stared at him and frowned, realizing she had just accepted Faren's explanation as the truth. More so, she was suddenly eager to learn more about this miraculous man.

"The medallion the Goddess bestows on her knights enables us to travel the world to many different places in time."

"How exciting." She paused and stared into his dark-blue eyes. "Do you get lonely?" she asked gently. "Have you family?"

He laughed shortly and ran a hand over the back of

his neck. "You know, that is the first time anyone has ever asked that. If I am lonely, that is." He smiled. "I appreciate it. And if you are asking if I am married, no, but I do have parents, whom I visit when I can, and…a younger brother."

She saw something akin to sadness flicker in his eyes but could not analyze the expression before it faded. "Go on," she urged. "Tell me more of the thirties and your sighting of Iraj."

Faren hesitated. "I have never told this story to anyone, not even the king." He paused for a moment, breathed deeply, then began to speak slowly. "As I said, it was in the thirties, 1931, to be precise.

"I had Iraj's identity. He was masquerading as a mobster during Prohibition. He had many men at his disposal; however, he grew desperate. The pyramid had shifted, and the movement made him careless. He needed a blood sacrifice in order to enhance his powers for a leap through time.

"I tracked him to an old factory in Chicago. What I found in the factory fair turned my stomach—a boy of about sixteen, strapped naked to a table. Iraj saw me and fled, but I could not move. I was riveted to the scene by a pair of pale-gray eyes so filled with pain and helplessness my heart wept.

"Iraj had placed a spell on the boy to stop him from crying out. His flesh had been peeled back from his chest, his ribs splayed, and his heart still beat, ready for Iraj's final act of depravity. I cut the cords from the boy's feet and hands, knowing I could not leave him to his pain. Knowing when it was over, Iraj would be long gone. I held the boy's head to my chest, and being aware there was no medical technology that could save him, I put my knife through his heart."

Faren cradled his head in his hands as tears formed in his eyes. "It is one thing to kill grown men in battle, another to have to take the life of a child left to rot by a madman—a creature so inhuman you could not begin to understand his depravity."

Silverdawn left her seat and knelt before him. She removed his hands from his face. "I have read the book, remember? I know what that monster is capable of. You did everything you could."

"Did I? I did not catch the boy's murderer."

"No, but you will this time."

He sighed and gathered her hands in his, bringing them to his lips. He smiled gently. "You almost have me believing you. Why is that?"

She freed her hands and brought them up to cup his face. "Because I trust in you. I know that when I am with you, I am safe."

"Are you?" He breathed. "How can you be so sure?" He leaned forward and captured her lips with his. He lowered her gently back onto the carpet, supporting himself above her. Their mouths ground together in intimate savagery. His lips left her mouth to cover her cheeks, eyelids, and throat, and then he took her mouth again in a searing kiss that sent the blood racing through her veins.

She gloried in the taste of the sweet fruity wine on his tongue. Her head swam with unfulfilled dreams and forgotten longings. Her hands went to his shirt, and she dragged it from his jeans. She splayed her fingers beneath the cloth to explore the muscled planes of his back. She felt the scars of several wounds, attesting to the fact that he was what he said he was—a warrior, battle hardened, yet gentle in her arms.

He took his mouth from hers, dragged his silk shirt over his head, then reclaimed her lips with a drugging kiss that filled her with wanting. His hands searched for the buttons on her blouse, and they seemed to melt beneath his deft touch.

Silverdawn was unable to—did not want to—stop him. It was as if she had waited for this man all her life. Was that why no other had ever seemed good enough?

He spread wide the edges of her blouse and bathed her in his admiring gaze. His fingers went to the front fastening of her bra, and she placed her hand over his, meeting his stare, silently pleading with him to take her, but also pleading for it to mean more than a night of lust. He met her look with his deep, azure eyes, and she was helpless to resist. Yet it was by choice, not from the power he was capable of wielding. She removed her hand from his, allowing his fingers to expose her breasts to his gaze, his palms whispering over her already sensitized nipples.

He lowered his head and took one rose-pink bud into his mouth, drawing on it with gentle pressure, then teasing it with his tongue. He repeated the movements with the other.

He sought her lips again, and his hands crept down over the flatness of her stomach, around her hips to clutch her buttocks in his hands and draw her intimately closer.

Silverdawn could feel his hardness straining against her—wanting her, needing her as she needed him.

He ran his lips in a butterfly trail from her breasts to the button of her jeans, then swirled his tongue around her navel.

Her hands went to his hair. She couldn't breathe.

"You know I want you," he said, raising his head. "I want your body wrapped around mine. I want to fill you until I can fill you no more. I want you as my woman."

She smiled softly in answer.

His fingers went to the fastening of her jeans, and with meticulous care he slipped the denim down her legs, leaving a trail of small kisses in his wake. He eased the last inch of fabric over her toes, then rose to rest his head in the valley of her breasts.

She pushed her hands through his coarse dark hair, then down over the hard muscle of his shoulders, feeling his unleashed power beneath her fingers. Her hands trembled as they skimmed his back, feeling the hard warmth of his flesh beneath her palms. She willed him to go on—willed him to stop.

Faren took her lips in a gentle kiss. Then he lowered his head, reverently placed a kiss on each nipple, and began to trace soft, wet kisses down to the top of her white lace panties. His hands went to the elastic sides, and he inched the scrap of lace down her legs, then nuzzled the golden curls within. She stiffened as his tongue found entry into the core of her womanhood. He lifted her legs over his shoulders and pressed his lips to her softness, sucking until she writhed with pleasure. Then he drove his tongue inside her and flicked it in and out. He tortured her with pleasure as he stroked his tongue back and forth across her cleft.

Silverdawn clenched her fists, and she forced herself not to cry out. She whimpered, tossing her head from side to side, then grasped at his shoulders, holding on.

Never had she felt anything so painfully exquisite. She had not imagined these sensations existed. Her insides clutched, as if she were being wound tighter and tighter. All thought and feeling spiraled from that one place he touched.

She rode the crest of a wave, growing higher and higher—climbing a mountain that had no summit. With a rush, her mind reeled, and her body gave way. Wave after wave of intense pleasure rippled over her skin, making her incapable of movement, making her want something or someone to ease her torment. She lay for a moment, reveling in the feeling, then she reached for Faren, but he withdrew from her touch, lowering her legs to the floor. She watched him, silent, bemused, her breath coming in short, sharp gasps. Aching for him to come to her, aching for him to fill her as no man ever had.

He rose, and in the muted light of the bed lamp and the dying embers of the fire, she watched his hands go to the fastening of his jeans. He flicked open the top button, and their eyes met. He paused, running his gaze over her body, then cursed loudly and swung toward the window, threading a hand through his hair. "I am sorry. I cannot do this." His voice came like the crack of a whip in the silence.

Her face burning with embarrassment, she reached for his raw silk shirt and pressed the dark cloth against her breasts. She sat with her knees raised, her head bowed, her hair falling forward around her face. "Was it something I did?" She turned from his gaze, unable to meet the blueness of his eyes now circumstances had changed.

****

Faren turned. Her skin was so fair, so beautiful, against the ebony of his shirt. The sight of her distressed face made his heart weep—a fair rose he had almost defiled.

"Was I too forward?" she asked in a small voice. "Is it because I allowed you to do that? I know I am probably different from the women you have known…" She left the sentence hanging.

Faren hurried to kneel before her and framed her face in his hands. He pushed her damp tousled hair back from her cheeks. "Never think that. You are perfect. It is I. I feel nothing but loathing for my own weakness. I made a promise to myself, which I have now broken. I should never have let this go so far. I am but a knight in your father's court. You are the Princess of Rastehm, perhaps one day to be queen. Your father means too much to me for me to besmirch his daughter."

"And I mean too little to you to love," she said, tears glistening in her eyes.

He wiped the tears away with his thumb, then released her and rose to move to the window. He stared into the night. Funny how the brilliance of the stars reflected none of the pain that he felt.

The sharp claw of desire clutched at his gut. He was so hard with the wanting of this woman he thought he would burst. Yet he could not bring himself to take her. As much as his mind and body screamed to do so, his head told him it would go against all his teachings as a Knight of Palladia. "I know little of love, Silverdawn. I have never had time for matters of the heart. I am but a rough soldier. I do not know if I understand what love is."

****

Silverdawn donned his shirt, which came just below her thighs, and snaked her arms about his waist. She pressed her cheek to the hard warmth of his skin. "Then, Sir Knight, I shall teach you." She felt a tremor run through his body as her breasts pressed against his back.

He stepped away, putting distance between them, and turned to face her. "Perhaps, but you are still who you are, and I am who I am."

Her heart clenched. What could she say to stop his words of rejection? Stop him from walking out of this room and never touching her again? Even the thought was too painful to contemplate. "And never the twain shall meet?" she asked softly, almost flippantly, while the knife pain in her breast twisted a little more. "What of Guinevere and Lancelot?"

"And to what end did they come?" he countered dryly. "He a monk and she a nun."

"You don't know that for certain."

He raised a dark brow. "If I could change the proof, I would, but to refute the truth is akin to holding back the waning of the moon." He gave a bow and reached for her hand, then brought it to his lips.

The gesture seemed to Silverdawn only to distance them more, slotting her neatly into her place—princess to his knight, far beyond his reach.

"You are a stubborn man, Faren Malaan."

"Good night, Princess." He rounded to stride to the door.

She found her voice as he reached for the handle. "One question."

He stopped but didn't turn.

"Does that dragon on your arm bear any significance?"

He glanced down at the red dragon that scaled his arm from elbow to shoulder, then turned, his eyes locking on hers. "All Knights of Palladia receive the dragon on the day of our investiture. It is our insignia."

"And are damsels not sacrificed to temper the dragon?"

He pulled the door wide. "Not this time, my lady, not this time." The door closed softly behind him.

Chapter Ten

A land of gods and giants, Silverdawn thought as she stared out across the sloping, rock-strewn field. Standing stones of every shape and size littered the ground. The sun was rising over the low-lying mountains, and the crisp morning air touched her cheeks as she climbed from the rover.

She spotted Emile Rousseau supervising the excavation work about fifty paces away. She called to him as she neared the edge of the site. He smiled, waved back, and grabbed up his shirt. Pulling the garment over his head, he loped toward her and her party.

"It can be hot work wielding a pick for an hour." Emile grinned, wiping a dirt-covered hand across his brow and pushing the long dark fringe from his brown eyes.

She had to smile at the brown smudge left behind. He hadn't changed since college. He never was one to be conscious of appearance. "A pick, Emile? I thought you would be a little more delicate in your methods."

"We're breaking new ground. Some of it is mighty tough work." His words carried a slight French accent. "And, as you see, we have a little problem with rocks."

She gave a short laugh. "That's a bit of an understatement, I'd say."

The ice broken, she introduced Faren, Todd, and Pen. She explained that Emile had been born in France but spent his school years in Australia, his family moving back to France after he graduated from the university.

The men shook hands, and they wandered forward to examine what the excavation had uncovered. The site was outlined with white tape. A trench twenty feet by twenty feet and approximately two-and-a-half-feet deep was being opened up. The tapes were numbered in one-foot intervals, and she knew that Emile would have cross-referenced his notebook to the markings on the tapes. Tools and tarpaulins covered in earth surrounded the fenced site. On the edge of the site lay the fully exposed skeletal remains of a warrior and his horse. The warrior was in full battle regalia, and the skeleton and armor were in perfect order.

****

Faren leaned forward to get a better a view of the skeleton. A tingling feathered along the base of his skull, then spread down his back. A violent cord tugged at his mind. What was it he must remember?

A searing pain flashed through his head, then a brilliant light before his eyes. He staggered and pressed a hand to his temples. Stepping back from the trench, he rammed his hands deep into his pockets to cover their shaking. He swallowed the bile that rose to his throat. He felt violated.

"The warrior's sword," he asked, a nervous tremor to his voice. "Where…where is it?"

He felt Silverdawn's stare but didn't turn her way.

"It's been shipped to the village museum for proper cleaning," Emile answered, seeming to sense nothing out of the ordinary. "The blade unfortunately was broken, but the hilt is still intact. Marvelous piece of work from what I could see. The hilt is made of a type of hardened metal, shaped into a serpent with roses entwined."

He staggered again, and Pendragon shot him a worried glance. Astute as always, the old man had noted something amiss.

"Have you put a date on the warrior yet?" Silverdawn went on before Faren could open his mouth to ask.

Pendragon moved to Faren's side and laid a discreet hand on his arm. "Are you all right, boy?" he asked quietly.

"A headache, nothing more." He swallowed down his nausea and listened to Emile's next words.

"No. No date as yet. Carbon tests are still to be run. But we believe somewhere in the vicinity of 500 BC."

Silverdawn ran her hand down Emile's arm. "This is fabulous, Emile. Do you think there may be more?"

"It's likely. This was found when a group of three standing stones toppled. A farmer came across the remains while he was rounding up his sheep after the storm. It's lucky he was astute enough to contact someone at the museum." He met Todd's gaze. "I believe you want to take some photos?"

The young man nodded and held up the camera he had slung over his shoulder. "The rest of my equipment is in the four-wheel drive."

"Fine," answered Emile, "just don't get too close to the workers."

Todd nodded and hurried away in the direction of the car.

Faren stared out at the rocks in the distance. "Pendragon and I would like to wander around, if that is all right. We have never been this close to this many megaliths. Do you believe there were any dolmen or *allee couverte* here before the quake?"

"Two upright stones roofed by a third, and upright stones placed in rows. Very good, Mr. Malaan. You have knowledge of megaliths?"

"Merely an amateur's knowledge." Faren winced inwardly at the lie. He had buried enough of his friends and family in such places to know them well. "The warrior's armor is more my forte," he said, keeping his voice even. "I hope to get a chance to examine your find a little more closely."

"I will arrange it. What part of France did you say you were from? Your accent seems unfamiliar."

"I didn't say."

Emile went silent for a moment, then nodded. "Sorry if I was being nosy. Must be the archaeologist in me." He dug his hands into his baggy drill pants, stared over at his men working in the trench, and shouted out an order.

He seemed to be eager to get back to work.

"We'll see you for lunch, then," Silverdawn tossed over her shoulder as she took Emile's arm and let him lead her away.

Faren frowned as he watched her and the gangly professor pick their way around the edge of the site to where his three assistants were working.

"What is it?"

"Does she have to be so forward with that man?"

"This is the modern world, lad, and she has known him a lot longer than you. The women of this world are not like the women of our time. Everything here happens much faster."

He felt the cold steel of the dagger strapped to his shin. "With those two it does not."

"He is merely a friend. Did she not say they attended university together? And in any event, from what you told me last night, you have taken our princess off your list of damsels." Pendragon raised a snowy brow. "Something about not being worthy, was it not?"

Faren glanced Silverdawn's way and cursed as she tossed her hair back over her shoulder and laughed at something the French archaeologist whispered into her ear. She caught him watching and waved. He could have sworn the minx was deliberately flirting with the other man to make him jealous. And from the itch in his palm to snatch up his knife and put it through Emile's heart, he knew her ploy was working. "I am more worthy than that one," he said, disgust lacing his words as he turned away. "Am I not the king's First Knight?"

Pendragon smiled. "That you are, my lad, that you are—now about our mission. I suggest we start with the stones on the perimeter of the northern slope and work inward."

He strode up the hill in silence, choosing his next words with deliberate care. "Did that skeleton strike you as odd?"

Pendragon stopped, putting a hand to his chest to catch his breath. "Odd, in what way?"

He met the old man's gaze. "I had the uncanny feeling I was looking—" He shrugged. "Ah, forget it."

"At yourself," finished Pendragon.

His jaw clenched. "Aye."

The old man shook his head. "'Tis only that the man was a knight, and that the burial was conducted in the way of our people. You know the Celts borrowed their custom of burial from our culture. That is all there is to it. But if it would make you feel any easier, ask Emile if you can examine the sword. He said the hilt was still intact. That way you will know one way or the other. For a Knight of Palladia's sword is his signature."

All thoughts of Silverdawn and the strange warrior drifted from Faren's mind as he laid the medallion on the first toppled stone and closed his eyes, concentrating solely on the music of the earth. Whispers of a heartbeat came softly to his ears. Then music only he who listened could hear. The sound of beauty. In his mind's eye, he stepped through a rocky passage and through a door. The door closed behind him. He was warm. He was in a lovely wood. Snowflakes formed a carpet beside a little river, which ran chuckling over the stones beneath a narrow bridge. Silver birch and rowan trees were coming into leaf, while the first new green shoots of honeysuckle and briar unfolded.

All around was the sound of birdsong. He crossed the bridge and found a path. On either side were stones covered with lichens the color of jade, coral, and amber. The smell of warm honey, violets, and wood anemones came to him on the breeze. To the left was a marshy place where willow shoots gleamed golden in shafts of sunlight. An alder grew on firmer ground, still with its black cones from the previous year. He followed the path through an orchard of old crabapples with their pink and white blossoms. Small creatures scurried about their business...

Faren broke from the Otherworld as Pendragon shook his arm.

The old man held tight. "I know it is easy to get caught up in the Magick, boy. Earth Magick is strong. But we must hurry. We have a lot of ground to cover and not much time in which to do it."

Faren pulled back from the sorcerer's touch and rubbed a hand over his eyes. "I know." He moved to the next stone and settled on its edge. "But I did not expect such…"

"Beauty?"

He sighed. "Aye. That it was."

"And dangerous."

He frowned. "I sensed no danger."

"No, you would not. Have you not heard the story of Merlin? It was Earth Magick that Vivienne, the Lady of the Lake, was reported to have used to lure poor Merlin to his doom. 'Tis easy to become lost in the Earth's Song if one listens too long. I caution you—be careful."

He pushed from his rock and held the flat surface of the medallion to the next stone. "I will take heed, to be sure. It was beautiful, but I would not want to live the rest of my days there. I fear it could become quite boring." He grinned. "What with no battles."

Pendragon gave a short laugh. "Humph! I can imagine *you* would think so."

The next few moments passed in silence while the men moved diligently among the rocks.

"Over here," Faren called softly, breaking the quiet.

"What is it? Have you found the pyramid?"

"Not sure. In this rock I find no music."

"Listen harder. Are you certain?"

He closed his eyes and concentrated. No sound. No painting of beauty, just cold, shattering emptiness rising up and threatening to engulf him, then…he reared back.

"What happened?" The old man hurried to help him regain his balance.

He put a hand to his head and tried to stop the shivers

that wracked his body. "A cold emptiness that weighed on my heart. A cry like a thousand lost souls." He shook his head. "I cannot explain."

"I think you have. This is one of Iraj's fakes. Only the Goddess knows what foulness he uses to conjure them. We must be wary. Touch the stones for a moment only. For both types of stones—the earth stones and Iraj's offerings—now hold danger."

He nodded and moved on, and the two men worked methodically until midday when they returned to camp to eat with the others. They shared a sober meal of sandwiches, sausage, cheese, fruit, and cider, then returned to their exploration, always being careful that they were not observed too closely.

****

A week later, Silverdawn stood in the darkroom of the hotel, waiting for Todd to set up the equipment. The pungent smell of photographic chemicals attacked her throat and eyes as she adjusted to the infrared light. She moved closer and watched as he dipped an undeveloped eight-by-ten into the developer and waited while the first photograph came rapidly to life. The photo showed Emile, a brilliant grin on his swarthy face as he held a warrior's helmet above his head. She chuckled and watched Todd dip the photo into water, fixer, and water again, then hang it to dry.

He peeled his sweater over his head. "I'm soaked." He laughed shortly. "You would think with all these years of practicing photography, I would have learned something. I always forget to strip off my sweater before I begin."

Silverdawn gave a short laugh, which ceased immediately on seeing the tattoo running the length of

Todd's arm. "Nice tat," she said, biting her tongue as other words threatened to follow—like *"Faren has one the same. When did you become a Palladian Knight?"* Her mind reeled with possibilities. Could the essence of Kalden, Faren's brother and fellow Palladian Knight, be buried deep inside of Todd? Or worse still, was Todd in reality Iraj?

The thought disturbed her greatly, and although it could be dangerous, she decided to probe. "Where did you get it?" she heard herself ask after she stopped freaking. "It's a beauty. Did it hurt?"

Todd finished struggling with his sweater, then tossed it onto a stool in the corner of the tiny darkroom. Now dressed only in jeans and a black T-shirt, he set to work on developing the next photo. "I know this might be hard to believe." He turned his head to meet her gaze. "I don't understand it properly myself. Perhaps you can make sense of the matter."

"Go on."

"It happened mid-June. I was invited to a bachelor party for a guy I went to college with, down at one of the bawdier taverns on the waterfront." He finished hanging another photo on the wire running above their heads, then pushed a hand through his fair hair. He gave a wry grin. "I'd had a few drinks but didn't think I was that bad. It was about three in the morning when I left and decided to take the shortcut through the alley to the taxi stand. The next thing I knew, something struck me."

"You were attacked?"

He shrugged. "That's what's so hard to explain. I awoke early the next morning with a stinking headache and a great scab up my arm. I checked my pockets. There were still over fifty pounds in my wallet. I crawled to my feet and caught a taxi home." He held up his arm. "A week or so later when the scab peeled, I found I was the owner of this beauty." He grinned. "What do you think? The victim of the Phantom Tattoo Artist?"

Silverdawn played along and smiled. "Could be."

They continued to develop the photos in silence for the next few moments until Todd spoke again.

"What do you know about this Malaan chap and his friend? Mighty curious, I would say. What are they doing all day poking around those standing stones?"

"Perhaps they're checking for more artifacts. Faren did confess to be a bit of an amateur archaeologist."

"Mmm, but you would think that Emile would have already checked out the surrounding countryside."

"I'm certain he has, but you never know. He may have missed something. As long as they stay out of the fenced-off area, I can't see that they are doing any harm."

"I guess you're right." He shrugged. "I must have a suspicious nature." He turned and put a hand on her arm. "I care about you, Silverdawn. I don't want to see you getting hurt. I've seen the way you look at Malaan."

She moved from his touch and busied herself washing the next photograph. "Is it that obvious?"

"Not to the ordinary person. But to a man you told two weeks ago you had no interest in men, it could appear irregular."

"Perhaps I've been waiting for the right man to come along."

"And this Frenchy, he's the right guy?"

"You think he's French?"

"Well, I guess. He was taking care of the French Armor Exhibition, wasn't he? But I couldn't really say. My French is pretty rusty. You're the linguist. What do you think?"

She pondered his question. Faren said Rastehm was another name for France, so she wouldn't be totally lying if she agreed with Todd. "As you say, his accent does sound a little French. I hadn't really thought about it."

He gave her a small pat on the back. "Then French it is."

They spent the next few minutes putting away chemicals and cleaning up, then parted company with a promise to meet later in the restaurant for dinner.

****

Todd stared at the telephone in his room as if it were a snake and might strike him. With a deep breath for courage, he quickly dialed the number that would connect him with the curator of the museum. He had put off the call for three days.

He heard the receiver being lifted, then a soft, feminine voice spoke from the other end. "Yes?"

"Serena, is that you?"

"Todd, you must help me." She was whispering, but her tone sounded desperate.

"How are you? Has he hurt you?"

"You know?"

"I know I will find a way to take you away from that monster."

"How chivalrous of you, Mr. Haversham," a deep voice rumbled from the other end of the line. "I will count the days. Now, what news have you? You are late in reporting."

Todd remained silent for a moment, contemplating his next words. "There is nothing to report," he answered steadily. "And you touch a hair on Serena's head…"

"And you will do what, Haversham? Your threats

137

are like empty vessels, and you are in no position to fill them. Serena is in my house, and you are over a thousand miles away. I feel you have not been trying hard enough in your quest. Serena is such a delicate woman, such lovely white skin…"

His fist tightened at his side as he imagined Waymer stroking his gnarled fingers down the length of Serena's soft cheek.

"You have followed Dr. Peterson and subtly questioned her. Have you found nothing?"

"I can barely get near her. She brought two men with her. They never leave her side, and when she's on-site, she is always with the professor."

There was a pause at the other end. "These men, what do they look like?"

"One is the keeper of the armor exhibition. I thought you would have known he was with us."

"No. Malaan sent someone to take his place at the museum. The replacement told me the Frenchman had been called away on urgent business. And the other man with you, who is he?"

"An elderly man by the name of Pendragon. I believe he owns an antique shop on the West Bank."

"Pendragon. I should have realized he would not be far behind. What have they been doing while you work?"

"It's strange. They spend their days walking and rummaging among the standing stones."

Iraj let out a heated curse, then silence fell on his end of the line.

"Something wrong?"

Out of nowhere, a hand sprang from the mouth of the receiver to grasp Todd's neck.

He jerked back as he fought the gnarled fingers

closing painfully around his throat.

"I want that key, and I want it fast. Do you hear?"

Todd could hear all right. The booming voice vibrated through his head and along his nerve endings as he gasped for breath and struggled for release. "I…hear."

"I hear who?" the disembodied voice lashed.

"I hear…you, sir."

"Master!"

"I…hear…you…Master," Todd croaked. Lights swirled before his eyes. Was he about to die?

Then the hand and voice were gone as suddenly as they appeared.

He sagged to the floor and leaned against the bed, staring at the receiver as if it were a rearing snake. He dared not touch the handset to place it in its cradle.

What just happened here? Was he crazy? Had a disembodied hand really materialized from the telephone in an attempt to choke him?

Gingerly, he poked at the receiver with his foot. When nothing untoward occurred, he picked up the handset and replaced it.

He was convinced he was mixed up with something supernatural, but to whom could he turn? He had no choice but to go along with the man professing to be Peter Waymer. He was certain now the professor had been possessed. But by what creature? Todd had never believed in the paranormal, but after tonight he had no choice. He would have to do whatever he could to find the elusive key the man desired, if not for himself, then for Serena.

And may God help Silverdawn, if the creature had chosen her as his next victim to torment.

****

Julie A. D'Arcy

It was a balmy night considering autumn was ending. Silverdawn sat closeted in her hotel room with Faren and Pen.

She folded her hands in front of her and looked at Faren. "So what have you found?"

"Nothing," he growled, moving to the window. "And we have neared the end of our search."

"We still have the west slope. That should take us another two or three days," put in Pen.

She grimaced. "I hate to tell you this, but Emile has decided to start digging elsewhere."

Faren turned, a dark frown marring his brow. "Let me guess, the west slope."

She nodded. "Right the first time."

"Well, there is only one thing for it." Pen scratched his beard. "We will ask him if he has seen the pyramid."

"And how do we explain the device?"

"I'll tell Emile that I have been tracing the pyramid through history." Silverdawn munched on a biscuit she'd taken from a plate on the table. "That it is Egyptian. That it was stolen by the Romans and believed to be located in the same time and location as the warrior's skeleton."

Pen raised a snowy brow. "Will he not know that you are lying? He is an archaeologist."

"No. Emile majored in medieval history and, if I remember correctly, never did have an interest in Egyptian."

"Fine." Faren moved to the minibar to slosh a dash of brandy into a snifter. He offered the others a drink, but they declined. He raised his glass, tossed back the contents, and placed the glass on the counter. "I just hope this does not backfire."

She stood and moved to the window. Night was

140

falling, and she scanned the riverbank, deep in thought. She spied Todd down below. Earlier that evening he had complained of a headache and retired to his room. It had given her and the others a chance for this impromptu meeting. He now stood alone, directly opposite the hotel, staring up at her room. He seemed surprised to see her but regained his composure and lifted a hand in greeting. She smiled, waved back, and then turned to Faren who had come up alongside her. "There is another matter I'd like to discuss—your brother. I think I've located him."

He spun and grasped her arms. "You have news of Kalden?"

"You mentioned you thought he had landed in another's body. As hard as I find it to believe, I think that person might be Todd."

He released her. "If this is your idea of a jest, I am not laughing."

She laid her hand on Faren's arm. His skin was warm and firm through his shirtsleeve. For a blink of an eye, a vision of their bodies entwined on the lounge rug flashed through her mind. She squeezed her eyes closed, then opened them again, forcing herself to return to the present. "Don't dismiss this, Faren. I am serious."

Pen met Faren's gaze as the knight turned toward him. "You could at least hear what she has to say, lad."

He nodded. "Go on."

"This afternoon, after returning from the dig, Todd and I were in the darkroom together."

Faren appeared about to say something, but Pen shook his head, and the knight remained silent.

"Todd accidentally splashed chemicals onto his sweater, so he slipped it off. And what do you think I saw? A large red dragon tattooed on his arm."

141

Faren stared at her for a moment, then shook his head, about to turn away, but she stopped him.

"Don't ignore this, Faren."

"No. It's too much of a coincidence." He pulled his shirt over his head and held his arm up level with her face. "Are you certain the picture is the same?"

"As sure as I can be." She forced her gaze from his bronzed chest to examine the tattoo.

Pen leaned forward in his chair. "Does he remember getting the tattoo? Did he mention it?"

"When I questioned him, he told me that he had been attending a bachelor party. He developed a migraine and left in search of a taxi. He cut through an alley a friend told him led to the taxi stand. Before he reached the end of the lane, he was struck down. When he awoke, it was morning, and he had a large scab on his arm. A week or so later, it revealed itself as a dragon tattoo. The same as Faren's."

"He wasn't robbed?" queried Pen.

"He says no."

****

Faren turned to stare into the night and rested his forehead against the coolness of the glass pane. "It is too easy," he said, his mind awhirl. Could this be true? Could Todd really carry within him the essence of Kalden?

He thought of their childhood and that day so long ago, when his father had brought to his home a tiny, fair-haired baby to raise. Faren's father had explained that Kalden's parents had been involved in a carriage accident. His father had been killed, but his mother gave birth before she died. The wee babe had no living relatives. An old woman near the site of the accident had placed the babe into his father's arms, then abruptly vanished. Not knowing what else to do, Faren's father had brought the baby home.

Kalden had been the brother Faren's mother could never bear. He missed the other man like life itself. They had shared their boyhood and grown to manhood together. He had not seen his adopted brother for over twelve months.

Now at last, hope. But was it real, or would it be snatched away again on the whim of the Goddess?

Pendragon spoke into the silence that had descended upon the room. "Ours is not to question, lad. Just be thankful the Goddess has been kind and given us this sign."

Faren watched Silverdawn move across the room. She bent and struck a match to the kindling in the grate. He followed her, crouched beside her, and began to build the fire.

"So what do we do now?" she asked, sitting back and allowing Faren to take over.

"We must find a way to nudge Kalden into remembering his name."

"Can't we just tell him?"

"*No!*" Pendragon and Faren shouted at once.

"That is something you must never do," cautioned Pendragon. "For two souls cannot inhabit one body without one being driven to insanity. 'Tis all very complicated and has to do with powers beyond our reasoning."

"So we need to make it seem as if he is remembering of his own accord?"

"Precisely," said Faren.

"But how? If your brother is inside Todd, and Todd is not even aware of it, then these memories you speak of must be seriously deep."

" 'Tis not hopeless. I have heard of it being done," said Pendragon. He clasped his hands in front of him. "Think, Faren. What are the things Kalden would feel most strongly about?"

He ran a hand through his hair and released a long sigh. "His home…his horse…his status as a knight of the order…"

"I could sew a tapestry," offered Silverdawn.

"Fine thinking," praised Pendragon, slumping back into his chair. "However, there is not enough time. But you could sketch the design—the plan."

"Brilliant. I have seen some of Silverdawn's work. I am sure she could do it." Faren rose, held out his hand to her, and pulled her to her feet. He turned her to face him, both hands on her shoulders. "How soon could you start, and when could you have it finished?"

She studied his face. "I could start tonight. I brought paper and pastels with me. They are in the car. I thought I would begin a new design while I was away. You will have to stay and help me with descriptions and colors."

He squeezed her shoulders in a friendly gesture, then released her. "Come. We will fetch your equipment."

"That sounds like my cue to leave." Pendragon came to his feet. "It has been a long day for an old man, and I am weary. I shall see you in the morning." He reached out and patted Faren's shoulder. "I am certain all will be well, lad. Just give Silverdawn what help she needs and put your faith in the Goddess. She knows what She is about."

Faren gave a half laugh and saw the old man to the door. If Deharna knew what She was about, Rastehm would not now be torn apart by wars of Her making. And

Kalden would not be in the predicament he was in. But Faren would keep his own counsel on that matter. He took Silverdawn's arm and led her to the door. "Now, where are these pastels of yours?"

Chapter Eleven

Silverdawn climbed the last step to the first floor. In all it had been a satisfactory day. Emile had decided to do an artist's reconstruction on the warrior's skull. When finished, it would give a realistic representation of the man's features. Due to the exciting discovery that morning of another skeleton only a few feet from the other, he had delayed his change of site and extended his original dig by ten extra feet on each side.

He had taken several hours to study the bones and pronounced the skeleton female—perhaps the wife or concubine of the warrior.

After the discovery, she returned early to the hotel with Emile, leaving Todd out at the site to catch a ride back with the archaeological crew.

As for Pen and Faren, she hadn't seen them. But she was certain if they discovered the pyramid, they would contact her.

She unlocked her room, pushed open the door, flicked on the light, and froze.

The room had been ransacked. Her bed was torn apart, covers and pillows tossed aside. The notes and sketches she had worked on last night spilled onto the floor. The contents of her bedside drawers were upended onto the bed. Even her toiletries were scattered into the bathroom basin.

The bitter taste of bile coated her tongue. She felt

literally sick—overwhelmed. She closed the door and sank to the floor, burying her head in her hands. Why? Why her? What had she done to deserve these attacks? Why wouldn't they leave her alone?

She had no idea how long she sat there, trying to gather her strength, before a knock sounded at the door. Dragging herself to her feet, she moved warily, clutching her handbag in her hand like a weapon as she inched the door open.

Faren stood in the hallway. She stared at him, unable to bring herself to speak—to tell him what had happened.

"Silverdawn, you are as pale as a specter. What is it?" He pushed past her into the room and gazed around, taking in the chaos. "By the Goddess, what happened here?"

"Who would do this to me?" she murmured.

He reached out and brought her into his embrace. "I think you know who. Our friend Iraj."

She allowed herself the comfort of his arms for a moment. Her legs felt as shaky as a newborn foal's.

"Have you the key somewhere secure?"

Reluctantly, she pulled from his arms. "In the hotel safe. I wasn't foolish enough to leave the device in my room once you explained what it was."

"Good girl." He stooped to pick up a group of reference books, which had been swept to the floor, placed them on a small side table, and returned his gaze to her. He raised his hand to stroke her cheek. "It must be hard for you. Coming from a different world, I am used to violence. Even expected it. I surmise you have led a relatively sheltered life." He smiled gently. "Do you have a headache potion—I mean powder? You are still shaking."

Silverdawn found it hard to meet the brightness of his eyes. "I'll be fine. But shouldn't we call the police?"

"It would only complicate matters."

"Then should you tell Pen?"

"I will, but not right now. You need me here." He gave her shoulder a gentle squeeze, then started to move around the room, retrieving various items tossed haphazardly to the floor. "Are you sure nothing was stolen?"

She sighed. "Pretty sure. I never leave valuables in hotel rooms." She walked to the bathroom, removed her cosmetics from the sink, and splashed cold water over her face. She retrieved an aspirin from her toiletry bag and washed it down with a glass of water. She returned to find him gathering a handful of lacy underwear from the floor.

He glanced up and gave her a wry smile. "Where do you want these?"

She snatched the scraps of lace from his hand. "I'll do that. You fix the bed," she answered tersely.

He gave a brief laugh and stared down at her. "Glad to see some color in your cheeks."

She gave him a small smile and knelt beside her dresser while he moved to straighten her bed and retrieve her papers.

Faren picked up the sketch she had rendered the night before.

He had given her a few brief ideas of the colors, insignia of Kalden's armor, and a description of the man himself, then left her to her own devices.

"You are more talented than I anticipated," he said. "You have captured Kalden's likeness to perfection. Long, ash-blond hair, square jaw, green eyes, silver dress armor of the Palladians—red dragon on his shield—indigo cape thrown over his shoulder."

He shook his head. "This really is amazing. Castle Baltimore in all of its majesty, and my brother's gray stallion in the full trappings of a knight's mount. You even captured the rolling green hills of the Rastehm countryside."

He crossed to Silverdawn, holding out the drawing. She was still on her knees beside the dresser. "I wish I knew how to thank you more."

"Thank me for what?" she answered softly. "For doing something I love anyway. I'm glad I could help. You have given me so much."

He shook his head, about to move away, but she captured his hand.

"No. You must hear me out." Her tone was grave. "You gave me my identity. The knowledge of who I really am helped me realize the visions that plague me are not signs of madness but glimpses of another world. You saved me from that creature in my apartment. Now you have given me the strength to face this latest crisis. No, Faren, it is I who should thank you."

"It is my duty as a knight to serve you," he stated, staring past her.

She sighed. "So we are back to that? You the brave knight, and I the princess."

"What else is there?" he asked stoically, pulling his hand from hers.

She came to her feet and stood on her toes, her hands going to his face to force him to look at her.

"Kiss me, Faren. I can't stand to have you so close and not have you kiss me. I need you to kiss me. I need your warmth. Your tongue touching mine. Your

149

strength. Especially now. After this…"

He grasped her arms and swung her around to back her against the wall, then clasped her hands above her head. His mouth came down over hers with savage hunger, his body imprisoning her against the wall, their tongues melding.

She thought she would surely faint with the overwhelming sensations that he evoked. Then, abruptly, she was released, and he stepped away. Her legs gave way beneath her, but he captured her again against his chest.

"Are you all right?"

She nodded, and his lips came down over hers once more.

Silverdawn had dreamed of this since he first touched her. In fact, since he first appeared in the park. She ran her hands through his hair, over his shoulders, and down his back until she found the edge of his shirt. She slipped her hand beneath the fabric to touch his skin. His flesh was heated and firm, just as she remembered. A shiver ran through her body as he touched his lips to her eyelids and cheeks, then skipped around to nip her earlobe.

"I shouldn't be doing this," he murmured, breath hot against the small pulse in her throat.

She frowned and stilled. "Why?"

"You are my princess." His words—rich, vibrant, seductive.

"Yes, I am *your* princess. And as your princess, I order you to do what you feel…*your* princess would like."

He laughed softly. "You are a wicked princess."

She pushed both hands down to clutch his buttocks

through the cloth of his jeans and pulled him into closer contact with her body. She felt him swell against her. "I could be *very* wicked if you would allow me."

Faren hooked a hand under her knee and brought her leg up around his hips, pressing his straining manhood to the junction of her thighs. Then, supporting her with his other hand, he leaned her back to give his lips better access to her throat and the shadowed valley between her breasts, trailing hot, wet kisses across her sensitized skin. Then he lowered her leg and pushed her back against the wall, his hand again clasping her hands above her head. "Was that wicked enough for the princess?"

Silverdawn could only stare at him wide-eyed, her breath coming in short hot gasps.

"Or would you like more?"

She nodded. "More." She breathed. Not caring what he thought, only knowing that she needed him.

He transferred both her hands into one of his, then, with painstaking slowness, eased her shirt from her jeans and began to unbutton it. When the last button was unfastened, he nudged the soft cotton fabric aside with his teeth and covered one lace-encased nipple with his mouth, drawing on the sensitive tip through the fabric of her bra.

Never had she imagined anything so erotic. She squirmed beneath his touch. Tiny shivers swept down her stomach to lodge in her navel, then traveled on to that part which made her a woman. Beneath the heat of his warm, wet mouth, her nipple puckered and begged for release.

He again captured both her hands in one of his and used his free hand to unclasp the front clip on her bra. Once more he used his teeth to move the fabric aside, and when his mouth went to her tortured nipple between his teeth and drew it into the exquisite haven of his mouth, she thought she would surely perish for the want of him.

She needed him against her flesh, to crawl inside his soul and never let him go. She struggled with the hand that held her.

Faren raised his head, and their gazes met. His eyes were the most brilliant shade of blue. So deep a blue she felt that if she stared into their depths for a moment longer, she might never want to return from that place to which they drew her.

He released her. "Wicked enough?" he whispered.

She smiled softly and brought her hands down to unbuckle his belt, her gaze never wavering from his.

He covered her hands with his own. "Are you sure this is what you want?"

"I know you are the one. I knew it from the moment I saw you in my vision."

"What if reality does not match the dream?" He put a finger to her lips. "No, do not answer that." He reached to push her hair back from her neck, to give him better access to her throat. As she finished with his belt, he bent and swept her into his arms. He was halfway to the bed when a knock sounded at the door, and he stopped, a frown marring his brow.

Her hands tightened around his neck. "Don't answer it."

He strode the rest of the way, lowered her onto the bed, and came down over her, taking her lips with his. She pushed her hands beneath his shirt and up his chest to trace over the jagged scars on his back.

The knock came again, more persistent.

"Silverdawn, are you in there?"

Faren lifted his head and groaned, touching his forehead gently to hers. "Pen."

"We could pretend we're not here."

"He knows already. He is a sorcerer. He knows everything."

She grimaced. "Everything?"

"Well, nearly everything." He chuckled.

She sighed and pushed on his chest. "I suppose you had better let him in."

He matched her sigh and rolled from the bed. He redid his belt buckle and with set features strode to the door and wrenched it open.

She came to her feet, hastily re-clipping her bra and buttoning her shirt. She just managed to fasten the last button before Pen stepped into the room.

He raised a snowy brow and gave her a knowing smile as he took in her disheveled hair and clothes. "I believe your blouse has a button missing, lass."

Silverdawn glanced down and flushed. She had accidentally pushed the last button into the wrong hole.

Pen ambled around the room, poking at this and that, looking into drawers and under the bed. "I can see what you mean about the mess, but this was not Iraj's doing— none of the usual signs. Looks like the work of an amateur." He took a seat in the padded chair by the fire and stretched out his hands to the warmth. "Did they get the key?"

Faren ran a hand back through his hair, pushing it from his eyes. "No, Silverdawn has it in the hotel safe."

Pen's gaze went to Silverdawn. "Good girl."

She perched on her bed and began to brush the tangles from her long, fair hair. "I must admit this gave me a bit of a scare. It was lucky Faren arrived, or I wouldn't have known how to handle the situation." She glanced around the room, looking at anything but Faren.

Pen gave her a studied look. "Mmm, yes, lucky."

"There was something you needed, Pen? Your reason for wanting to see Silverdawn?" asked Faren.

"Ah, yes. I was wondering how the sketch was coming along—our plan to free Kalden."

Faren picked up the sketch. "We were just discussing that same matter." He passed the drawing to Pen.

"Is that so?" Once again Pen's brows shot into his hairline. He threw a look at Silverdawn, and she flushed and laid her hairbrush aside.

"Yes, Faren was just thanking me for my help. Is not that so, Faren?"

A small muscle flickered at the side of his jaw as he met her gaze, and the emotions that raced across his face made her want to cry out in denial. Defiance, anger, and the most hurtful of all—regret. She dropped her gaze and turned to Pen, a lump forming in her throat at Faren's rejection. "What do you think of the sketch?" she asked, trying to lighten the mood.

Pen studied the drawing a moment longer, then glanced up at her, an unreadable look crossing his face.

"Something wrong?"

The wizard broke from his reverie, shaking his head. "Wrong? No. Nothing is wrong. Of course, I have never seen the man, but it is a very good likeness of the castle and the countryside. I am sure if Faren gave you a description of Kalden, it is close to perfect."

He bent to retrieve some papers lying on the floor and stacked them on her dresser. Faren and Silverdawn followed suit. Half an hour later, the bed was made, furniture straightened, and not a paper out of place.

"Now, my dear." Pen turned to her. "I thought I would take my meal early tonight. I am old, and I feel that all of this outside activity is playing havoc with my bones."

Faren headed for the door before Pen finished speaking. "I'll go with you. We need to go over our plans for tomorrow."

The old man pursed his lips but said nothing, and Silverdawn nodded, unable to find the words to make him stay. She watched the door close behind him, an empty feeling in her stomach.

What had made him leave like that? Was she pushing too fast?

She wondered if he was still holding to his same objection—he the knight and she the princess. She knew she should take things slowly, but she was afraid that if she did so, it might be too late. He was in her dimension for a limited time, and then he would return to Rastehm. She had to make him want her. She sighed and threw herself down onto the bed to stare up at the ceiling. "If only he loved me. Then he would stay."

****

Faren followed Pen into the room and slammed the door. He strode out to the balcony and smashed his fist onto the wooden rail. "What in the name of the Goddess is wrong with me? Why cannot I leave her be?" He swung around and stared at Pen standing behind him. "She has bewitched me. When I am with her, I lose all reason."

Pen spoke calmly. "Can you not recognize the problem?"

He shook his head impatiently. "What problem? She is my only problem. She only half believes us. She says she has no intention of going back with us, yet I cannot seem to keep my hands off of her. If Mikkasah knew about this, he would have my head. If it had not been for your timely intervention, I probably would have—ah." He gazed heavenward to the stars, allowing the cool evening breeze to wash over his heated face. "What has she done to me, Pen?"

"You ask me a question man has been asking throughout the ages. The answer is always the same. You are in love, boy. Nothing more, nothing less."

Faren grasped the balcony rail, squeezing until pain ripped through his fingers. "No. I will not allow it. I am here for three reasons. To free Kalden, to recover the pyramid, and to take Silverdawn to her father." His words, even to his own ears, seemed more a chant than words spoken to the other man.

"If you believe that, you are a bigger fool than I thought you were."

He grasped Pen by the front of his navy sweater. "You dare to call me a fool, old man. I have killed men for less."

"If you speak as a fool, so shall you be named."

He gazed into the old man's golden eyes and saw nothing but compassion. He released the sorcerer and swung back to stare out across the moon-streaked river. "If she will not travel with us, then I will never see her again. If she does travel back with us, her father will eventually marry her off to some foreign prince. Either way, I will lose her. It is best we cut the ties now."

Pen shook his head. "Mikkasah is no fool. He is aware that his daughter grew up in a different age and her customs may differ from those of our people. Somehow, I cannot see Silverdawn standing back and allowing herself to be sold off to the highest bidder. Speak with the king. Tell him how you feel. You told me he treats you like a son and has hinted at making you his heir—why are you so sure he will object? We know that his daughter means everything to him. Perhaps he will see the match as an advantage."

Faren shrugged. "Perhaps. But for the time, it is best that this courtship goes no further."

Pen sighed and turned away. "If that is what you wish. But know this. Chivalry can only play so much a part in a man's life, then that man must be true to himself or be lost."

Chapter Twelve

Todd took a deep breath and swung his leg over the balcony of Silverdawn's room. He had waited several hours until he was certain she was asleep. He had never imagined himself a cat burglar. If his father found out about this, he would definitely be disinherited.

He struck his kneecap as he dragged his other leg over the rail and bit down on his lip to stifle his cry. Waiting several moments for the pain to subside, he prayed that Silverdawn hadn't heard him.

On the move again, he fished in his pocket for a key, which he fitted into the lock of the glass balcony door.

In the event that he needed to return, he had made an impression of the key when he'd broken into her room the day before. He'd been lucky yesterday. She had left the balcony doors open, and he'd slipped into her room without detection. Would he also be lucky tonight?

Todd was certain, having had her room ransacked once, Silverdawn would be careful to check all windows and doors before retiring.

He was right. The door was locked. He turned his key in the lock, and it gave a soft click. Cautiously, he inched open the glass double doors. They made more noise than he anticipated, and he stilled.

Silverdawn slept on.

He really hated doing this, just as he had loathed ransacking her room. Although he had worn gloves, he'd been certain some shred of evidence would connect him to the deed.

He found it hard to believe his good fortune this morning when Silverdawn had not even mentioned the incident.

Snapping from his reverie, he used the moonlight filtering into the bedroom to creep to the chair beside her bed. His heart sank. Her handbag was not where he had seen it earlier that night when he made an excuse to come to her room.

Where else would a woman put her bag?

He took a small flashlight from his pocket and pointed it away from the bed. She groaned and rolled over. A bead of sweat trickled down his spine. His heart beat so loudly in his ears he was sure that noise alone would wake her.

He bent low to search under the bed and spotted his quarry on the other side. He switched off the flashlight, shoved it into his pocket, and lowered himself onto his stomach. Careful not to touch the bed, he slowly slid beneath it, thinking he would be less likely to be detected this way. But Lady Luck was not to be with him tonight.

"Is someone there?" Silverdawn's voice sounded hesitant.

Todd paused, too afraid to release his next breath should the sound be detected.

"Is someone there? I know someone is there!" Her voice grew louder, firmer. "You'd better show yourself."

He released his breath in a rush. He was sunk. His only chance was to make a dash for it.

He wiggled farther under the bed until his hand closed around the bag. Then, with a final push, he was free on the other side. He was halfway to his feet when something struck him from behind. As he staggered, he realized it was a pillow. Silverdawn swung again, this time hitting the side of his head. Todd lost his balance and almost fell. Another pillow hit his back.

He sprinted for the balcony with her screams for help ringing in his ears.

Not stopping to see if she gave chase, he swung over the balcony, lowered himself as low as possible, and dropped the rest of the way to the grassy bank below. He landed awkwardly, and a sickening pain shot through his ankle. He dropped flat, rolled down to the water's edge, and lay panting in the darkness.

From his vantage point, he watched her room light go on and two more people step out onto the balcony. Pen and Faren, he surmised.

He had to hurry back to his room. How would he explain his absence in the morning if they found him missing tonight?

Cautiously, he rose to his feet, groaning as pain shot up his leg.

To top things off, his ankle was sprained. Just one more thing that would need an explanation. He just hoped whatever was in the handbag he clutched was worth all this pain and risk.

****

Todd knew the moment he looked into Silverdawn's eyes over the breakfast table that she suspected him. With his bandage and crutch, how could she not? Nevertheless, she said nothing. She just stared at him with her big, sad, green eyes—as if to say, "Why did you betray me?"—gave him his assignment for the day, and told him to take it easy. What better way to make a man feel guilty?

Out of guilt, he paid a young street boy ten pounds to return her bag to the reception desk. She must have it by now.

His phone call to Waymer had been bad enough. Reporting he still had not unearthed the mysterious key.

Waymer, to say the least, was not happy. Yet he had controlled his temper, which was one thing in Todd's favor. The man was so unstable it was hard to tell how he would react.

Now, as he stepped from the elevator and traveled the few paces to her room, his heart filled with dread. He glanced at his watch, four o'clock on the dot. He peered at the number ahead of him—242—and couldn't have felt worse if the number jumped off the door and ripped out his heart. He straightened his back to fortify his courage and knocked on the door. It was opened immediately by Faren. He had not expected the Frenchman, though he supposed he should have. When he and Pen were not wandering among the rocks, Faren was invariably at Silverdawn's side.

Todd smiled briefly and limped into the room.

"Sorry about your ankle," said Faren stiffly, eyeing Todd's bandage.

His smile felt as if it were pasted to his face. Pen sat across the room in a lounge chair. The old man stared at him with his strange golden eyes, unsmiling.

"Todd hurt his ankle last night while wandering along the riverbank," explained Silverdawn.

Faren pursed his lips. "Oh. And what time was that?"

"Around eight. Why?" Todd shot back with a defensive note to his tone.

"And you waited until this morning to tell us?"

161

"I could see no reason to bother you." He glared at Silverdawn. "I resent these questions. What's going on here?"

The Frenchman answered for her. "Someone broke into Silverdawn's room last night and stole her handbag. He jumped from her balcony."

"And you think *I* did it?" Todd threw a desperate glance at the handbag resting on a side table and pointed. "Isn't that Silverdawn's bag right there?" He drew a deep breath in an attempt to settle his nerves. He knew these people could prove nothing. They had only their suspicions.

She rose and offered him her chair. He hobbled forward and sank into it gratefully, resting his crutch against the arm.

"We think nothing of the sort, Todd. We consider you one of us and thought you should know."

He frowned. "One of us? I don't understand."

"Of course you do. We are all working together, are we not?" She settled on the other arm of the chair beside him and laid her arm lightly across the back of the seat. "My bag was returned this morning. Nothing was taken. I just thought I should fill you in on the details." She rose, crossed to the minibar, and poured three small glasses of brandy. She handed him the first glass.

He thanked her politely and leaned back into his chair. Relaxing, he cast his gaze around the room, searching desperately for a new topic. He saw some artist's pastels resting on the desk and a covered canvas standing beside it. He stood, reached for his crutch, and hobbled toward the sketches. "I didn't know you were an artist, Silverdawn."

She cast Faren a glance.

The knight nodded.

"Would you care to see?" she offered.

He grinned, relief turning his voice jovial. "Very much. I like to paint in my spare time. Perhaps we could exchange ideas?"

She gave him a warm smile. "I wouldn't call myself an artist. I merely dabble."

Very carefully, she unveiled the canvas and passed the picture to Todd.

He was amazed at the detail she had captured in the image. The knight was arrayed in black-and-silver armor, an indigo cape thrown over his shoulder. Beneath him, a mighty warhorse. Todd gazed into the knight's green eyes. There was something familiar about them. A slow humming began to pound in his head, growing in volume. "Do you hear that?"

"Hear what?" someone murmured. He couldn't distinguish who.

It was as if he were peering into his own soul. As if something or someone within those green eyes were calling his name. But it wasn't his name they called. It was the name of another. Or was it him? Kal…Kalden.

The humming grew louder still. He pressed his hands to his head, dropping to his knees. The pastel drawing receded as if it were spinning. Or was that him too? The canvas dropped from his fingers. The humming turned to a roar. His hands went to his ears. He had to block out the sound. He fell to all fours as faces flashed before him. Images raced fleetingly through his mind. A castle with high gray walls and bedraggled pennants. A large, silver-gray warhorse. A man with an iron beard and a woman with white-gold hair—like his own? All conscious thought vanished. He was falling—falling into a deep dark abyss…

****

Silverdawn made to rush to Todd's side, but Faren dragged her back. "No. You must not touch him. To wake him now could be disastrous."

She stared at Todd in dismay, and in that instant, a brilliant yellow aura encased his body. She watched, partially fascinated, partially horrified, as a ghostly image rose part of the way from Todd's recumbent body. The specter sat and gazed around sleepily, as if waking from a dream.

She opened her mouth to speak, but Pen cautioned her to silence with a shake of his head.

The apparition peered from one occupant of the room to another. When his gaze alighted on Faren, a look of recognition entered his eyes. Frowning, he rose and stepped from Todd's reclining body to move toward the other man. "Faren, is that you?"

"Aye. I am Faren. But who might you be, sir?"

"Surely, you jest. Do you not recognize me? I am Kalden, your adopted brother, friend, and Palladian Knight of Rastehm."

On those words, Kalden's body solidified and became whole—once more a man of flesh, blood, thought, and laughter. He slapped Faren on the shoulder and grinned. "Good it is to see you, Brother, but where are we?" He ran a hand back through his long fair hair.

Faren took his brother is a brief hug, then released him. " 'Tis good to see you too, Brother. I thought I had lost you. We are in France, and there is much to tell, but not now. First let me introduce you to my friends." He drew her forward. "This is Silverdawn."

She let her gaze trail over the tall, rugged man before

her. He was every inch the medieval knight. Then he turned, and their eyes locked. For a split second she saw in his eyes the likeness to her own. Stunned momentarily, she could do nothing but stare, then realizing her *faux pas*, she gave a small, nervous laugh and shakily held out her hand.

It was as if the knight had stepped from her painting—complete with white-blond hair and black riding boots. She had never met him before, but for some uncanny reason she felt drawn to him. He was handsome, yes—with his wide shoulders and regal bearing—but that wasn't it. There was something familiar about him. She felt a vague attraction, but not sexual, more sisterly. She curved her lips into a smile. "Pleased to meet you, Sir Kalden."

He gave a chuckle as if she had said something amusing, took her hand, and brought it to his lips, then released it. "My pleasure, Silverdawn."

His voice was deep-throated with the same rich accent as Faren's. Had she not already given her heart to her dark knight, that voice alone might have been enough to sway her. Kalden turned, and Faren stepped forward and embraced his foster brother, tears coming to his eyes. He wiped them away impatiently. "You had me worried. For months now you have been trapped within this man's body." He glanced down at Todd.

Silverdawn was placing a pillow beneath the sleeping man's head.

Kalden ran a hand through his shoulder-length hair, obviously taking a moment to come to terms with Faren's words. "I body crashed. So that is why you asked me who I am and why I can't recognize this place. I was wondering where and how I got here. The last thing I remember, I was holding the medallion over my heart, wishing for London, in June of the allotted year of the Third Dawning. I was to go in search of the pyramid." He slapped his hand to his forehead. "The pyramid! Have you found it?"

Faren shook his head. "No luck yet, but Pendragon and I have a lead."

Pen gave Silverdawn and Kalden a pensive look, and she sensed something was going through the old man's head that had nothing to do with what they were talking about. She held her tongue, and the look vanished as the old man caught her watching him.

He smiled and took the knight's hand. "Well met, young knight."

"Pendragon? Not the fabled Pendragon of His Majesty's court?"

Faren laughed. "The same, I am afraid. And still up to his old tricks."

"Tricks. As in Magick?" Kalden frowned.

"Harmless, I assure you." Faren slapped his brother on the shoulder, changing the subject.

They spoke for a few moments, then Kalden turned to Silverdawn. "And this lovely lady, where does she come into all this?"

Faren reached down and drew her to her feet, bringing her close to his side. "Silverdawn is responsible for bringing you back to us."

The knight took her hand again, this time keeping it cradled between his two. His eyes were a deep forest green, and he stood silent, staring down at her. "Have we met? You seem most familiar."

She smiled and tried to pull away. "I don't think so, but Pen and Faren say I resemble my mother."

"And do I know this mother?"

"She is Aurelia and Mikkasah's daughter. And I think the lady would like her hand back, Brother." Faren's voice held an edge.

Slowly, the knight released her. "Pardon if I caused offense," he said. "I feel it has been an age since I last saw a pretty maid."

Faren slapped his brother's shoulder in a friendly gesture. "Later, I will show you a place where you can purchase a maid for a night of pleasure."

Silverdawn felt a stab of jealousy that Faren should know of such a place. "Drinks?" she asked weakly, crossing the room. She sloshed three more brandies into glasses and handed them around.

Kalden threw his head back and downed the drink in one swallow. "Faren assures me you are responsible for my saving. It seems you have achieved the impossible. Never have I heard of anyone surviving such an incident without both minds going insane."

She settled on the edge of the overstuffed chair near the fire and tossed a helpless glance at Faren. "Really, it was Pen and Faren's idea. I only played a small part."

Faren perched on the arm of her chair while Kalden took the chair opposite. Faren went on to explain their plan about the painting. When he finished, he gave her shoulders a brief squeeze and met his brother's gaze. "And so here you are."

"And where exactly is that again?"

Faren laughed shortly and passed the conversation over to Pen. The old sorcerer detailed what they were doing in France, about Iraj, and how they suspected him of creating the fields of standing stones to cover the whereabouts of the pyramid. He then explained how, on

167

the morrow, they were going to confront Emile and ask him if the pyramid had been found. He also detailed their suspicions about Todd and the ransacking of Silverdawn's room.

She stared down at Todd, still deep in slumber on the floor. "I think we should be getting him back to his room, don't you?" She glanced across at Pen. "Will he be all right?"

"Perhaps a little disoriented with a massive headache, but he will be fine, I am certain. Perhaps Faren could carry him to his room and put him to bed."

"Allow me," said Kalden, rising. He squatted to gather Todd into his arms as if he weighed no more than a pillow. "It is the least I can do for the man, considering he has been carrying me around inside him for several months."

Faren searched Todd's pocket for his room key and found it. He picked up the crutch, hooked it beneath his arm, and bent to touch his lips lightly to Silverdawn's cheek. She gazed at him in surprise but remained silent.

"One thing," said Pen before the two men reached the door.

They both stopped and turned.

"It might seem strange to the hotel staff to see Kalden running around dressed like a medieval knight."

The large man glanced down at his chain mail, breastplate, and dagger, then at Faren's more modern garb. "I do feel a little foolish."

"Wait," said Pen. He waved his hand in a series of intricate movements and uttered three guttural words. With a flash of light, Kalden's clothes were transformed to black jeans and black woolen sweater, which replicated Faren's.

Kalden laughed out loud and followed his brother down the corridor, with Todd in his arms. "I see what Faren means about the Magick," he tossed over his shoulder.

Chapter Thirteen

Pink and mauve streaked the sky as Silverdawn followed Emile into his tent. She pulled her coat more closely about her body to ward off the chill lingering in the morning air.

"I'm sorry, Silverdawn, I never knew you were interested in the piece. You should have mentioned it sooner. We found the pyramid last evening." He lifted a fax from his desk and handed the paper to her. "It's funny, but your employer, Professor Waymer, sent me this fax the day you arrived, stating specifically that, if I located the pyramid, it should be shipped directly to him. About five o'clock this morning, we transported it to England. I automatically assumed you knew of the request."

Her mind whirled as she returned the fax to him. They were too late. "I had no idea the professor knew of the pyramid. Let alone that he would ask for it."

"I guess you are both after it for the museum, so all worked out well." He paused. "Bizarre object, that."

She stilled, her gaze going to his face in alarm. "Why is that?" She tried to maintain an even tone. "I'm certain you have uncovered more unusual artifacts in your travels."

"Nothing like this. We lifted the pyramid from beneath tons of dirt and rock, yet it was as bright and shiny as a cut-glass decanter, and light. You could even have lifted it without effort. You said you had studied its history. Have you any idea what causes those unusual blobs of color to writhe within, even when the piece is stationary?" He pushed a hand through his already tousled hair. "I wish I'd had time to investigate the pyramid myself, but with my workload, not a chance. Perhaps you could send me a copy of the notes on your findings."

As Emile spoke, she felt the color drain from her face. She smiled weakly. "Yes. Yes, of course."

He could not possibly know that the blobs he spoke of were Iraj's undead creatures. Or that those same creatures, should they be released, had the power to systematically move across the world, spreading plague and wreaking havoc on the unsuspecting population.

"Pity, though…"

She broke from her thoughts. "About what?"

"The pyramid had a crack up one side."

"I expected some damage. How bad is it?"

"It looks as if the apex was sheared right off. We searched, but there is no sign of it. Also, as I said, there is a crack that extends halfway up the side. But the artifact is still a fabulous find."

Silverdawn nodded, and Emile went on innocently.

"And your friends. They did not come with you this morning." His words were more a statement than a question. "Faren rang earlier and asked if he could examine the armor and sword at the museum in the village. I explained he was just in time, as we were about to ship that exhibit to your museum this afternoon as well." He took a seat at his desk and waved her into the hard-backed chair across from him. "There is one thing, though, I wished to discuss with him…"

"Yes?" she prompted as he slid a scrap of paper from a folder on his desk and bent over it intently. She smiled inwardly as she remembered his old habit of starting conversations and forgetting to finish them.

He looked up and flushed. "Umm. Sorry about that. What was I saying?"

"You wanted to speak with Faren."

"Ah, yes. Do you know where his ancestors were from? I'd love to get a sample of his DNA. My forensic pathologist has done a full facial reconstruction on the warrior's skull using a plaster mold, clay, and computer, and has come up with the most striking resemblance to your friend."

A shiver traveled down her body, but she covered her uneasiness with a small laugh. "How…interesting. I must remember to mention it to Faren." She knew she wouldn't. She couldn't think of Faren as dead. He was so vital, so alive. Yet Emile's words brought home just how far apart she and Faren really were. Worlds apart— in time, customs, and way of life. How could she ever have imagined they could be together? He was from a medieval world, steeped in Celtic-like tradition. Even if she could travel back with him, could she live like that? Without running water, sewage, or electricity. And no central heating. She shivered at the thought. And she already knew his answer to living in her world. He hated it here. "It is too fast," he had said. "Too impersonal."

"Have you put a date to the warrior's origin?" she asked offhandedly. "You said around 500 BC?"

"I know that was what I said, but it wasn't even close. Strange, we can't seem to get a true fix on the warrior's skeleton, but we feel it is much older. One of the pathologists seems to think 4000 BC." Emile laughed shortly. "I told him he was insane."

Silverdawn frowned. "Would that even be possible? For the warrior to have lived that long ago?"

"4000 BC? I think it unlikely, given his equipment."

"What if he weren't Celtic?"

He stood. His gray eyes were serious. "Of course, he was Celt. Everything points to it. He has the armor—the horse was buried with him. That is how the Celts buried their dead, is it not?"

She glanced away, unable to meet his probing look. "Of course. What was I thinking?" She pretended to read the cover of an archaeological magazine on his desk. When she looked at him again, he was already intent on studying a map beside her, his mind supposedly engrossed in the next part of his project.

She leaned over to drop a light kiss on his dark-stubbled cheek, and he glanced up in surprise.

"Sorry, was I doing it again?"

"Never mind, and I love you too," she called over her shoulder, heading for the exit. "I'll be in touch. Thank you for allowing me to tag along."

He raised his hand in farewell as she stepped into the sunrise and allowed the tent flap to drop back into place. For a moment, she stood still and gazed around the site, breathing in the fresh mountain air, admiring the lush green hills, saying goodbye to the giant monoliths that had been part of her life for the last three weeks. For the blink of an eye, she experienced a pang of jealousy. To be so single-minded about one's work like Emile must be amazing.

She laughed softly. She *had* been like that once. Funny how it seemed so long ago when in reality it was only a matter of weeks.

****

Faren, accompanied by Kalden, entered the small museum in the quaint village of Besancon. Faren had rung Emile earlier for clearance, so they passed untroubled through the double doors at the back of the building into the pathology lab where the relics Emile had unearthed were temporarily held.

A man in a white coat introduced himself as Dr. Verville and led them to an open wooden crate lying on a table in the far corner. Reverently, Verville lifted the remains of an ancient broadsword from the crate and held it out to Faren.

Faren's fingers trembled as he touched the hilt. His hand fitted like it were made for him, and a white-hot tingle of recognition ran up his arm and down into his gut.

Kalden stared at the etchings on the blade, bright now that it was clean of dirt. "Is that not—"

Faren silenced his brother with a hard stare and a shake of his head. "Do you think we could have a moment alone?" he asked Verville in an even tone, although inside he was anything but calm. He had the beginning of a headache.

The man grimaced. "I really shouldn't."

"I am certain Emile would say it was fine." Faren reached out and placed a hand on the man's shoulder. "You can ring him if it would put you more at ease."

"Perhaps I should ring him," said the man, trancelike, moving away.

"You used your power of coercion on him."

"I know that, and you know that, but by the time he realizes he had to move away to use the phone, we will have said all there is to say."

Kalden grinned, then nodded at the sword. "That is your sword, is it not?"

"Aye, it is." Faren raised the hilt to eye level to stare at the serpentine handle intertwined with roses. "You know why I chose this design?"

"No. I always wondered."

"Because it reminded me of Deharna. The beauty of a rose with the ice heart of a serpent."

"You best not let Her hear you say that, or any of Her other knights."

Faren met his gaze. "What of you? What will you do now that you know my impression of the Goddess?"

"Nothing. I have long held the view myself. She may have saved our world, but a lot of innocent people have died or been separated from loved ones because of Her decree. What happened with Iraj happened twenty-seven years ago. I think perhaps it is time for a softening."

"You would have a hard time convincing Deharna of that. But let us speak no more of it. I came here for a purpose, and that was to see if the warrior Emile uncovered is indeed I. This whole thing has brought home to me the fragility of my own mortality. For some reason, when you are our age, you feel you will live forever. Yet over there in a box somewhere are my bones. How did I die, I wonder? Was it sword, lance, or battle-axe? How old was I? Was it this year, the next—thirty years from now?"

"Stop it, Faren. You don't know for certain it is you. Perhaps the sword was stolen."

Dr. Verville hastened their way. "Excuse me, Mr. Malaan. I have spoken with Dr. Rousseau, and he agrees it is acceptable for you to view the sword alone." He frowned. "Which I guess you have…already done," he finished lamely. "He also wondered if you would be interested in examining the reconstruction of the skull. Emile is of the opinion that it bears a striking resemblance to yourself."

The cold hand of fear clenched Faren's heart. He staggered as bright lights flashed before his eyes and his temples pounded like war drums at the sides of his head. He pressed a hand to his eyes.

Kalden reached out and caught his arm before he fell. "I am sorry, but not today, Professor. My brother is ill."

"But Emile wished me to ask Mr. Malaan for a blood sample to compare his DNA," replied Verville, his hands gesturing agitatedly. "He believes Mr. Malaan may be related in some uncanny way to our warrior."

Kalden pried Faren's fingers from the hilt of the sword. He handed the broken blade back to Verville, then laid a hand on the man's shoulder. "No." The knight's voice held a note of steel. "My brother is sick. Another day."

The doctor nodded, seeming to sag. "Another day, then." He sighed, absently running a hand over the back of his neck. "I will tell Emile. Tomorrow?" he asked hopefully.

"Perhaps," replied Kalden, taking Faren's arm and leading him toward the door.

Cold air lashed Faren's face as he stepped to the edge of the cobbled footpath and jettisoned his breakfast into the gutter. He stood shaking, beads of sweat dotting his forehead. Head bowed, he took several deep breaths, trying to steady his jittering stomach. He could not look Kalden in the eye. He felt shamed. Never had he reacted so badly. He had fought weremons and never felt fear, but now, faced with his own mortality, he had squirmed and thrown up like an infant.

"You must think me a fool." He peered up at Kalden. His brother's face was almost as pale as his own.

"I probably would have acted the same under the circumstances. But who is to say you did not live a rich and full life? Were a woman's bones not uncovered as well? She may have been your wife. It may even have been Silverdawn. Have you thought of that?"

Faren straightened and wiped his hand across his mouth. "No. I am embarrassed to say I gave the woman no thought. She must have died with me. But it could not have been Silverdawn. She swore not to return with us."

"People change their mind."

"Not her. I have grown to know her. She is stubborn. When she makes up her mind, she sticks to her decision. But there is one thing to be gained in this. No woman of mine shall ever journey into battle with me."

"Stubborn like you?"

He chuckled, fished a handkerchief from his pocket, and wiped it across his brow. "You are good for my soul, Kalden. You know how to put matters into perspective. Perhaps something has been gained by this experience after all. I cannot fathom why Mikkasah chose me as First Knight and not you. You are wise in the ways of a king."

The big knight gave a short laugh. "I may be wise in the ways of kings, but you have a better sword arm." He slapped Faren's shoulder. "But as today you say I am wise, I suggest we collect Pen from that bric-a-brac dealer and find your woman. We are already late, and as has been said down through the ages, it is never wise to

Faren laughed aloud, regaining his humor. "Right again, Brother."

****

Later that evening, Todd again found himself sweating before Silverdawn's door. All day his conscience had stewed. Early this morning, he had rung the demon who possessed the professor. He had ceased thinking of the man as Professor Waymer after the incident with the telephone.

The demon had informed him that Emile had forwarded him the merchandise for which he needed the key that morning. It was now even more imperative that he found the piece.

The demon had forced Serena to the phone. Todd had heard her scream, then the line had gone dead. The demon's voice had reverberated in his mind. He'd ordered Todd to confess to Silverdawn. To tell her everything. He had not said why. Only that if he did not do as told, he would not see Serena alive again. And her passing would not be pleasant.

Todd balanced on his crutch and wiped his hand across his forehead. It came away damp. The hallway was cool, yet he was sweating profusely.

He had rested in his room all day after Silverdawn sent word she did not need him. She had only to see Emile and prepare for their departure tomorrow.

He knocked on the door, the sound almost inaudible. The door swung open. Pen stood staring out at him. It was as if the old man had been waiting on the other side for his knock.

"Come, boy. We were expecting you." He stepped aside. His manner was friendly enough.

178

Silverdawn came forward to greet him and maneuver him into a chair by the fire. "I believe you have not yet met Kalden, Faren's foster brother. Faren ran into him last night in the restaurant. He had no idea he was in this part of France. Kalden has decided to travel back to London with us."

Todd nodded at the man across the room. Tall, with white-blond hair pulled back in a tail and wearing a navy sweatshirt that stretched across his broad chest and biceps. He seemed a man not to be trifled with. Todd wondered what his reaction to the betrayal of his friends would be.

Silverdawn passed Todd a glass of bourbon on ice.

She must have remembered it was his favorite.

"You said on the telephone you had something to discuss."

He thanked her for the drink and took a large mouthful of the fortifying liquid courage. "What I am about to say may in some parts be hard for you to believe."

Pen smiled at him across the small table separating them. "We will be the judge of that, lad. We have heard some pretty amazing things and know most of your story anyway."

"You...do?" He spluttered, almost choking on his drink.

"We know you broke into Silverdawn's hotel room," said Faren, turning away from the window and speaking for the first time since Todd entered. "We know you were looking for something. What we don't know is, who hired you?"

Todd scanned the faces of every member in the room. All had an expectant look, testifying to the fact they did indeed know of his troubles. "Waymer," he blurted, unable to contain the knowledge any longer.

Silverdawn bounded to her feet. "No. You lie! It couldn't be the professor. It couldn't be."

"I swear it, Silverdawn." Todd ran a hand over the back of his neck. "The professor you and I once knew no longer exists. He has been possessed by some kind of...monster."

Still shaking, she settled back into her chair, and Faren crossed the room to stand beside her. He gave her shoulder a gentle pat.

"Then why do his bidding?" Faren asked, his tone as cold as chipped ice.

"Blackmail. He would never persuade me otherwise. He has pictures—terrible photos—of me with another man. I swear I didn't pose for those pictures, but he has them and threatened to show them to my father. When I said I would go to the police, he used some strange power to throw me to the ceiling. Then he ripped at my insides. I was in such terrifying pain I could think of nothing but releasing myself from the agony. This man can make a fist appear through the end of a telephone!"

He shook his head and took a mouthful of bourbon. "I know you don't believe me, but it's all true." He peered down at the melting ice in his glass. "The creature has me searching for some sort of key. I don't even know what the damn thing looks like."

Pen half rose, thumped Todd on the shoulder in a sympathetic gesture, then settled back into his overstuffed armchair. "We believe you, lad. But this is unlike Iraj. Why does he not do his own work?"

"Iraj?"

"That is the name of the sorcerer of whom you speak. The person possessing Dr. Waymer."

"Sorcerer?" Todd shook his head. "As in magic? As in fairy tale?"

"I know this is hard for you to understand, but there is more to this world than what you can see. We must ask you to suspend your disbelief and, yes, to believe in Magick."

He ran a hand over his eyes and bowed his head. "I do believe. I can do nothing else but believe with all the strange things I've seen lately. It's either I believe or I am going crazy." He met Pen's eyes. "But there is something else the matter with the professor. I think he's sick. He keeps muttering things like he is running out of time, he is getting weaker, and he needs the key to restore his power."

"We've known all along he was after the pyramid," said Faren. "But he must to be getting desperate."

Todd glanced from one man to the other. "Pyramid? What is going on here?"

"No time to explain. We will tell you later. What else did Iraj say?"

"He said that the merchandise you are seeking will be waiting for you in the museum's attic in a week's time—at ten o'clock on New Year's Eve."

"Winter solstice, when the veil is thinnest. He plans to use the pyramid to invade both worlds," said Faren.

Pen released a breath. "Do you know what that could mean?"

"The end of civilization as we know it. Death and destruction to every living creature and being."

Silverdawn shook her head. "We can't let this happen." She looked desperately at Pen and Faren. "*You*

181

can't let this happen. No matter what it takes. You must stop him."

Todd began to rise, then settled again. "Waymer said to bring the key. If you don't show, he will kill Serena."

"Serena?" Faren frowned.

"Professor Waymer's wife?" Silverdawn gave Todd a penetrating look. "She is still with him?"

"He holds her captive." Todd came to his feet, then winced as pain shot up his shin. He sank back into his chair. "We cannot let anything happen to her. She's an innocent." He pushed a rough hand back through his hair. "May God forgive me, but I love her. It is for her that I have been doing this."

She reached over and patted his hand. "We'll save her, I promise." She glanced at Faren. "Won't we?"

He nodded. "Of course."

Todd peered around at his comrades hopefully, noting their encouraging if somewhat worried expressions. "Then you forgive me?"

Silverdawn smiled. "That's what friends are for, aren't they?"

Pen gave Faren a pensive look. "It seems to me that if we are able to gain the pyramid and withhold it from Iraj long enough, this malady which ails him may do what you have not been able to do all these years."

Silverdawn took a sip of water and leaned forward, her glass cradled in both hands. "I knew the professor looked ill, but when I questioned it, he brushed my worry aside and told me it was an old ailment acting up. If we can rescue Serena, she may know what's wrong with him."

Faren nodded. "I will see to it."

"And I." Kalden came to his feet across the room. "My sword arm grows rusty without use."

"No!" Todd gulped down the rest of his bourbon and felt it burn all the way to his gut. In the alcohol's fire he found his courage. He had been a coward too long. Now was the time to act. "It must be me. The professor will expect me to report. I'll go," he heard himself say. And for the first time in a long while, he felt like a man again.

Chapter Fourteen

December 22nd

The train arrived in London at dusk the next day. Todd, who by now had discarded his crutch, volunteered to go straight to the house of the man he now knew as Iraj. Silverdawn and Faren had filled him in on quite a few details of the sorcerer's past, some of which were hard to accept. Yet, from his own experience with the sorcerer, he had no choice. He still couldn't believe how understanding Silverdawn had been about everything. He just hoped he could carry out his part of the plan without failing her.

The taxi pulled to a stop outside the old priory. The building looked as dark and forbidding as ever; the weather was as dreary as the last time he'd ventured here. He glanced at the top window and could have sworn the curtain moved.

He paid the driver and stepped out of the taxi, telling the man to wait. Dragging the collar of his overcoat closer around his neck, he began the long trek up the drive, his footsteps sounding ominous on the gravel. He reached the bottom step, inhaled deeply, and trudged up the stairs to rap twice with the knocker.

Almost immediately the door inched open, and he was surprised to see Serena standing before him. Her dress was dirty and torn. One of her eyes was bruised.

Her lip had been cut, and her beautiful mahogany hair lay in disarray around her shoulders. For a moment her face lit up, then all color drained away.

"What are you doing here?" she whispered. "If he finds you—"

"I've come for you," he whispered back, running a gentle knuckle down her cheek.

"He'll never let you take me. He is a monster." Her voice, though quiet, held a note of hysteria.

He took her arm and drew her through the door onto the open porch. "Go." He pointed down the drive. "There is a taxi at the gate. Wait ten minutes. If I'm not out of here, drive to this address." He pushed a folded paper into her hand. "The people there will know who you are. They will help." He leaned forward, touched his lips to hers, and then gave her a gentle push. "Run!"

He watched her sprint down the stairs, then straightened and turned into the house.

In the room where he had met the sorcerer for the first time, Iraj stood at the window. "Come in, Mr. Haversham," Iraj said without turning. His voice held no trace of emotion. "Sit."

Todd did as he was told, not wishing to antagonize the creature. Every moment he kept him occupied was a moment added to Serena's freedom. Iraj must have seen her leave. Would he allow her to go?

The other man turned. His skin was the color of parchment paper, and his face was more drawn than Todd remembered. Whatever illness he suffered was taking its toll.

Iraj limped toward the desk with the aid of a cane and eased himself onto a padded desk chair. "Do not let this body deceive you. My powers are as strong as they always were. I suppose by now Pendragon has explained who I am."

He nodded.

"And you are wondering what I will do next?"

He remained silent.

"I could kill you. I suppose."

Todd started to rise.

"But I won't."

He eased himself back into his chair.

"In a roundabout way, you did me a service. You relayed my message to my enemies." He paused, leaning back in his chair, and met Todd's gaze. "They have agreed to bring the key?"

Todd nodded.

"Speak up!"

"Yes…Master," he replied, barely able to keep the sarcasm from his voice.

Iraj mustn't have noticed, because he went on. "Good. Now you may take one more message to that old charlatan, Pendragon. Tell him that the winner takes all."

"Only that?" Todd frowned. " 'The winner takes all'?"

"He will know what I mean." Iraj rose to stand at the window, staring out at the drizzling rain. "Go! I must prepare myself."

He rose and was halfway to the door when the sorcerer spoke again. "May your *short* time with Serena be a pleasant one, Haversham. For that is all it will be—short!"

A chill ran the length of Todd's body, and he forced himself not to flee the room like a frightened schoolboy. But as his foot touched the bottom step of the house, Iraj's laughter floated through the open doorway after him, filling his ears and his heart with foreboding.

****

Iraj watched him go. *Fool.* The boy thought he had escaped. He wondered what Todd had made of his last message. Would he be forever glancing over his shoulder? He laughed out loud, a hoarse, horrible sound that turned to a racking cough. He touched a cloth to his lips, and it came away red. *Blood.* How he had once adored the stuff—the color, the feel, the taste. Now he abhorred it. For it was Waymer's blood, forever on his tongue. For the thousandth time he cursed the weak, useless husk of Waymer's body and the fate that had forged his path.

Iraj rested his forehead against the damp windowpane, listening to the patter of the rain and the beat of his heart. Soon he would rip out all of their hearts: Pendragon's, the knight's, Silverdawn's—just as he had her adoptive parents. He had felt powerful that day—victorious. So he would again once he freed his army.

He smiled inwardly, remembering better days when his army had marched across the breadth of Rastehm. Glory had been his, power and riches beyond counting. Death had marked his path, and his minions had fed upon the innocence and pain of the people. So it would be again on New Year's Eve. When he claimed the pyramid and Magick once more flowed in his veins.

Chapter Fifteen

Silverdawn awoke in the small bed in Pen's back room. Christmas was in two days. The thought beat a repetitive tattoo in her mind.

This year Christmas would be very different, spent with very different people. Again, the thought that she would not be sharing it with her adoptive parents brought a pang of grief, which she quickly squashed by cutting off the link to those memories.

She rolled from her bed and began to dress. She would get Kalden, and they would go find a tree.

She had struck up a great friendship with the big, blond-haired knight over the past week, finding in him a friend who shared similar interests. He had developed a fondness for classical music in his travels to the future. He also had a penchant for classic literature and art.

Last night they'd sat for hours discussing Shakespeare, Dickens, and the Brontë sisters. She saw the hard look Faren threw his brother before he retired to his room, his demeanor stiff and proud.

Kalden waited for the door to close, then burst into laughter. "If it was not so alien to his conduct, I would say my brother was cat-spitting jealous."

She laughed at his words and scooped her kitten onto her lap as he rolled a small yellow ball close to her feet. She ran her hand through his gray silky fur, held him to her cheek, then lowered him to her lap to ruffle his tummy. He had grown so fat while she was away.

"You feel it too, don't you?" Kalden asked, reaching over to pet her kitten.

"The bond?" She nodded. "Yes, I felt it from the moment I saw you."

"I cannot say why, but I feel we have met before. That we were great friends."

"I too." She laughed shortly. "Perhaps it was in another lifetime."

His brow rose. "You believe in reincarnation?"

She had nodded, and they'd enjoyed an in-depth conversation on the topic.

The barking of a dog in the lane outside Silverdawn's window snapped her from her reverie, and she hastily dragged on blue corduroy jeans, a white long-sleeve shirt, and a windbreaker. She left her room and found her way through the study into the kitchen.

Kalden had settled at Pen's small kitchen table with toast and coffee. He looked so huge and awkward beside the slight forms of Todd and Serena. Silverdawn gave an inner smile as she moved to the refrigerator to fetch a glass of juice.

"Faren and Pendragon have gone out," Kalden informed her.

She turned at his words. He had pulled his hair back from his face into a ponytail. He wore a navy sweater and tight-fitting navy jeans that stretched across his muscular thighs. Had she been any other woman, she would already be half in love with him. But to her, he was just Kalden, Faren's brother and good friend, nothing more, nothing less.

He offered her his chair, but she declined, leaning back against the counter.

"No, I won't be staying."

He opened his mouth to speak, but Serena, who had been gazing from one to the other from the moment she entered the room, blurted, "Do you realize how much you two look alike? You could almost be twins."

Silverdawn looked at her wide-eyed. Serena had mentioned feeling uneasy about encroaching on Pendragon's hospitality and the state of her appearance and had retired early last night. It was good to see her come out of her shell but—

Kalden gave Serena a handsome grin and a mock bow. "Thank you, lovely lady, but my ugly countenance could in no way be compared with anything as exquisite as the princess's fair face. Nor," he quipped, as he ran his hands down his sides, "my figure with one so svelte."

Silverdawn laughed outright. "And I don't think I could get my tongue around such false tales as he tells. Now, where are the others?" she asked, sobering.

"They left me here to guard you." He grinned wolfishly.

"Good. I couldn't have planned this better."

His eyebrows rose into his hairline. "Oh yes? And why is that?"

"Because, my fair knight, we are going shopping."

He reared back in feigned horror. "A Palladian Knight does not shop."

She leaned over him and poked him in the chest. "I am your princess, and I say this Palladian Knight does."

He put a hand to his breast in a false display of grief. "It wounds me that my lady would use her station in so dastardly a manner."

Todd and Serena looked at each other and smiled at the show.

Silverdawn gave Kalden a playful slap on the arm. "Enough. It is Christmas in two days, and I wish to purchase a tree."

The knight frowned and reached for his coffee. "A tree?"

"You don't have trees where you come from?"

"Of course, we have trees. What I do not understand is why you must purchase one."

"Don't you celebrate Christmas?" asked Serena, breaking into the conversation.

"Faren and Kalden's people celebrate in the Celtic tradition," explained Silverdawn, pouring a coffee.

"We do a lot of the same things you do," Kalden added. "There have always been miraculous children born at winter solstice; Jesus was only one of them. Dionysus, Attis, Mithras, and Baal were all welcomed to the world with song and dance in mid-winter—the time when Norsemen also celebrated the birth of Freya.

"Instead of a tree, we deck the house with as much greenery as we can, holly, ivy, mistletoe, boughs of pine or larch. We give presents and have a wonderful time." He smiled wistfully. "My mother used to spend a lot of time preparing special dishes, including a rum pudding, which she called 'Tipsy Cake.' "

"Sounds charming," murmured Serena. Todd had filled her in on everyone's background. "I think Todd and I should go shopping for food." She smiled hesitantly at Todd.

He reached over and placed his hand over hers, giving it a gentle squeeze.

"I'll cook Christmas dinner. It is the least I can do, considering what you have done for me," said Serena.

"Good." Silverdawn dragged Kalden to his feet. "I

hate cooking." She was glad the other girl seemed to be coming out of her shell. She had been worried about her. Last night she'd been very quiet.

"I have not completed my breakfast," Kalden protested, snatching the last piece of toast from his plate and cramming it into his mouth.

She headed for the door. "You can eat on the way."

He gave his companions a shrug and followed her. "You are a fiery woman, Princess. I am glad you are Faren's woman and not mine."

She tossed him a sideways glance as she reached for her trench coat hanging on the peg beside the back door. "Am I his woman? Is that what he told you?"

"Well, by the way you look at him and the way he looks at you, I felt that there was some fondness between you, yes. And he seems very territorial whenever he is around you."

"He has not said the words," she said softly, staring at the door handle.

"It has always been hard for Faren to show affection. I do not know why it should be so. Our parents were most loving." He reached out his hand and gently lifted her chin to stare down into her eyes. "Does Faren not show you with his smile that he cares for you? With the gentle touch of his hand? The manner in which he treats you. Sometimes words are not necessary."

She nodded and pulled away, a painful lump forming in her throat. Perhaps Kalden was right. Perhaps words weren't necessary, but they would be nice. She refrained from answering, took Faren's black wool coat from the hook, and tossed it to Kalden. He caught the garment with a questioning look.

"It's Faren's. I'm sure he won't mind if you borrow

it," she said gruffly. She waited for him to don the coat, then pulled open the door.

A cold blast of wind blew in from the alley, causing a quick shiver to pass over her body. The threat of snow hung in the air but still had not relinquished itself to the earth.

She hugged her arms to her chest, bowed her head, and stepped into the lane. The same lane she had stumbled through with Faren that first night, which now seemed so long ago, yet in reality was only a matter of weeks.

Silverdawn and Kalden strolled in silence for some time, scanning the icy streets for a tree salesman. Finally, she spied a potbellied man selling fir trees across the road. They waited for their chance, crossed the busy roadway, and entered the yard. It was as if everyone on the block had waited for this same time and day to purchase a tree. Women dressed in heavy coats and scarves, stern-faced men in woolen overcoats and hats, and laughing, squealing children in puffed jackets at every turn in the small muddy yard.

"This one," she decided after ducking in and around people and trees, checking the pines for freshness and sturdiness.

Picking a tree about five feet tall with a strong trunk, good color, and branch coverage, they waited in line for several minutes for the privilege of paying the potbellied proprietor. She wished the man a Merry Christmas, and Kalden hefted the pine onto his shoulder.

"Could you not pick a bigger one?" he joked as they left the yard.

"No. This one is perfect." She smiled as they waited for their chance to cross the road. "I think we'll go back via the front of Pen's shop. It will be quicker, and I have yet to choose a gift for Faren. Pen may be back by now, and if not, Serena and Todd can let us in."

She stopped as they approached the window of Pen's small antique shop.

Kalden lowered the tree from his shoulder. "Do you see anything you like?"

Pen had an array of medieval weaponry on display in the window. Gold swords and daggers, painted shields, crossbows, pendants, chalices, neck chains, and more. All of superb workmanship, all with their own special insignias.

"I noticed when I was in Faren's room that his shield carried the picture of a rose and a serpent. Do you choose your own insignia, or is it chosen for you by the king?"

"We choose our own."

"What does the serpent and the rose combination mean?"

"I think you should ask Faren that. I do not think he would be pleased with my telling you."

She smiled. "Perhaps I'll do just that. And what about yours? Why a dragon?"

"How did you know?"

"Remember the painting which helped bring you back? Faren described the dragon on your shield."

"Of course," he said, staring down at a shield in the window similar to his own. "I chose a dragon for its courage and because of its special significance to the Palladian Knights. You have seen our tattoos?"

"Yes. Are there really dragons in Rastehm?"

He laughed and turned his head to meet her gaze. "You will have to see for yourself."

Her lips thinned, and a lump formed in her throat.

"You must understand. I couldn't live like that—without electricity, sewerage, air-conditioning, modern medicine, and conveniences."

"Without pollution, murders, and the threat of nuclear war looming over your head," he countered dryly.

She turned from the condemnation in his emerald eyes.

He balanced the tree on one shoulder, grasped her arm, and pulled her around to face him. "Your father has waited twenty-four years to see you. Does that not mean anything to you? Do you know your mother has not spoken to him in all that time? That you have a chance of mending that rift?" His green gaze bored down at her. "Faren lives in hope that you will change your mind and return with us."

"And I live in hope that he will change his mind and stay," she answered stiffly, pulling from his viselike grip. She knew she was being unreasonable, that she had every reason to go and hardly any to stay. She loved Faren, and should he disappear from her life, it would be akin to tearing her heart from her breast. But she could not find within her the will to go with him. "I'll buy the Celtic cross," she said, changing the subject and pointing to a piece in the window. She tried to force a gay note to her voice. "He will like that."

"I am sure he will." Kalden's tone was dry, forced.

She ignored him and banged on the door several times, wishing only now for the privacy of her own room.

Todd answered the door, greeted them, and stepped aside for them to pass.

"But not as much as he would like you to go with

him," continued the knight, softly, as she preceded him into the store.

Chapter Sixteen

A dark and dirty night. The wolves of the wind howled, and tears from the heavens slashed against the windowpanes. The room was lit intermittently by sheet lightning. Faren lay awake, staring at the blackened ceiling. He flicked on the lamp and climbed from his bed to pull on a pair of loose-fitting pants. He needed to occupy his mind.

His hand went to his broadsword lying on the table, the hilt an exact replica of the one in the museum. He paused as a shiver touched his nape and ran down his spine. His grip tightened, defying the specter of death that constantly haunted his thoughts. He grasped the hilt with both hands and swung the blade through the air, imagining he was taking the head off one of Iraj's undead. As if by taking the head of death, he could conquer Death herself.

Was Death taunting him?

Would *She* be waiting for him in the shadows as he strode into battle against Iraj's minions? For if there was anything he was sure of, it was that Iraj would be putting all the strength left in Waymer's frail body to conjuring a mighty foe for this last deadly battle.

The necromancer had stated this contest was for all or nothing. What Faren and his friends would be facing in three days' time, their enemy would be brewing this night.

Faren worked his arms, lunging and blocking, diving to the side and rolling to his feet. He drove himself relentlessly until the rain ceased and tiny pinpoints of stars forced their way through the heavily laden clouds. Not a sound stirred in the small hours of the morn.

Bone weary and sweat drenched, he bathed, toweled himself dry, and crawled into bed. His hand had just touched the bedside lamp to kill the light when his door creaked open. Faren closed his hand around the hilt of his black-handled dagger beneath his pillow. The blade eight inches long and razor sharp.

"Faren?" Her whisper cut through the silence of the dark room.

He released the dagger, but his body tensed. "Silverdawn?" He paused, then spoke again. "Is something wrong?" His voice was soft, laced with concern. "What is wrong?"

****

She stepped into the room, and the door closed with a quiet click. She approached the bed in silence and slipped beneath the covers. "I don't want to be alone tonight."

He leaned over and turned her to cradle her spoon-fashioned against his body. She could feel his heartbeat against her back and his soft breath on her hair. The heat of his skin radiated through the fine cloth of her nightgown, and she realized he was naked. She squeezed her eyes closed, trying to block out the erotic thoughts flittering through her mind with his hardness pressed against her bottom.

"Neither do I." He spoke gently against her ear, as if reading her thoughts, and touched his lips to the top of her head. "Sleep now. Tomorrow is time enough for talk."

She smiled into the darkness and yawned. He understood her so well. Now was not a time for talk; now was a time for comfort.

She relaxed into the arms of the man she loved, saddened by the knowledge that perhaps this would be their last night together. She had come here to tell him she couldn't return with him. As much as she loved him, the cold, austere life of the Medieval Ages, with its hardships and wars, was his way of life, not hers. Could never be hers. She enjoyed studying history, but never had she wished to live it. Yet again, from the moment she had glanced into the deep azure eyes of this man, she had felt her resolve weaken. She sighed as his arms tightened around her waist, one hand going to her breast in his half sleep as if it belonged there.

Thoughts spun in her mind like a carousel. How could she let him leave? Could she make him stay? Should she go with him? And what of her parents? Could she live her life never having met them in person, knowing they were just one step away?

She closed her eyes, trying to gain some respite, and drifted into a restless sleep...

She ran through a garden. Birds cheeped in the boughs of overhanging branches. Blossoms hung thick on the trees. The sun was bright overhead, not a cloud marring the perfect blueness. She laughed, a happy sound that rang joyfully in her ears.

Suddenly, she came to a fork in the garden. Hedges lined both paths, and the ends of the paths lay in a thick cloud of mist. She hesitated, then shrugged, not allowing indecision to weaken her buoyant mood.

Running on, she found herself within the mist. Her

steps faltered. She glanced back the way she had come. Mist rose behind her. She gazed to the heavens, knowing already that the blue sky had vanished, along with the birdsong. Where was she? Where were her parents? They had planned a picnic at the bottom of the garden in the arbor.

She walked on, hesitant now, almost afraid. Her head ached with unanswered questions. Something was wrong. Something she should remember. Something that nagged at her heart. But she couldn't recall what.

The mist parted, and she saw the arbor. Trepidation now marked her steps. She approached slowly, knowing that there was a memory here. A memory that cried for release—that also cried for silence.

She stepped through the door of the sun house, and all thought ceased to exist—horror, blood, and a shattering sense of loss overwhelmed her. She tried to reach for her parents. But they were beyond reaching, and she felt herself falling. Falling down into a deep pit of despair where comfort was numbness and numbness was darkness, and if she were lucky, she would never have to return to the real world.

****

Faren heard Silverdawn's cry and felt her body begin to shiver uncontrollably. He switched on the lamp and rolled her over. Her face was the color of snow, and blue tinged her eyelids and lips. He forced her to sit up, but still, she did not respond. She crossed her hands over her chest and began to rock back and forth.

He shook her, but nothing seemed to tap into the dream world to which she had retreated. There was something terribly amiss. He had to act fast, or he would lose her. Magick touched her, and Magick could be deadly when used in the wrong manner and drawn from one who was evil.

Gently, he laid her back on the pillows and leaped out of bed. He dragged on his breeches and raced for the door. He would fetch Pendragon. The sorcerer would know what to do.

He sped down the corridor, then took the stairs two at a time. The old sorcerer had miraculously transformed the settee into a double bed. Todd and Serena were sharing his own bed.

Pendragon opened his eyes as Faren entered the study.

"Quick! Silverdawn is in trouble."

The sorcerer grabbed his dressing gown and raced up the stairs, displaying the energy of one much younger. Belying his great age. How he knew she was in Faren's room instead of downstairs in the back room where they had set up an extra single bed, Faren could only guess. He pushed open the door, and Pendragon squeezed past.

The princess still rested where Faren had left her, if possible, even paler.

"In the right-hand top kitchen cupboard, there is a blue pouch. Fetch it."

Pen needed to say no more. Faren took the stairs two at a time and entered the kitchen, found the pouch, and raced back up the steps.

The old sorcerer had dragged the rug from the center of the room and laid Silverdawn on the floor where it had been. Beside her sat three lighted blue candles. Faren wondered what the old man was about but did not have to wonder long. He tossed the pouch to Pen, who caught it nimbly and poured a portion of yellow powder into his palm. He then bent to sprinkle a circle around the sleeping girl.

"What are you doing? What is wrong with her?"

"Iraj has stolen her mind. He has taken her to a place from which she cannot, or will not, return. I must find her and bring her home."

"Can I not come?"

"Not this time, boy. Now, no more questions. Move aside, and I warn you, do not speak or touch me, or you may lose us both. And do not let the candles go out."

Pen knelt on the floor in the circle beside Silverdawn. He took another handful of yellow dust and blew lightly until a golden sheen covered her from forehead to toe. Then he took up one of her hands, closed his eyes, and began to chant.

****

Pendragon knew the moment his astral body lifted from his physical body. A lightheadedness and sense of euphoria descended over him. He sped away through the ceiling of his house, higher and higher into the night sky. The rain had ceased, and the sky was clear. The stars hung like jewels in the sky. They seemed so close he could reach out his hand and touch them. He rode the soft wind from the city and swept over forests, mountains, and flat gray moors. Stark, rugged coastlines came into view, and he followed. Ruins of ancient castles cried their mournful lament. Blocking his ears to their untold tragedies, he changed direction and veered out to sea.

Below he spied a school of tuna skimming the surface of the wild, moon-burnished water, and among them a single white dolphin. The spirit who was Pendragon dipped lower, his voice asking and seeking from the creature riding the waves. The dolphin's song rang out, sweet music to his ears, knowledge to his mind.

Absorbing all that one of his kind could accommodate, he rose again, drifting on the air currents back to the mainland.

He glided low over fields and houses, searching. But searching for what? What was it he must find? He delved deep within the recesses of his mind.

He saw himself as a boy, fishing on a riverbank. It was spring, and an old man stood beside him, lecturing him on the way to bait a hook. He chuckled. Things had been so simple then. He delved deeper. There was another young boy, but this time he was the teacher. He was lecturing the boy on the ways of life, the ways of war, and the ways of a king.

He watched for a while, reliving those majestic days before Guinevere, before Lancelot, before Morgana.

Then there was Camelot.

That magnificent golden city. Days of glory, when hearts were pure, life was grand, and women were more beautiful than the first blossom in spring. Knights were valiant and strong, and chivalry was still a song to sing. Before Nimue had come and his honor was lost, Arthur betrayed by Mordred, and the sword returned to the lake.

Once more he tried to find that which he sought.

Ah yes! Two babies born. One stolen away and one sent to the future.

As he flew the sky and dipped over the night-silvered plains of the English countryside, a face appeared in a vision before him.

Of course, the girl! The one taken.

With that thought etched in his mind, his astral body began to spin. No longer could he control his movements. He lost all sight. He soared at a terrible speed, closing his eyes, trying to block the nausea; the bile he knew couldn't possibly rise to his throat, but it was doing so anyway.

His descent slowed. He opened his eyes. He was passing through a dark tunnel, the end shrouded in wan light. He landed gently on his feet, feeling as if they would go from beneath him. Drawing a deep breath, he straightened. The strength returned to his limbs, and his body rejuvenated. Retaining all the wisdom of the ages, he was young again, with fair hair and the strength of youth.

And the young man stepped forward.

He was in a large room, the floor covered in soft white mist. It was as if a curtain were drawn aside, and in a corner of the room sat a young woman, warming her hands by a fire as she stared into the flames.

Pendragon approached, but as he did so, a gigantic wyrm reared out of the mist—luminescent green in color, yellow slime hanging from its jaws, and a wicked twisted horn jutting from its head.

He peered within its maw, and a blackened face with red eyes and white, jagged teeth glared back at him.

"You shall not take the girl. She is mine!" it snarled.

For several heartbeats, the tight fist of fear clutched his heart, then it was gone. "You shall die trying to keep her!" he shouted.

He envisioned a sword. Not any sword, but the mighty sword that the Lady of the Lake had once bestowed on a king. The sword appeared in his hand, and with one mighty blow, he leaped forward and rammed the sword into the maw of the beast.

The creature screamed and reared back, black-and-crimson blood running in a constant stream from the corner of its mouth. The creature's head swept down in attack. Its great fish-like fins folded back against its neck. The force of the strike knocked Pendragon from his feet. He rolled, losing sight of all, as the mist flowed over him. He grasped the sword of power in both hands, feeling the Magick flow through his blood. He rose from the mist, strong, ready. The wyrm struck again, this time horn first.

He leaped to the side, and the sword arced down in one fluid movement to take the head from the beast.

The body fell back into the mist, its giant coils rising from the cloud of white in a macabre dance of death. The creature writhed once again, then, with the mist, was no more. Pendragon raised the sword high. Another mist descended from above him, eldritch in color. A light shone down, engulfing the sword. And from the cloud above his head reached the slender arm of a woman. The young Pendragon relinquished the sword into her grasp, whispering words that wrenched his heart. Heartfelt words, belonging to another time, another place. A time he knew that, should he think of it, his heart would surely break. "Thank you, my love," he whispered.

Pendragon crossed to the young woman and took a seat at her small fire.

"Why have you come here?" she asked, hugging her arms to her waist, rocking back and forth.

"You know why I have come."

"I will not go back. I am happy here."

"Yes, nothing can hurt you here, can it, Silverdawn? Yet you would inflict hurt on others."

The young woman looked up, her huge green eyes filled with the pain and innocence of a questioning doe before it succumbs to death from the arrow in its breast. "Hurt others? I hurt no one," she whispered. "I wish only to be left alone, so be gone from here, old one."

"There is a man waiting for you. He would gladly journey into hell for you, but you have not given him that option. You have traveled to a place he cannot reach to help you. A place of warmth, comfort, and darkness. Yes, this is a place where you could quite happily remain for the rest of your days until your heart gave up the struggle and your body became a tired, burned-out shell."

"Your words are cruel. You are cruel!"

"No, this place is cruel." Pendragon cast out his arm. "Cruel to that man who loves you. Cruel to the friends you have made. Cruel to your body and heart, which cry out for life and living."

Tears filled the young woman's eyes. "I don't want to return. I will die there." Her hands rose to cover her face. "My mother…my father, they—"

"No. You don't have to remember. There is no need for words. Just take my hand, and we will journey together. I promise I will shelter you. This will soon be over, and we will all be safe."

****

Silverdawn closed her eyes and reached out to Pen. Her arm passed through the fire, yet she felt no pain, only a numbness around her heart. When she opened her eyes, she was lying on the floor in Faren's room, and he was looking down at her.

"Welcome back." He smiled gently.

She shivered and struggled to sit. "Where is Pen?"

"He thought we would like to be alone."

"He said that you loved me, that you would march into hell for me."

He gathered her into his arms. "So I do, woman, and

so I would. I think it is time I showed you."

He strode the several paces that separated them from the bed and laid her gently on the counterpane.

Her arms rose to encircle his neck. "Make love to me so that I think of nothing but you, feel nothing but you."

Faren lowered his head, his fingers tangling in her hair, his lips touching hers in a gentle kiss. In his eyes she read the words. Words passed down through the ages, female to male since the conception of Eve. She smiled shyly, and he moved over her, his thighs touching hers, his weight bearing down on his elbows.

Her legs tangled around his, and he kissed her eyelids, lips, and the small pulse below her ear, then slid down to her waist. He paused to study the small dragon-shaped tattoo just above her navel and frowned. "I have seen a tattoo like this before." He traced the small pinkish mark with his tongue.

"Mmm?" she asked, not really listening.

"Nothing." He slid from the bed to strip off his breeches and reach for the light, but she stopped him.

"No, leave it on. I want to see your face. I want to remember this night always."

She ran her gaze over the hard bronze length of Faren's body. So strong, so powerful. Muscles bulged in his shoulders and chest. She could not force herself to drop her gaze lower. Instead, she held out her arms.

He came into them willingly and rolled her over until she lay atop him. Then he pushed her silken nightgown up over her head and dropped it over the side of the bed.

She giggled. "If that is how you roll maidens back where you come from, Sir Knight, I think you must have a few notches on your shield."

He laughed. "On my sword, don't you mean?"

She frowned for a moment, then, getting the joke, brought her fist down on his shoulder.

He laughed again, then sobered. "This is not the time for bawdiness, wench. This is the time for business."

She tilted her head to the side. "What business might that be, Sir Knight?"

"The business of love." A deep, sensual note entered his voice. He brought her forward so that her breast settled into his mouth and drew on her nipple.

Her head went back, and her neck arched, and she wished him never to stop, but he did. Momentarily, she was set free, then his lips fastened to her other breast, repeating the exquisite torture. Moisture gathered between her thighs. He had not even touched her there, but just the thought of him entering her had her wet.

Again, he pulled away, and she heard the sound of a foil wrapper being ripped open. A condom? She hadn't realized he would know about such things having come from a medieval civilization, but on second thought he'd been visiting the modern world for years.

Then his hands were on her again as he lifted her hips and slowly lowered her onto his body. She fought against the pain, and it forced a cry from her lips.

He stopped and rolled them both over, his lips going to her ear. "I'm sorry, I wasn't sure—"

"Take me. I want nothing more than to be yours." Her arms went around his neck, and she brought his lips down over hers as their bodies joined. Her cries were lost beneath his kiss.

He entered her fully, then stilled until her body lay passive beneath his, accepting his weight, his thickness.

Then he began to move. Slowly at first, building to a gentle rhythm. Silverdawn hid her face in the crook of his neck, her hands clutching at his back, her legs tangling with his.

Faster and faster, higher and higher, they seemed to climb. She forgot the pain and could only think of the pleasure. Heat coursed through her veins. Every part of her came alive. Delicious sensations raced and danced along her nerve endings. She was being drawn toward something, but what? Her breath came fast, ragged.

Faren's chest heaved above her. His skin was slick with sweat as she scraped her fingernails down his back.

Then it happened. He went very still. A cry broke from his throat, and it was as if something burst inside of her. He thrust into her again, harder. Her body whirled away. She was floating in a world of sensation. For long moments she remained there, small convulsions traveling her body, then gradually she returned to Earth.

Faren rolled onto his back, staring at the ceiling for several long heartbeats, then he leaned onto his elbow and smiled down at her. He lifted a handful of her hair and let it glide through his fingers. "Silk," he said. "Glorious silk, just like your skin." He dropped a small kiss on her shoulder, and she stretched like a luxuriant cat.

"How do you feel?"

"Wonderful." She traced a finger down the line of his cheek and across the bridge of his nose, as if trying to memorize his face. "Wonderful. But tired."

"Good." He smiled gently and gathered her into his arms. "Now you shall sleep."

And she did.

****

As sunlight touched Faren's bedroom window with its first weak rays, Silverdawn came awake and stretched languidly. For several minutes she lay, quietly savoring the warmth and strength of Faren's body against hers, the reassurance of his presence. Then she turned onto her elbow and looked down at him.

He was already awake. "Morning." He grasped her around the waist and rolled her over so that he had the advantage. "How did you sleep?"

"Wonderful."

Faren kissed her brow and ran a gentle fingertip over the lines in her forehead. "Then why this?"

"I must tell you of my parents. My adoptive parents."

"You don't have to."

"But I do. If not for you, then, selfishly, for myself. I can't keep it bottled up any longer."

Faren lay back on his pillow, and Silverdawn settled into the crook of his arm. "If you must, then speak, but at any time should you feel you cannot go on, I will understand."

She reached down and squeezed the large hand that lay across her waist. "I know."

Her first words came softly—hesitantly. "It was the first day of my summer vacation from work. I had arrived at my parents' holiday house in the South of France that morning. They seemed on edge, not at all their normal jovial selves, and after lunch they called me into the lounge and sat me down.

" 'It is time we told you the truth,' said my father. 'You know how much we love you. You have been the most wonderful daughter we could have possibly imagined. So know this—we never meant to hurt you in any way.' He knelt in front of me, his hands taking mine. 'We are only telling you this because we believe you to be in grave danger.'

" 'What kind of danger?' I shook my head, unable to comprehend. What was he so worried about? 'I am sure whatever you are going to tell me will not alter the way I feel about you or mother.' I looked over at my mother and smiled.

" 'You are adopted,' said my father. 'Illegally adopted, when you were two.'

"I sat silent, stunned. I had heard of this happening to people before, but never had I imagined I would be one of them. My whole life had been a lie—my whole existence. I stood, and my father stood. I looked at my mother—my kind, gentle mother—and my heart swelled with love, but I couldn't speak to her. Not yet. The hurt was still too raw. I walked out of the room. I knew I was being unreasonable. I knew they loved me, and I loved them. But at that moment I felt betrayed.

"My father called me. 'Silverdawn, come back. You are in danger! We must talk.'

" 'Later,' I called back.

"But there never was a later. I left them in anger. Two wonderful people who had never caused me a moment's grief and who had doted on me for twenty-two years.

"When I returned, they weren't in the house. I searched the grounds, calling their names, until I came to the arbor. My father had the arbor built so we could sit and read and enjoy the sun. Even before I entered, my heart started to pound. I knew there was something wrong, but I couldn't have imagined what.

"As I climbed the three steps to the entrance, I saw

smudges of red on the marble. I stepped through the door, and horror struck me like a physical blow. My mother was thrown at an awkward angle across the table, her chest gaping, her throat cut, and her lifeless blue eyes staring accusingly at me. My father had been nailed to the wall. His shirt was stripped from his body, and his ribs splayed. His heart was missing. Blood still dripped from the wound, pooling on the polished boards at his feet. I think I fainted, because when I came to, I was back at the house in my bed with a doctor bending over me. Apparently, the gardener had found us, carried me to the house, and called the police."

"Did they find the killers?" Faren's voice sounded gruff.

"No. There were no leads. No fingerprints, not even a strange footprint. I called the detective about a month ago. He said they were still on the case, but nothing new as yet." She turned over to stare down into Faren's brilliant, blue eyes. "Do you think Iraj killed my parents?"

He sighed and remained silent for a few moments. "Yes…I do."

"He was looking for the key, wasn't he? He tortured my father."

He nodded. "Either personally, or through his minions."

"Do you think my father knew the small pyramid I brought with me as a child was the key?" Tears filled her eyes, threatening to overflow. "Did he die to protect me?" Her voice sounded strained and hoarse to her own hearing, and she drew a deep breath.

Faren grasped her shoulders and rolled her back onto her pillow to stare down at her. "I would say, yes, your father did die to protect you. He did it because he loved you. And I am positive he would not wish you to torture yourself like this. You wanted to speak of the matter, and I allowed you to, even though I knew it would upset you. You cannot bring your parents back. No one can, not even the Goddess. But understand this. I swear on my own blood that the man responsible for your parents' deaths will himself dwell in the deepest darkest pit of hell by midnight of New Year's Eve."

She pushed at his chest and sat up. "And know this, Faren Malaan. I will be at your side that night to meet him, and I will put him in hell before you."

"No! It is too dangerous."

"You have no say in this. I am my own person, and don't bother using any of those mind powers on me, either."

His face ran through a gamut of emotions, and he glance away, then back at her. "What do you know of mind powers?"

"You have had me agreeing to all sorts of things I would not usually agree to. Did you think I wouldn't realize something was amiss? I asked Pen, and he filled me in on your powers of coercion."

A half smile formed on his lips. "Did he now? I will have to speak to that old man." He tried to turn her over, but she refused to budge.

"I shall hold you safe while you sleep," he said, frowning.

"No."

"No?"

"No, you are right. No one can bring my parents back. But I don't want to sleep."

"You don't?"

213

"No. Not when there is so little time left to us. Not when there is so much more we could do." She gave him a sensual smile.

He lay back on his pillows and stretched. "Oh yes, and what is that?"

She moved to cover his hard-muscled body with her softer curves. Her breasts pressed against his chest.

He grinned. "Ah, I see."

Chapter Seventeen

Three nights later, Silverdawn sat on Faren's bed. She wore the nightgown Pen had given her, and while she brushed her hair, she stared across at Faren as he burnished his shield. He then laid it aside and picked up his sword and whetstone. She sighed impatiently, wishing only for him to come to bed and hold her as he had the night Pen had rescued her from Iraj's Magick.

"Can't that wait?" She cast a look at the antique clock across the room. "It's twelve o'clock. Come to bed."

He continued to work on his sword. He didn't look up. "Get some rest. You must be tired after all that training today."

"So that's it." She frowned. "You still don't want me to go tomorrow night." She crawled from the bed and stood before him. "I have been practicing for three days now. You said yourself that I wield the battle-axe Pen gave me like I was born with it in my hand. I know I can hold my own with Iraj."

Faren stilled in his task of sharpening his sword and met her gaze. His eyes appeared more brilliant than usual. "I already agreed you can go. That has nothing to do with this."

"Ah. So there is a *this*?"

He released a ragged breath and took up sharpening his sword again. "Just go to bed."

215

"No." She stood watching him as the tension between them intensified—the only sound the scraping of the whetstone.

She broke the silence. "What does it mean?" she asked, tracing her finger over the painting of the rose and the snake on his shield.

He glanced up in askance.

"The insignia on your sword and shield—the dragon and rose. It has a meaning, doesn't it?"

He met her gaze, his eyes cold, hard. "It is my representation of the Goddess."

She raised a brow.

"A fair rose for her beauty. And the ice-bitch heart of a serpent," he replied bluntly.

She stared straight at him. "You liken me to her. Don't you?" She laughed shortly and turned from the condemnation in his eyes. "It's because I won't go back to Rastehm with you, isn't it?"

He glanced away.

"We have been through this, and yet you still condemn me. I couldn't live like that, Faren. You cannot expect me to give up the trappings of modern life for the hardships of a medieval world. I would go crazy." She pushed a hand through her hair. "You were raised in that life; I was not."

He laid his sword and the whetstone aside, stood, and grasped her shoulders. "It is not that bad, really. You would get used to it." But even as he spoke, she shook her head.

"No. I could never get used to it. They don't even have running water, for goodness sakes, or proper toilets."

His hands dropped to his sides. He resumed his seat

216

and turned back to his task. When he spoke, his voice sounded dull, lifeless. "Go to bed. I will join you shortly."

She turned and trudged across the floor. Guilt weighed heavily on her shoulders. "I know you think I don't love you, but this goes both ways, Faren Malaan. If you loved me enough, you would stay and send Kalden back with the pyramid." She climbed into the lonely four-poster bed and pulled the covers to her chin.

His sword clattered to the table, and he strode across the room to stare down at her. "You know that is impossible. People depend on me. And without a male heir, Mikkasah has hinted that I am next in line to the throne. Also, I am a sworn knight of Rastehm, and although I do not hold with some of Deharna's beliefs, I have pledged my life and allegiance to the Goddess and my king. And that vow I will not break. So as you see, my reasons are many, whereas you only have one."

He reached for the bedside light, and darkness filled the room. She heard him move to the other side of the bed. Heard the soft rustle of his shirt as he pulled it over his head, and his jeans drop to the floor. The bed sank beside her, and he reached to pull her into his arms. The heat of his large body flowed over her through the flimsy cloth of her nightgown, and she smiled into the darkness and turned into his arms. His breath was hot on her face. He didn't move.

"Make love to me," she whispered. "So I have something to remember you by when you are gone."

He lay silent—uncannily so. She put her lips to his, but he didn't respond.

"What is it?" She drew back, trying to read his face in the moonlight streaming through the window.

"Do you think I have no feelings, woman—that I am a man made of stone?" He breathed harshly. "It would please me if you would turn over. I will not be making love to you tonight—or ever again—unless it is with your father's blessing."

She couldn't answer because of the lump in her throat. Tears welled in her eyes, but she refused to let them fall. She rolled over, and his powerful arms wrapped around her waist, drawing her back against the comfort of his body.

"This is blackmail," she said quietly into the darkness after finally finding her voice. "You're using my love to force me to go with you."

He groaned and turned her again quickly. His lips came down over hers in a kiss that held all his pent-up longings, which echoed hers. And she knew her words were a lie.

****

It was a dark and stormy night. How appropriate those old words seemed. Silverdawn saw a bolt of lightning streak above the museum. Never had she thought the museum eerie, but tonight the gothic building, with its rows of gargoyles decorating the fringes of the turreted roof, appeared to come straight from a horror movie.

She stood at the park gate with the others, staring across the road. Her hands trembled, and she thrust them into the pockets of her leather breeches. It was a quarter to ten. They had two and a quarter hours to retrieve the pyramid and assemble back here so that Faren and Kalden could meet their deadline to be transported back to their own time. Two hours to the new year. Silverdawn wondered if she would live to see it.

She stared across at the small window at the bottom corner of the museum—Professor Waymer's office. She felt an overwhelming sense of sadness. She had liked the man. He'd been her mentor for the three years she had worked at the museum. The fact annoyed her that she'd not known the difference between him and Iraj after spending so much time in the professor's company.

She supposed she couldn't feel too bad. Serena was his wife, and she hadn't even known Iraj's identity until it was too late. She glanced at Serena, secure in Todd's arms, several feet away. They were saying their last goodbyes.

Todd had chosen to come with them. Serena was to take a taxi back to Pen's store and wait, then meet them back here at midnight, should everything go as planned. Silverdawn met Todd's gaze as he smiled at her over Serena's head. He wore blue jeans and sneakers, a blue tunic belted at the waist, and a sleeveless chain-mail vest beneath. A short sword supplied by Pen hung at his waist. He was a most unlikely knight, but she admired his bravery.

He had already experienced a sample of Iraj's power. Yet still he insisted on accompanying them. He told her early last night that he had to go with them to prove to himself that he was still a man. Iraj had taken his confidence and sense of worth from him; tonight, he would gain it back.

"Are you sure you want to do this?" asked Faren, reaching down to take her hand. "You know I would rather you stay with Serena."

"I can't do that, Faren. I must do this for all those I have loved. That monster took my parents. Now I will take something from him."

He gathered her into his arms, gave her a brief hug, then slowly set her aside.

She smiled sadly and ran her gaze over his large body. Tonight, he and Kalden had both dressed in the full garb of Palladian Knights—black tunics beneath chain mail, black leather pants, and ebony boots. They carried an array of weapons. Swords were secured in leather scabbards on their backs, daggers strapped at their waists, another slipped into a special pocket inside their boots. Their shields, each bearing their own special insignia, hooked to their arms—Kalden's, the fire-breathing dragon—Faren's, a serpent entwined in roses.

Faren had chosen Silverdawn's clothing as well. Black tunic and chain-mail vest, knee high, flat-heeled boots, and soft, woven leather pants the same as his.

She was brought from her reverie by Pen's touch on her arm.

"Stay in the center, Silverdawn, so you can advise us where to go. Faren and I will lead, then you and Todd. Kalden will take the rear."

She nodded and smiled inwardly at Pen's attire. He was dressed as she had first seen him—long robes with a cowl pulled up around his face, his strange golden eyes aglow within the dark depths. But this time, he held a five-foot rosewood staff. "Come," he beckoned. " 'Tis time."

She took a few steps, then glanced back to see Todd drop a kiss on Serena's cheek. The young woman watched them as they crossed the slick black asphalt toward the museum. Serena raised her hand to Todd who had risked so much for her. Then she turned to cut through the park toward the taxi stand as arranged.

Silverdawn smiled and turned to catch up with her

220

friends. What a strange procession they must appear to anyone who witnessed their passing. The streets were unusually quiet, with most of London's population probably attending the New Year's Eve festivities on the banks of the River Thames.

In silence they climbed the marble stairs leading to the double doors of the museum. At the entrance, all was darkness. The lantern-shaped lights that usually burned above the doors were suspiciously absent.

Pen pushed at the door. It was locked.

"What do we do now?" she asked. "I thought Iraj would have left it open, since he knew we were coming."

"Allow me." Faren moved forward and pushed on the door. It opened with ease. "He was expecting me. We are old foes."

The five moved into the foyer. All was silent except for the ticking of the grandfather clock around the corner from the door. Silverdawn felt for the light switch and gave it a flick. Nothing.

Pen moved from behind her. "My turn." He spoke several words in a deep guttural language more ancient than any artifact held within the museum. Words unfamiliar to Silverdawn.

A light sprang up around the wizard, and a soft, phosphorescent glow lit up the floor within a ten-pace radius. "I apologize. This is the best I can do for the light, but I have also cast a protective spell around us. However, I would suggest we stay close."

She nodded. "Straight ahead is the staircase that leads to the first floor. Since the electricity is out, the elevator will be out of order."

"I would not trust the elevator with Iraj in the building in any case," put in Faren. "It would prove too easy a trap."

The others agreed, and they progressed across the black-and-white tiled foyer to the staircase that lay about twenty feet away. They began to climb, their boots echoing ominously on the polished wooden steps.

****

Each moment seemed like an eternity. Faren glanced behind to catch a glimpse of Silverdawn's face, lit by Pen's eldritch light. What, he wondered, did Iraj have in store for them?

Would the attack be hard and fast, or would it be a long, drawn-out affair—a test on their nerves? And would Pen's protective glamor hold?

He did not have to wait long for the answer. He topped the last step, and a dark shadow swooped toward him.

"Duck!" he shouted, dragging his sword over his shoulder and bringing it down hard across the neck of the beast as it reached him. Body and head toppled to the floor.

Kalden raced up the last few steps, followed by Pen, Silverdawn, and Todd. "Who or what was that thing?" Kalden nudged a large falcon's head with his toe. A human body garbed in Egyptian clothing lay a mere foot away.

Silverdawn crouched to examine the decapitated figure at her feet. "It's Horus, Egyptian God of War. His statue once stood in that corner." She pointed into the shadows and grimaced. "This is so lifelike. It's like a real being."

Pen nodded. "Iraj has the power to bring inanimate objects to life. This is the perfect battleground for him."

The sound of falling rubble arose from across the

room. Pen moved closer, his body encased in light. Before them stood a large Egyptian tablet, depicting a mural of ten royal guards from the tomb of Queen Haiti. Even as they watched, the life-size paintings metamorphosed into flesh-and-blood beings and broke from the wall to march ominously toward the party. Their mesmerizing golden eyes glowed eerily, their extended swords glinting in the dim light. Scanty, white-pleated skirts and heavily muscled chests completed the picture.

Silverdawn froze, as the figures changed course and headed toward her.

Faren leaped forward and rammed his shield sideways into the first guard's head as the creature slashed at Silverdawn's throat. The Egyptian fell backward. Faren righted his balance and finished the guard with a sword point to the heart. Black blood sprayed into the air, and he reared back.

One of the Egyptians grabbed him from behind, trapping his sword at his side. He kicked back, slamming his boot into the guard's kneecap. The man toppled to the floor.

Silverdawn snapped from her daze, dragged her axe clear of its holster, and glanced around. One of the guards held Todd by the throat, pinning him to the hieroglyphic wall, slowly choking him. Todd's sword was trapped between the man's ribs.

She buried her axe deep into the Egyptian's back. The creature screamed and fell forward, and Todd pushed the body aside.

Several feet away, Faren landed a powerful left to a guard's jaw. The man staggered, then came again, and another Egyptian joined him, jabbing at Faren with his sword. The second figure blocked Faren's thrust and grasped at his arm with his free hand. The first guard lunged at him. Faren twisted and landed a savage kick to the Egyptian's gut. The creature fell, and Kalden ran in and finished him with a disemboweling thrust and cut.

But Faren was still held by the second guard. The strength of Iraj's conjuration was prodigious, and the hand wrapped around his arm burned like a thousand searing fires. He stifled a cry and dropped his sword, which was useless at close range, fighting to keep the guard's hands from his throat.

He was being forced back, inch by inch, toward the wall. Then suddenly, he was released as the guard fell forward onto him, then sagged to the ground. Pen stood before Faren with his rosewood staff, a grin on his wrinkled face.

Faren turned to see Kalden finish the last of the guardsmen. And as he crumpled, all of the bodies miraculously crumbled to dust and dissipated, no evidence of existence remaining.

He gathered his friends close, his jaw clenching. "All of you did well. But I fear this is just the first phase of our quest. Iraj was testing us." He added an edge to his tone. "So watch yourselves and the person before you. I promise things will only get worse!"

****

Iraj cursed and flung his goblet of red wine at the wall above the hearth. The glass shattered into a thousand tiny slivers and fell noisily to the marble tiles below. The liquid ran like ruby blood down the white wall.

Blood! The word pounded through his head. It should have been *their* blood. All of them should be

224

dead. He had underestimated them. He'd thought that his Egyptians would at least finish the girl and that weakling Haversham.

He groaned and gripped his stomach as deep pain ripped at his insides. Then, when the pain subsided, he raised his head to stare into the standing oval mirror on his desk. With a touch of his hand, the mirror reverted to a normal looking glass, and the face that peered back at him haunted him. Impatiently, he pushed back his cowl—skin a ghastly shade of gray, eyes dark and sunken.

He appeared so emaciated; it was hard to recognize Professor Waymer's suave face in the specter staring back at him. Pain tore again at his abdomen, and he groaned involuntarily. Frantically, he searched the pockets of his cloak for the tablets the doctor had given him. At first, he had refused to take them. Now he realized they were the only concoction that would kill the pain—even if only temporarily.

He poured another goblet of wine and washed the pills down. Then he slouched back into his chair to await their effect. After several minutes, a dream-like languor washed over him, and he gained some small respite from the pain.

He thumped his fist onto his desk. How could matters have gotten so out of hand? All seemed so simple. Find the key, find the pyramid, and release his demons. And with his demons would come his power.

He laughed, an ugly sound that rattled in his throat. So far Malaan and Pendragon had gotten the better of him, but tonight, he would be victorious. He would see them beg. See them *all* beg. He smiled, an evil smile that lit up his sunken ebony eyes as he stared into the mirror.

Perhaps he wouldn't kill the girl. Perhaps he would use Silverdawn as his blood sacrifice to Samioa, Goddess of Death. He bunched his fist. Tonight, all of his dreams would be realized.

He reached forward, touching the mirror's glass, and watched his reflection transform. Within the frame, Faren, Silverdawn, and their friends trudged up the stairs to the next level.

Little did they know what awaited them.

Chapter Eighteen

Todd squinted as he peered into the darkness ahead of Pen's guiding light. He wondered what would attack them next. They weren't that lucky that nothing would be waiting for them in the darkness. "So what is on the second level?" he asked Silverdawn. "I don't think I've ever come this way. I usually take the elevator or the northern staircase."

Silverdawn didn't turn but answered as she climbed, speaking loudly enough for them all to hear. "When we reach the top, we will enter a hallway lined with paintings from the Renaissance period. Then we will turn into the Amazon Jungle Room, at the end of which lies a room holding an exhibition of Japanese pottery and statues from the Kamakur Era, spanning 1192 to 1333 AD."

"That room connects to a staircase leading to the third floor." Todd groaned. "Great. We are either to be attacked by creatures from a Renaissance painting, killed by wild animals and natives, or slashed by samurais."

"Just stay close to me," said Kalden from behind him. "I'll watch your back."

"I'll do that and return the favor."

"You just get yourself home in one piece to that pretty lady you have waiting, or she has promised she'd have my guts for garters."

He frowned. "She did?"

Kalden laughed. "Well, not in so many words, but she implied it."

Todd chuckled. He couldn't imagine Serena even thinking such a thing.

Faren called a halt as they reached the landing. As Silverdawn had said, a long, dark hall stretched out in front of them. Pen nodded, and they continued on.

Todd didn't tell them of the skeletal hands that reached from gilt-edged canvases in the shadows as they passed by. A chill flickered down his spine, but there was no need to worry everyone for no reason. Apparently, the creatures in the painting couldn't escape, or they would already have done so.

****

As they rounded the end of the corridor, a living vine reared out of the darkness. Thick as a man's wrist, the vine latched onto Pendragon's ankle and dragged him, shouting and struggling, down the hallway toward the Jungle Room.

Faren charged after him, to see the old man hoisted into the air toward the gaping maw of a violet, bell-shaped bloom. He leaped and slashed down with his sword, severing the vine. The giant flower reared back, its petaled mouth snapping shut and its long red tongue retracting.

The old man fell with a thump to the floor and lay panting. Faren reached down and helped him to his feet as their comrades fumbled through the darkness, guided by the wizard's wan light.

"You best not move any more than necessary," Pendragon cautioned, gaining his balance and his breath. "If you have not noticed, we are surrounded."

Faren froze, becoming suddenly aware of hundreds

of vines hanging from the ceiling and useless light fixtures as Pendragon's Magick light intensified.

It was hard to tell who the vines would attack first. Greenery writhed up and down walls, bringing each wooden panel to life. Flora slithered from the shadows, closing around him and his friends. Edging closer to their feet and legs, guided by Pendragon's eldritch light, which was turning the glow from companion to foe.

Faren noted that only one flower appeared visible, and all the vines seemed to stem from that main growth. Several plans filtered through his mind but were quickly discarded as he brought his sword down to slash at a vine threatening his leg. All thoughts of the vines disappeared, though, as a greater danger approached. The silence shattered as a loud noise ripped across his nerve endings.

The sound echoed through the dark room and rang out against the high, frescoed ceiling. It was a hacking cadence, like a wood saw cutting metal. He knew that sound instantly.

"What is it?" whispered Silverdawn with a tremor in her voice, laying a hand on his arm. Her eyes were wide in her pale face.

"Panther." He breathed, meeting her gaze with a chill in his guts. He squeezed her hand reassuringly, then released her to grip his sword with both hands. He swung around—scanning the edges of the dark periphery of their light—and glimpsed the cat. It had moved behind them, circling in. A large cat's most hostile maneuver— a predator circling its prey before rushing in for the kill.

He signaled to Pendragon. The wizened old man stepped forward and raised his hand. A shot of light equivalent to that of a torch beam flashed from his palm into the beast's golden eyes. For a moment the cold eyes of death stared back at him. Then, with one lithe bound, the creature disappeared behind a heavy curtain of vines and display cases—its growl of hatred reverberating through the darkness yet again.

"It is hunting us. We have to hurry, but be wary," warned Faren. He took the lead, Pendragon just behind. As they crept through the cavernous room, thoughts of the past played heavily on his mind.

On assignment in South Africa in the early 1900s, he had seen what a panther could do to a man. A black panther had mauled the man whom he had been sent to reprimand. He had been the first on the scene and recalled vividly the terrible injuries the beast had inflicted.

This flashed through Faren's mind as he made his way through the semi-dark room with his companions. Instinctively, he dragged down the bottom edge of his chain mail coat. It came to the center of his knees. He prayed, should the panther choose to attack, the cat would elect him or Kalden as its prey and not one of the others, for his other friends would be defenseless. The knights were the only ones dressed to battle such an animal and the only ones trained in real combat. Suddenly, Kalden groaned and doubled over in pain. A black-shafted arrow lodged in his flesh, below the line of his sleeveless chain-mail coat.

Faren watched a native with long black hair, dark skin, and red-and-white streaks staining his face leap from the shadows but wasn't fast enough. Kalden spun as the man reached him, grasped the warrior, and brought him over his shoulder hard onto the floor. "A bit of help over here!" he shouted as three more natives attacked from his left.

Silverdawn caught the first warrior across the gut with her battle-axe. He grunted and fell.

Todd raised his short sword to the second, but the impact of the man's leap knocked him to the floor. The young man fought desperately to keep the warrior's dagger from his throat.

Faren intercepted the third warrior as Kalden's sword was knocked from his hand and skittered along the floor. Faren grabbed the warrior's knife hand and forced it back from his throat, turning the dagger toward his opponent's chest. The man's eyes widened. Faren dragged him across his chest until the native was pinned beneath him and, with one powerful push, used his body weight to force the dagger point into the warrior's heart.

He shoved the body aside, hastily wiped the knife clean on the dead man's loincloth, then scanned the area for Silverdawn. She and the wizard were methodically dispatching the vines that were curling about various parts of their bodies. Silverdawn used her axe while Pen brought his rosewood staff into play, dissolving the vines as they made to tangle around his limbs.

Todd was locked in a deadly embrace with a native. Faren started toward him but caught sight of his brother, the arrow shaft still buried deep in his shoulder. Kalden stumbled, the veins standing out on his neck with the exertion of holding off the native he battled. He could sense his brother was weakening and changed course. Kalden was strong, but the pain in his shoulder would be agonizing.

In a final effort, Kalden loosened his hold on the warrior's hands and brought his fist down into the warrior's eye. The man barely flinched; the blow from

Kalden's injured arm had no power behind it.

Faren dashed toward him but was knocked off balance by an unknown force exploding from out of the darkness. He never heard the panther charge. The creature landed with all its weight and the full momentum of its attack in the middle of his back, between his shoulder blades.

Faren hurtled forward, but claws bit in and held, and for a moment he thought they were hooked into his flesh. However, instead of bringing him down to the wooden floor, the feline had slammed him into a thick wall of dead, hanging vines.

The vines cushioned the impact, but the pounding had driven the air from his lungs. They burned, and his ribs felt as if they had been crushed.

With the panther still mounted high on his shoulders, he staggered under its heavy weight, realizing that the animal's claws were caught in his hauberk.

Somehow, he managed to keep his feet and support himself by grasping hold of the vines. The beast's mighty heart pounded against his back—or was that his own heart?

He felt the cat gather itself, bringing up its back legs, coiling its body like a spring, ready to lash downward across his buttocks and the back of his thighs. His flesh would be opened to the bone, blood vessels and arteries sliced through, a crippling injury from which he would probably bleed to death in minutes.

He pushed off from the vines, both arms flailing backward. As he fell, he drew up his legs. The cat's back paws, claws outspread, struck the air, missing his flesh. Man and beast, with their combined weight, crashed to the floor.

He was a big man, and the panther was underneath him. A single, hissing snarl was forced from its lungs by the impact, and the animal released its claws from his hauberk. He twisted violently and, fueled by his terror, seized a thick fold of skin at the scruff of the panther's neck. He tore the creature free and hurled it against a wooden display case.

As he dragged his dagger from his boot and rolled to his knees, the panther rebounded at him like a rubber ball. Its jaws open to full gape, its extended front paws reached for his shoulders. As it smashed into him chest to chest, its back legs locked up in an instinctive disemboweling movement, and its head shot forward to sink its fangs into his face and throat. Faren countered with his dagger held sideways between both hands, thrusting it like the curb bit from a horse's bridle into the panther's open mouth. One of the creature's front fangs broke off completely as it struck the blade, and then he was on his back, holding the panther off his face with the dagger. It snarled, and a hot mist of spittle blew into his face and filled his nostrils with the stink of carrion and death, and something else—camphor. It was even more frightening to think this beast had been resurrected for the sole purpose of his demise.

He sensed a paw reach over his shoulder. At the same time the animal's back legs jackknifed up, claws fully extended to tear out the front of his stomach.

However, the back of Faren's head was pressed up hard against a deep pile of vines, and the animal hooked its paws not into his throat but into the wrist-thick vines beside his ear. Then the cat slashed down with both back legs together, but instead of slicing open his belly, the claws tangled in the heavy metal links of his chain mail.

233

For a moment the panther's attack was weakened. It ripped at the vines as its paws sank deeper into their foliage, seeming not to realize its error, and the back legs kicked downward spasmodically, tearing at Faren's hauberk with a metallic scraping sound.

As it struggled, the animal pulled back its head, trying to avoid the steel blade that Faren was still forcing deeply between its open jaws. Instantly, he whipped back the dagger, then drove it forward again into the panther's eye and through its brain.

The panther faltered, and he pushed and twisted the knife again and felt the beast release its deadly grip. He shoved hard, and the animal fell away from his body to lie unmoving upon the vines.

Exhausted, Faren lay panting, gathering his strength. He realized how close he had come to death and thanked the Goddess he had survived. Several long gashes ran along his arm, one in his thigh, and a graze on his cheek. He hadn't the strength to check their extent. All he knew was that they stung like hell. Finally, rolling slowly to his knees, he scanned the surrounding area and found Silverdawn making her way toward him.

"Thank the Lord, you are alive." She gasped. "I saw the panther take you down, but I couldn't break free of the vines." She extended her hand to help him stand.

Faren noted the unshed tears in her eyes. "There was nothing you could do," he answered, resting his hands on her shoulders. "And I am glad you stayed back."

She dabbed with the edge of her tunic at a deep slash in his arm, but he brushed her away.

"It is nothing. Is my brother all right?"

She stepped to the side, and Faren spied Pen bent over Kalden, helping him to sit. Todd stood, peering into

234

the darkness, his sword drawn in readiness.

Kalden glanced up and grimaced as Faren crossed to kneel at his side.

"Sorry." He grinned. "I let my guard down. Told you I wasn't as good a swordsman as you."

"You were not to know what was hidden in the darkness or the extent of Iraj's evil." He noted the black shaft jutting from his brother's arm, then met his gaze. "You know what has to be done?"

"Make it swift. You know I hate being wounded." Kalden peeled his glove from his hand using his teeth, then bit down hard on the thick black leather.

Faren glanced at Silverdawn. Her face was the color of tallow. "You best not look. This is no sight for the tenderhearted."

She nodded, reaching down to give Kalden's good shoulder a brief pat, then turned away to keep guard with Todd.

Pendragon moved behind Kalden to help support his back, and the younger man gave Faren a brief nod.

He snapped the feather end from the shaft and, in one fluid motion, pushed the shaft end through his brother's shoulder until it protruded through the other side. Then he dragged the arrowhead swiftly from Kalden's flesh.

The big knight sagged back into Pen's arms, perspiration coating his brow.

"I really need to attend this wound," said the old man, "but 'tis too dangerous here. What is in the next room?"

Silverdawn turned. "The Japanese exhibition."

"I hope it *is* only Japanese pottery." Pen dragged a length of linen from the confines of his robe pocket and wound the bandage hastily around Kalden's arm. He pulled the knot gently but firmly and straightened. "Faren, help me get him to his feet."

He did as Pendragon asked, and the party moved on through the last part of the Jungle Room. But even as they stepped through the exit into the next exhibit, the high-pitched howl of a jackal sounded through the silence, indicating that they had merely forestalled the inevitable. Evil still lingered within the darkness.

They entered the Kamakur Era exhibition, leaving whatever harm still lingered behind.

"Stay vigilant," Faren reminded his friends. "Be aware that danger could lie in wait but a step away."

All around them pieces of ancient pottery and intricately carved statues painted a scene of their own place in history, but nothing sprang to life.

Faren wondered if Iraj was tiring—if his illness had finally taken full effect. Maintaining the Magick of keeping the panther, vines, and native warriors alive would have taxed the strongest of sorcerers.

He asked Silverdawn if she remembered the length of the room and was told it measured roughly two hundred meters. After traveling what he reasoned to be about half that length, he called a halt.

"Rest for a moment," he ordered, turning to the wizard.

"I will see to Kalden's wound." The old man sank to the floor and began dragging a fresh bandage from his bag. "And what of you?" he asked. "Have you wounds from the panther?"

"Just a few scratches and superficial bites. When you finish with Kalden, you can deal with mine."

Pen nodded again. From the pocket of his robe, he

took a red velvet pouch, upended it, and poured a substantial amount of the white powder onto the lacerated skin around the back and front of Kalden's ruined shoulder.

The knight winced as the powder seeped into his flesh but relaxed as the mixture began to take effect. He sagged back against the wooden display case behind him, and his eyes widened in amazement. "The pain. It's gone. What is that stuff?" He grinned. "I will have to take a pouch into battle next time."

The wizard dragged a clean section of white linen from his pocket and wound the cloth around Kalden's arm. Then he turned to attend to Faren's wounds. One long scratch down his left forearm was particularly deep and still wept blood. Faren grimaced as Pen wiped it clean, applied the powder, then carefully bound it.

"Unfortunately, this concoction can be deceiving," the wizard lectured both men. "It will kill the pain but not heal the flesh. I am afraid both your wounds are still severe. You just cannot feel them. So try not to tax yourself overly much."

Kalden pushed to his feet. "Try I will, but it may be hard without the pain."

The old man gave the young knight's good shoulder a gentle squeeze. "You do that, boy. I would not like to see you bleed to death."

Chapter Nineteen

Iraj shoved his scrying mirror aside and fell forward to rest his face on his arms. Chills racked his body, but his flesh was afire, and perspiration beaded his brow. The power to hold the panther and other sorceries in place had taken its toll. He felt as weak as a babe.

He'd thought he had them when the panther attacked Malaan—Mikkasah's First Knight was by far Iraj's biggest worry. The other knight was not to be scoffed at either but had not the battle skills of the First Knight.

Iraj reached for his tablets. His hand shook as he unscrewed the lid, and the jar dropped, scattering small blue tablets across his desk. With trembling fingers, he scooped up several pills and popped them into his mouth, then proceeded to wash them down with a gulp of water. He had discarded the wine, knowing that to win this battle he would need his full wits about him. He straightened in his chair and placed his hands to his temples.

He had to think, but it was becoming so frustratingly hard. His body ached in every joint, and his head thumped as if it had a major concerto playing in his brain. He prayed to his demon lord the medication would soon take effect. He needed to concentrate, but how could he do so in such agony? He was certain had he been an ordinary mortal, he would now be in a hospital bed with a multitude of tubes and drips hanging from various parts of his anatomy.

He slammed his fist onto his desk, knocking several of the pills to the floor. Nothing must interfere with his concentration. If only he could release his demons so he could use them in the ceremony to restore his powers.

He should have captured the girl and used her in a blood sacrifice. At least then, some of his power would have been restored. But he had been too overconfident, and now it was too late. His physical body had deteriorated so much over the last few days he hadn't the strength to achieve such a feat.

He had felt triumphant when the pyramid arrived from France. Little did Emile realize what he had set in motion. When Iraj held the pyramid in his arms, he'd felt an immediate influx of euphoria. Unfortunately, it had died with the sound of his creatures' plaintive cries— silent to any of mortal hearing, torturous to one of his kind. His darlings had squirmed beneath the surface of the crystal, begging for release—release only the key could give. The *key*!

Iraj pressed his palms to his temples, squeezing, willing the pain to wane, willing there to be an easier way to obtain the key. But the only way he knew was through the demise of these five people. And dead they certainly would be when they entered the next level.

He reached for his mirror and waved his hand across the flat, luminous surface. The glass shimmered and revealed the five people he most despised in the world as they stepped onto the landing of the third floor. The last level—the winner-take-all level.

****

"Great! That's all I need to hear—dinosaurs!" Todd's hand curled around the hilt of his sword.

239

"Just a skeleton of a Brachiosaurus and a reconstructed Albertosaurus," placated Silverdawn from beside him. Todd seemed to be becoming more skittish as they moved farther into the large chamber.

"An Albertosaurus? Only the fiercest of all dinosaurs next to the Tyrannosaurus rex. And what else is up there?" He shot back.

"A statue of a griffin," she answered weakly.

"How the hell did a griffin get mixed up with a Jurassic display?"

"The statue is being held here until the Greek exhibition opens next week. The third floor has the highest ceiling."

"How convenient for Iraj." He grumbled.

Faren rounded and threw Todd a hard look. "Get off her back, Haversham. Silverdawn is not responsible for the doings of this museum. Iraj has probably been planning this confrontation for weeks."

The young man ran a hand through his fair hair, mussing it even more, then reached out and touched Silverdawn's shoulder. "Sorry. Faren is right. I guess I'm letting the pressure get to me. So what else do we have up there?" he asked, more composed.

"Apart from those, a couple of fossilized dinosaur eggs. A few other miscellaneous fossils and what we think may be a Piltdown Man. We are waiting on verification."

"Piltdown Man?" asked Faren, half-turning. "Explain."

"I can answer that one," ventured Todd. "Last century, someone planted a skull made from a human cranium and an ape jaw in an excavation site, and a scientist thought that he had found the 'missing link.' "

"Then there are 'Jenny Hanivers,'" continued Silverdawn. "Which are mermaids made by sewing monkeys and fish together. Dead ones."

Todd squirmed. "There are some sickos in the world, all right."

"Where we come from, there is no need to make mermaids. We have the real thing," cut in Kalden from behind them.

"Real mermaids!" Todd sighed. "That's one sight I'd like to see."

Silverdawn stopped on the staircase as Faren turned and glanced back, but instead of meeting Todd's gaze, he looked at her. "All kinds of wonders inhabit our world," he said. "Dragons, selkies, and real griffins, to mention a few. Creatures your historians put down to mythology because there is no scientific evidence to support their existence. Our world is indeed a world of mystery and wonderment. A place that must be seen to be believed. But you will never see it, will you, Silverdawn? Because you will not take the risk."

Guilt and hurt cemented a lump in Silverdawn's chest. She looked away, unable to meet the accusation in his eyes.

Pen, who had been leading, turned to grasp Faren's wrist. He spoke gently but firmly, and his eyes were filled with ancient knowledge. "There is no time for this now, lad. Personal problems must be laid aside to be dealt with should we survive. We have but an hour left to find the pyramid, and we must still face Iraj's greatest challenge. For, fear not, he will know by now that if he does not stop us this time, there will be no stopping us at all. So fortify your courage, people, and band together, for we can have no petty differences between us now."

He glanced at each of his companions in turn. "I am hoping we will prevail, but there may be those of us who do not survive this quest. Just know that I regard you all as friends and have been honored to stand beside you."

He put his hand out palm down. "I think this old Rastehm custom would be appropriate here." Faren placed his hand on that of the old man. Kalden moved up the couple of steps that separated them and laid his hand over his brother's. She and Todd joined in.

"May we all survive to tell the tale to our grandchildren," said Kalden.

They all agreed and once more took formation to move up the last few steps to the landing. But even as they stepped onto the third floor, a horrific roar sounded from out of the darkness of the thirty-foot-high chamber.

Silverdawn stopped, her hand going automatically to the battle-axe strapped to her hip. "I think it's at the end of the chamber."

Faren moved to stand beside her, his lips close to her ear. "How long is this room?"

"At least six-hundred-and-sixty-feet long."

"Good, that will give us a little time—however, I think you had better tell us more about what we face."

"Perhaps we should form a circle. The least noise the better," cautioned Pen.

When they'd formed a circle, Silverdawn began to speak softly. "The Albertosaurus was a small dinosaur about three times the size of a man in height and twenty-five feet long. Its remains were found in the forests of North America. Its hind legs had three long, sharp claws that pointed forward, one smaller one that pointed backward, and two arms that ended in two miniature claws.

"Its jaws are massive and lined with rows of knife-like teeth." She grimaced. "If one of us is taken, we don't have a prayer."

They all stood silent.

"Tell me," asked Kalden. "Does this beast have any weaknesses?"

She took a moment to think. "Unlike bone-frilled dinosaurs, Albertosaurus has no protection around its neck. Its veins stuck out when it was in full action, shaking its head to catch or kill its prey and tear off pieces of its flesh."

"Let us hope none of us becomes its prey," replied Todd, heartfelt.

****

Kalden grinned across at Faren. "A little like the old days, fighting rogue dragons, aye, Faren?"

Faren relaxed and met the glint in his brother's eye. Kalden had the most marvelous way of relieving tension, of taking the seriousness out of life-threatening events. He had forgotten that trait of his brother's but was now grateful for it. "You could say that, but in those days we had the aid of lances."

"And dragons breathed fire, so I would say we and the beast are about even."

Silverdawn peered into the darkness. "You think if we had spears, we would stand a better chance?"

"It might help. If dinosaurs are anything like dragons, the scales on the underside of their bellies and neck are thinner than those on their backs."

Another low roar sounded through the black room. This time closer.

"Follow me." Silverdawn took Pen's arm and led her friends across the room to a tall, narrow door in the corner. "We may be able to improvise. This is the cleaner's storeroom."

She pulled on the handle, but it was locked. "I have no key, but if you could open it with your Magick, Pen, there are brooms and mops we could fashion into spears."

"Allow me." Faren moved in front of her. "Will this room hold all of us?"

She grimaced. "I can't remember, but there should be enough room."

He nodded. "When I break the lock, the beast may come to investigate. We'd best move quickly into the storeroom." He slammed into the door twice with his shoulder. The lock gave way, and the door broke open.

They moved within the safety of the small room, and Faren turned to prop the door closed with a mop under the handle. In the confined space, Pen's enchanted light burned bitter-bright, giving them plenty of illumination by which to work.

Faren reached for a broom, flipped it upside down, and struck off the end with Silverdawn's battle-axe, then passed the stick to Kalden.

"If ever you had to produce anything from that bottomless pocket of yours, wizard, do so now. For we are in desperate need of copper wire."

Pen's weathered countenance dissolved into a grin. "You have only to ask, lad." He delved into his pocket and pulled forth several lengths of flexible copper wire. "But I think you should show Todd how to do that. Kalden's wound is bleeding again. I need to see to it."

Kalden glanced down at the damp staining the arm of his tunic and agreed.

"I can help too." Silverdawn took a doctored broom

handle from Kalden's hand. "Just tell me what to do."

Faren instructed Silverdawn and Todd in the ways of attaching an eight-inch dagger to the end of a five-foot broom handle using wire.

When they each had a satisfactory weapon, the small band of companions moved out of the cleaner's closet into the dark room housing Iraj's latest challenge.

****

"Lower the light," Silverdawn heard Faren hiss. "Use only the slightest measure. If we are careful and skirt the edge of the room, we may have no need to battle the beast."

They moved on through the semidarkness, not speaking. If they were anything like her, Silverdawn thought, scarcely daring to breathe lest the dinosaur that dogged their steps and searched the shadows for prey caught their scent.

Through the darkness came the rapid pounding of heavy footsteps. Then a terrible, awful scream that reverberated through Silverdawn's head and filled her mind with dread. She searched the darkness behind her. A darkness that should have been occupied by Todd. A darkness that was now empty.

The scream became her own. "Todd! My God, it has Todd! Todd's gone!"

Faren rounded, his hand closing over her mouth as she tensed to scream again. "Take a deep breath. We have no time for hysterics."

He released her, and she sagged against his chest. It felt warm, safe, and secure in this world of turmoil, but he gripped her shoulders to hold her at arm's length. "What did you see?"

"Todd! He was right behind me!"

Another cry echoed through the room, and she stiffened.

"It is all right," he soothed into her ear. "We will save him."

Faren looked at Kalden. "What did you see?"

"He was there, then he was gone. I saw—I thought I heard something…" The blond knight shook his head.

Faren released her, then picked up his spear from where he had leaned it against a cabinet. "Right—quick, no time for talk. Pen—your light!"

Pen raced after Faren into the darkness, she and Kalden close behind.

"Stay back," urged Kalden as he sped past her. "Let Faren and me handle this!"

Like hell! There was no way she was staying behind.

Another of Todd's screams tore through the darkness, spurring her on. Where there was sound, there was life, and she would not leave her friend in peril.

She halted with the others in front of a tawny-colored dinosaur illuminated by Pen's light. The grisly sight had her stomach lurching and her blood freezing in terror. Todd wasn't dead, but his face was ashen and his cries no more than mewls of pain as loss of blood and exhaustion took their toll. The Albertosaurus shook him back and forth, trying to tear his leg from his body. Blood that could only be Todd's dribbled from each side of the dinosaur's wicked jaws and down the young man's trouser leg.

Faren hurled his homemade spear. It missed Todd's head by a hand's span and lodged in the dinosaur's chest. The giant reptile roared its pain. Todd dropped from its jaws to be caught by her and Kalden.

Unfortunately, Kalden took the bulk of Todd's body

with his one good arm and was knocked backward by the force of the impact, taking her with him. The beast, seeing more prey, bent to attack, but fire flashed from the end of Pen's rosewood staff into the reptile's head. The creature reared back, giving Kalden time to gain his feet and, with her aid, drag Todd clear of danger.

The knight released the injured man into her care, took steady aim, and hurled his six-foot spear toward the reptile's throat as Faren leaped onto its back. The dinosaur spun at the intrusion and swept its curved tail across the floor, trying to dislodge the knight.

Kalden's spear went wide, missing the creature completely. The beast's powerful tail slashed and caught him across the ribs, knocking him to the ground and sending him skidding across the polished floor.

****

The dinosaur tried to reach over its shoulder with its tiny arm to dislodge Faren from its back. But its arm wasn't made for such a long reach. He dragged his dagger from his boot and punched it into the Albertosaurus' tough hide. Using the dagger as a handhold, he hauled himself farther up its back. The reptile went wild. Forgetting about all other threats, it crashed into walls and display cases in a desperate ploy to remove the thing from its back.

Faren held on for dear life, praying that the dinosaur would tire long enough for him to reach its neck and drive home his sword.

From the corner of his eye, he saw Silverdawn run at the Albertosaurus and hack at the back of one of its legs with her battle-axe, then duck quickly out of the way as the beast lost balance and slammed into the skeletal remains of another dinosaur.

Bones fell, toppling all around. One struck Faren a painful blow to his left shoulder, and another struck Silverdawn a savage blow to her hip as she tried to dodge out of the way.

Faren almost lost his balance, but he caught himself just in time and held on grimly. The great reptile staggered. It was the opening he needed. Using his dagger, he dragged himself onto the reptile's shoulder, then up onto the neck where he drew his sword over his shoulder and drove it down into the thinner skin at the base of the dinosaur's skull. The reptile faltered, falling sideways as Faren freed his sword and leaped from its back.

Pen ran in, and his staff flared, sending fire bolts into the beast's eyes, and Faren rammed his sword into throat of the dinosaur till it hit bone. The reptile opened one blinded eye, tried to rise—then fell back. All life extinguished.

Faren pulled his sword and dagger from the beast and dropped both blades down beside him. Exhausted, he sank to the floor to lean against the dinosaur's cold hard carcass. Pen dropped down beside him. They glanced at each other in silence. For several moments they remained like that without speaking. However, Faren realized he had to find out what had happened to the others. He extended his hand to the old wizard and drew him to his feet.

Slowly Pen straightened, and a weary smile lit his eyes. "Well, we did it."

Faren gave a mixture of a sigh and a half laugh and ran a hand over the back of his neck. "Yes, old friend, we did it. But at what cost?"

Faren found Silverdawn huddled beside Todd in the

far corner of the room.

He bent and cupped her cheek gently with his hand. "Are you all right?" he asked, meeting her eyes.

"Fine." Her voice cracked, but she coughed to cover it. "Todd's not so good; he'll lose his leg."

Faren nodded. "Most likely, but he has his life. Kalden?"

"I don't know. Sorry, but I—"

He squeezed her hand. "I know. Everything happened so fast."

She nodded, but her face was uncommonly pale. He guessed this battle was taking its toll on all of them. He bent to examine Todd.

"He's alive but unconscious," Silverdawn murmured beside him.

He felt for a heartbeat and found one, albeit erratic. *Just as well*, he thought. His leg was a total mess. One glimpse had been enough to have even his stomach churning. The bone was completely snapped. The leg was hanging by no more than a mess of sinews, nerves, and lacerated muscle. Even if they could get him to a hospital, he doubted the doctors could save the leg. It would take a miracle. The leg was no more than mangled flesh.

"Stay here." He gave Silverdawn's hand another gentle squeeze. "Pen and I will find my brother."

Faren found Kalden seated between a wrecked display case and a pile of gigantic white bones from the ruined dinosaur skeleton. "I think a couple of my ribs are broken. How are the others?" he asked, his tone grave.

Faren crouched beside him. "Silverdawn is shaken. Todd is unconscious. He will lose his leg."

"Pity. He is a good man. I like him. I hope it makes

249

no difference to his woman."

"I think you will find Serena is of sterner mettle than you think. She'd have to be to survive all those months with Iraj."

The big knight nodded. "Perhaps you are right. I hope so. I have known women who cannot cope with such injuries in their man and end up leaving, but that is neither here nor now." He looked at Pendragon. "So, old man, what now? We won this round. Will Iraj give up the pyramid?"

The wizard shrugged his frail shoulders. "If the man is as sick as we believe, he may not have a choice. However, he has lived for thousands of years on his wits. I would not underestimate him." He leaned over Kalden. " 'Tis good you wore chain mail, or your injuries could be worse." He produced a section of white linen and proceeded to bandage Kalden's ribs with Faren's aid. Pendragon tightened the bandage, then Faren helped Kalden to his feet and followed the old wizard back to the others.

Faren crouched beside Silverdawn. "I have given this some thought and feel it best if you, Todd, and Kalden stayed here while Pen and I go for the pyramid."

"Iraj will try something else, won't he? You don't trust him to keep his word."

"Of course, I do," he lied smoothly. "There is no need for you to come the rest of the way, and Todd might regain consciousness."

Kalden and Silverdawn spoke together. "No way!"

Silverdawn scrambled to her feet and folded her arms over her chest. "I have not battled irate Egyptians, killer vines, resurrected natives, and dinosaurs not to go the distance."

"And I took an oath to Mikkasah, just as you did. I will see this through." Kalden turned his hard green gaze on Faren.

Faren came to his feet to stare down at his brother. "Now, look—"

"No. You look, Brother—" Kalden pushed to his feet to stand eye to eye with him.

"There is no time for this," Pendragon broke in. "This leg has to come off. The boy is bleeding to death."

"Then stand back." Faren gritted his teeth and pulled his sword from its scabbard.

Silverdawn stepped to block his path. "No! You can't just hack off his leg, like a…a wounded animal. In fact, you wouldn't do that to an animal." She searched his face. "Would you?"

He clenched his jaw and held her gaze, then with a ragged breath, slipped his sword back into its sheath. "Damn, woman. Do you think the decision was made lightly? Pendragon examined the leg. Nothing can be done. You said yourself that Todd would lose his leg."

"Yes. But a doctor—"

"There's no time, and we have no doctor, and be as it may, I would put my faith in Pendragon's medicine before any of your modern physicians. Now move aside, woman, or I shall have Kalden physically remove you."

Silverdawn glanced across at Kalden and met his steady gaze.

"Sorry, Princess, but I agree with Faren on this one."

With a heavy sigh she stepped aside and turned from the scene.

Pen placed a comforting hand on her shoulder and gave it a gentle squeeze.

"Have faith, lass. It is for the best. You will see."

"If you are going to do it, get it over with!" she ground, teeth clenched, eyes squeezed closed as if to block out Todd's pain.

Faren raised his sword above his head and with a two-handed stroke brought the blade down swiftly, just below the knee, severing the leg with a clean cut. Todd jerked and screamed, springing momentarily awake, but Pendragon quickly moved to place a cool, soothing hand on his brow, and the young man settled into a dreamless sleep.

Faren sheathed his sword and turned to the old man. "The wound will have to be cauterized."

The old man nodded. "I know," he replied gruffly. "Move aside."

The wizard mouthed three words of power, "*Quindus, Nimou, Daldah.*" The last six inches of his rosewood staff began to glow. He knelt, then drew the edge of the staff slowly across the weeping wound of the stump, sealing tendon, ligaments, and tissue. The stench of burning flesh filled the air. Pendragon mouthed three more words of power, and the staff reverted to normal, and he laid it at his side.

Taking a pouch of the same magical powder he had used on Kalden from his pocket, he sprinkled the contents onto the cauterized wound and carefully and swiftly bandaged the stump with clean white linen. "I can do no more. Todd's recovery is now in the hands of the Goddess." He touched his staff to the young man's amputated leg, and the limb turned to a pile of silver ash, then moments later vanished altogether.

Faren wrapped a hand around Silverdawn's arm, but she flinched away and turned to pick up her battle-axe from the floor. Averting her gaze from the wounded man, she swept her hair back from her face and secured her ponytail. She straightened her back. "Faren, you take Todd back to the storeroom and leave him there where he will be out of harm's way, then we'll go on."

He stared at the stubborn set of her chin, so like her father's. He realized there would be no softening. He replied as hard and tight. "As you will." He reached down and helped Kalden to his feet, then bent to scoop Todd into his arms.

Chapter Twenty

Ten steps. Ten steps to the attic door. Faren stood with his friends, staring up at the brown polished door with trepidation. Having crossed the Jurassic Room's great expanse and survived everything Iraj had thrown at him and his friends, he felt almost afraid to see what lay behind the final door.

Leaving Silverdawn and Pendragon to help Kalden, he cautiously took the first step, waiting several moments, testing for signs of a trap. Nothing. One, two…the number of steps reverberated in his head until he reached the small landing at the top of the stairs.

Stretching out his hand, he was careful not to touch the door in the event of a trap. He tested the handle, then turned to his companions and mouthed the words. "The door is locked."

Pendragon nodded, then he and Silverdawn helped Kalden up the stairs.

The old wizard pursed his lips. "We should have realized he wouldn't make this easy."

"No. But no door will keep me from gaining that for which I have fought!" Faren raised his foot and, with all the force of his frustration, crashed his boot into the wood. The door splintered and flew back on its hinges.

"Come in by all means." A deep voice sounded from within the shadows on the room's far side.

The four companions stepped through the doorway.

As they entered, light flooded the huge attic, but instead of the room being laden with old exhibits, paintings, and bric-a-brac, it was filled to capacity with six-foot mirrors, each mirror holding a living image of the dark sorcerer, Iraj. An ebony cowl shadowed his face, and his full-length black robe swirled to the floor to brush across his shiny ebony boots. Faren watched Silverdawn retreat a step and caught her arm for reassurance. She gave him a tremulous smile and straightened to her full height.

Pen, on her other side, also patted her arm. "Do not fret, lass. 'Tis merely an illusion."

The sorcerer's cruel laugh rang through the room. "Is it, old man? Is it?"

There was a pause and a momentary silence, but Pendragon once more broke through the quiet. "Show yourself, you villain!"

"It seems we meet again, Pendragon. It has been too long—almost a millennium in fact in this time frame, or twenty-seven years in Rastehm. Yet I still remember the day you betrayed your own kind and joined with that bitch Deharna to trap me!"

"I was never one of—*your* kind." Pendragon turned and spat on the floor as if to emphasize his words. "Always, you were a dark depraved thing without pity or conscience. And now you are beaten yet again. But this time for the final time!"

"Am I beaten?" The sorcerer curved his hand into a claw and aimed it at Pen who cried out and clutched at his chest, doubling over in pain.

Faren swept to his aid, but Iraj changed tactics, and a narrow ray of green energy flew from his fingertips straight at Faren. He ducked and rolled as the cutting ray flared past his ear to bore into the wall behind him, leaving a black smoldering hole.

Iraj tossed back his head and laughed. "Even near death I am invincible!"

Silverdawn gasped.

The cowl had fallen away from the sorcerer's face, and the face beneath was even worse than Faren had anticipated. The features were completely emaciated—the flesh gray, the eyes sunken and black with the flat patina of a dead man. A great flap of dry ruined flesh hung from his left cheek.

"A pretty sight, am I not, Silverdawn?"

Faren watched her take in the multiple mirrors and the horrific images, and she shook her head.

"You have lasted longer than I anticipated, girl. Perhaps you do have something of Mikkasah and Aurelia in you after all. Did Pen tell you your mother fought alongside Mikkasah in the war against me?" He straightened, and his voice grew stronger. "My army was mighty then."

"But not so mighty now," she replied sweetly. "I will have Faren relay your compliment to my mother and father when he hands them the pyramid." Her resolve seemed to have strengthened at the mention of her parents. She seemed determined not to allow the creature to intimidate her.

The necromancer's face twisted in a cruel sneer. He made to reply, but Faren cut him off. "Enough! Where is the pyramid?"

"Where you will not find it!" A small lightning bolt streaked from the sorcerer's hand and then another of the green rays, this time aimed at Silverdawn. She dropped and rolled as Faren had taught her. A quick succession of two more lightning bolts flashed at Kalden. He leaped aside just in time.

"The mirrors!" shouted Pen, charging one of Iraj's look-alike mirrors, smashing his staff into the glass, shards flying haphazardly across the room. "Destroy the mirrors. All of them! 'Tis through them that he wields his power. 'Tis an old conjurer's trick!"

"No!" Iraj cried as the first mirror broke. Lightning streaked from his fingertips, but the companions ducked and rolled and managed to avoid the rapidly fired bolts. Kalden brought his sword down into two more mirrors. Silverdawn made a dash and slammed her battle-axe across the face of three more, being careful to avoid flying glass. Kalden moved slowly but still managed to dodge Iraj's rays and lightning bolts.

Whether the sorcerer was tiring of keeping up the rapid succession of fire or his illness was taking its toll, Faren did not know. But Iraj's aim was deteriorating, and his fire was sparse.

The companions systematically smashed the mirrors until only one was left standing in the far corner.

Iraj gave up his defense and for one moment appeared to sag. His image shrank, then grew again and loomed with menace. He swooped away from the mirror and hovered above them in the air like a dark specter of doom. "You think you have beaten me! You think you can defeat Iraj of Istani! You will never crush me. Never!" His hand raised, his eyes narrowed and took on a reddish cast. In a final act of defiance, he spat out words in an unintelligible language.

But the spell was never completed—

Faren palmed the dagger from his boot and hurled it across the room. The mirror shattered, splintering the sorcerer's last image. The specter above them vanished, leaving only a black cloak, which floated slowly to the floor to lie at their feet.

And behind the mirror sat the pyramid.

****

All stood dazed, especially Silverdawn. In all of the movies she'd seen pertaining to mirrors, the archenemy had always been revealed behind the last mirror to be finally vanquished. Iraj had disappeared completely.

She turned to Pen, who also stood staring at the shattered glass slivers pooling like crushed ice at the foot of the last looking glass.

"Where is he? I thought he would be there. How could he do that and not be here?" Her tone held a hint of hysteria.

Pen took her hand and gave it a gentle pat. "Make no mistake, lass. Iraj was a mighty sorcerer, but he allowed his power to overtake him and corrupt him. There is no drawing from Magick to such an extent without paying a price. That is what almost destroyed Rastehm and what the Goddess guards against still. For all his power, I can quite confidently say Iraj is dead. Contrary to his last words."

She was still unconvinced.

"Or he is in his office downstairs, too weakened by disease to lift a hand to do more Magick?" offered Kalden.

"Or this last spell may only have been an elaborate illusion. Perhaps Iraj was already dead, and this"—Faren gestured at the mirrors around the room—"could have all been set in place before he died, as one final act of retaliation."

He came toward them. In his arms he held their

prize—the crystal pyramid of Rastehm. Silverdawn wondered fleetingly at the weight of the piece as Faren did not seem to be struggling to carry it at all, but the thought slipped from her mind as he crouched and placed the pyramid gently on the floor at her feet.

"Have you the key?"

She undid her belt and lifted her tunic and light chain-mail vest. Strapped to her waist was a red velvet pouch.

Pen's eyes darkened as he noted the birthmark on her stomach but held his tongue. Now was not the time for the questions that struggled to be born.

Silverdawn undid the cord holding the pouch and upended the contents onto her palm. The pyramid key flared bright blue in her hand. She reached out to place it in Faren's hand, but Pen called a halt.

"You must do it, Princess. You are the guardian of the key. That is why Iraj tried so hard to stop us. You had the power to heal the pyramid. Any other attempting to unlock it would release Iraj's demons."

"Then do it," urged Faren, "for we must hurry. It is almost the witching hour."

Silverdawn fitted the key into the triangular-shaped grove at the top of the pyramid, locking it into place.

"Turn it!" urged Pen.

She twisted the key counterclockwise. A humming sound erupted from the pyramid, gradually getting louder. The companions hastily stood back, and a golden light burst forth from the apex of the pyramid to encompass the whole of the crystal. The glass cleared, and for a moment only, Iraj's demon minions were revealed in all their ghoulish horror, pressing miniature faces against the glass. Then, as fast as they appeared, they were gone. The long crack that had run down one face, allowing black goo to ooze from within, began to fade until not a trace of the heinous substance remained; the magical pyramid had healed itself.

Quickly, Faren gathered up the pyramid and headed for the door. With a swift glance over his shoulder at the glittering carnage of their battle, he stepped through the door followed by the others, only to be met with another surprise.

It was as if the battle had never been. Light flooded the building. Not a prop was out of place. Display cases were as they had always stood. The dinosaur skeleton was intact. The reconstructed Albertosaurus occupied pride of place in the center of the room.

The only one who could have told the tale of what had happened in that room was Todd, but he was still unconscious in the closet. Unfortunately, although all inanimate objects had reverted to their previous forms, the four companions' injuries still remained—Todd's leg still missing and Kalden's arm still wounded and his ribs broken.

Faren handed the crystal pyramid to her. "Do you think you can manage?"

Her arms closed around the pyramid. It was three-feet high and, being smooth-sided and taller than it was wide, awkward to handle. But she marveled at its light weight.

She'd thought it would be much heavier. It was almost as if the paperweight she'd carried all these years was the only part of the pyramid that bore any weight. Perhaps it was because it was the key and had the weighty job of activating the crystal. She shrugged mentally—and maybe not. Perhaps one day she could ask her father.

"The elevator might be working, now that everything seems as normal," she put forth, breaking from her reverie.

"You are right," Pen said, rising from beside Todd. "We need to get Todd to a hospital. His pulse is low, and he has lost a lot of blood."

Faren wasted no time. He scooped the young man into his arms and strode toward the elevator, leaving the others to hurry behind.

****

The companions stepped from the museum into the night. Holding her watch up to catch the glow from the lantern-shaped light above the main glass doors, Silverdawn read fifteen minutes to midnight. Faren descended the stairs with Todd, while she and Kalden waited for Pen to pull the doors closed with a resonating bang.

As the doors locked, all lights in the building died.

She met Pen's golden gaze speculatively in the dim light still radiating from his body, and he shook his head.

"Do not ask, lass. Some questions are better left unanswered."

She frowned but nodded, knowing that if she lived to be a hundred, she would never have the answer to any of the Magick she'd witnessed here tonight. She waited for Pen to go ahead with Kalden, then picked her way carefully down the stairs with the pyramid. She smiled as she saw Serena waving from across the road. The young woman leaned against a taxicab—such a haven of normality against the unreality of the night.

She hurried toward them as Faren took the last step onto the footpath. He strode past her to the taxi, and

Serena raced ahead to open the door. "Is he dead?" she asked, wringing her hands, staring at Todd.

"No." Faren lowered him onto the seat. "But get him to a hospital, fast. He is very weak."

Serena's face took on an ashen hue, and she stifled her gasp with her hand. Drawing a deep breath, she straightened as if firming her resolve. "He will be sorry he missed saying goodbye. I know he thought of you as his friends." She stood on tiptoe and dropped a small kiss on Faren's cheek. As Silverdawn approached and gave Faren the pyramid, Serena took Silverdawn into her arms and gave her a brief hug. "I'm glad you gained your prize."

She nodded. "We'll talk later," she promised. "Just make sure you get Todd to the hospital."

"I'll look after him."

"I'll see you at Pen's place later tonight. What about him?" She gestured at the driver, who was avidly listening to the conversation and viewing Silverdawn and Faren's clothes with undisguised suspicion.

Serena pulled a wallet from her handbag and handed the man what looked like a couple of hundred-pound notes. The driver accepted the money with a grunt and swung back to stare out of the windshield in silence.

"I returned to my house while you were busy and found where Iraj had hidden Peter's money and bank books. I figured the creature owed me."

"That he did, my friend. He owed a lot of people, but most of all you. He owed you a husband and someone who cares about you a lot." She glanced at Todd. "However, *he* will not be worrying you ever again."

Serena's eyes widened, and she leaned in closer so that the driver would not overhear her words. "He is dead?"

"Pen says so."

"You believe him?"

"I have no reason to doubt him."

"Then it's good enough for me." Serena squeezed Silverdawn's hand. "I want to thank you...for everything."

"Hurry!" Pen called from the park gates. "We have not much time."

Serena leaned over, kissed Silverdawn's cheek, and climbed into the taxicab beside Todd. "Good luck," she said, rolling down the window as the driver revved the engine. "And goodbye, Faren." She waved.

Faren raised his hand, and Silverdawn watched as the taxi drew away.

"Coming?" Faren asked, picking up the crystal pyramid from where Silverdawn had placed it on the ground and turning briskly toward the park. "You are going to say goodbye, are you not?" His terse tone cut through the night with a note of finality, such a cold comparison to Serena's friendliness.

The time she dreaded had arrived.

Light snow began to fall as they crossed the park. A short length away, they halted in front of a towering standing stone. Silverdawn had passed it many times on her walk to work, but she'd never given a thought to the megalith's significance.

Pen took her aside. Faren and Kalden withdrew the golden medallions hanging within their tunics in readiness for their journey.

"I will be going with them. I must see the king on a matter of urgency, but feel free to make my home your home."

"But, Pen, what—"

"It is not for me to tell you. If all goes well, you shall know on my return."

Faren joined them, and Pen took the pyramid from his arms.

"I will see how your brother fares. I think, perhaps, you would like a word alone with the princess."

Pen moved away, and Faren drew her into his strong arms, and he held her close, the warmth of his body surrounding her. His scent, pine and sandalwood, invaded her senses. She wanted nothing more than to stay lost in his comfort and warmth forever.

He held her at arm's length. "You will not change your mind?" His face was set, no emotion in his words.

"Who would look after Todd and Serena?" she asked, trying for flippancy but failing miserably.

He released her abruptly. "Todd and Serena, be damned!" He turned and smashed his fist into the tree trunk beside him. "Who will look after me?"

She ran a hand up his arm, unable to free the words crying for release.

He swung around and grasped her shoulders. "Damn it, woman, I love you. I have never loved another woman in my life, and I love you. Does that mean nothing?"

She opened her mouth to speak, say something, anything to break this horrible tension, but Kalden approached, and Faren released her as abruptly as he had seized her. However, his gaze never left her face.

Kalden bent to kiss her cheek. He gave her a brief smile and ruffled her already mussed hair. "It has been a pleasure, Princess. Perhaps somewhere in the future, we might meet again." He grinned and met her eyes. "I will miss our talks."

She gave a brief nod. "Look after yourself." Holding back tears, she watched the big blond knight move to join Pen. She saw him take off his medallion and hold it to the heart of the rock. A light flared up around the two, and Kalden's gaze met Faren's over the head of the old man.

"Ready, Brother? 'Tis time to return home."

Faren rested his hands on her shoulders and stared into her eyes now brimming with tears. She wondered if he was using his power of coercion. Was he willing her to relent? She felt a weakening, a softening in her attitude. Her whole body cried out for him. A silent plea. His aura surrounded her. Then it was gone, to leave her with an overwhelming feeling of bereavement.

He dropped his gaze and swept her into his arms, then took her lips in a fierce kiss that held all the frustration *she* felt. All the longing she would ever have. And all the goodbyes she could not say.

Then he released her and, without another word, tore off the medallion hanging loosely around his neck and strode over to take his place beside his brother. He refused to look at her, although she willed him to do so. Her want and need for one last look was almost palatable. Vibrating through the air. But if he felt it, he didn't acknowledge it. His countenance was that of frozen granite.

He wouldn't look at her. Why wouldn't he look at her just one more time? She watched as the light encased his strong beautiful body and his image began to fade, knowing there would never be another man like Faren Malaan. Her savior. Her black knight. Knowing that her one chance of happiness was fading as his image was fading. Knowing that she had never once told him she loved him. Or not enough.

"Wait!" She raced forward. Her words, dredged from a great distance. She dived for his outstretched hand…a flash of light, then deep abiding darkness…

Chapter Twenty-One

Silverdawn hit ground and rolled gently down a grassy slope until she came to a halt. Stunned, she lay for a moment, regaining her breath, staring up at white fluffy clouds in a perfect blue sky. What had just happened? It had been night in the park. Bright sunshine now filled a lush forest glen, and she was slap-dang in the middle of it. She pushed herself to her knees, and as she did so, someone bent over her and plucked a dry strand of grass from her hair.

"Greetings, my lady."

She glanced up. A man stood above her, his expression grave.

Sun filtered through the branches overhead. Tiny red-and-white toadstools dotted the grass alongside multicolored wildflowers. "What is this place? Where are Pen and Kalden?"

Faren ignored her first question. "Gone ahead. Kalden's wounds ail him. I told them I would wait for you. I saw you leap toward me as the light faded. Why did you do it?"

She took the hand he offered and allowed him to help her to her feet. She glanced away, unable to meet the brilliance of his azure gaze. "Surely, you know."

He cupped her jaw with his hand and turned her face to stare down into her eyes. "What foolish games do you play here, Silverdawn, Princess of Rastehm?"

She hesitated. "No game, Sir Knight. I came to see my parents. Is that not reason enough?" She squeezed her eyes closed, breathing deeply, taking in the scent of him. "And I came to be with you, because I know there will never be another man who can make my heart sing, my blood burn hot in my veins, and make me feel as if my very soul would perish if I never looked upon his face again." She opened her eyes.

All the love she thought she had lost was aglow in his brilliant blue eyes. He gathered her into his arms, and his lips came down over hers, promising, taking, remembering all and everything they would ever be to each other.

When he released her, he was grinning like a young boy. "Come," he said, taking her hand. "It is time I took you home."

A magnificent old oak, its new leaves tipped with scarlet, stood at the top of the bank. As she approached the tree, she had the overwhelming feeling it was reaching out to her, blanketing her with warm protection. Somewhere ahead she heard a clear, high birdsong—a liquid melody of incredible beauty. She had the uncanny feeling it was calling to her and that they must follow. Farther along the path the sound merged with the songs of thrush and blackbird.

They scrambled up another bank and were met by an archway of thorns, then passed through a grove of great armored beeches. Looking up, she spied the most delicate tracery of nature and the bright blue of the sky. She had left behind winter and found autumn.

A jay—blue and buff with striped wings—sped overhead.

Faren gently squeezed her hand. "It is said that our

ancient oak forests were planted by the jay."

"So this is Rastehm?"

"Not quite." He smiled and drew her along.

The woods changed character again. The light began to fade as the forest grew denser. The birdsong stopped. She could hear small creatures scurrying about their business and caught sight of a small white tail before it disappeared into a patch of dense greenery. Sycamores turned bronze, and through a light mist, a gold-and-silver birch glowed like a lantern. Silverdawn spied a hedge of holly. An unearthly light showing through the gaps in the foliage displayed the red berries in their regal splendor. Pen and Kalden, their faces highlighted by the mystical light, waited beside an arch, which appeared to lead through the hedgerow.

Pen stepped forward to welcome her. "Lass, you have come. Glad I am that you decided to join us." The old man gave her a brief hug.

Faren helped Kalden, who had been resting, rise gingerly to his feet. "I never doubted you," he said with a wide grin on his handsome face.

"It may only be temporary," she reminded them. "I have first to meet your Goddess."

Faren's hand dropped to his sword, and his tone turned grave cold. "I will deal with Deharna if and when the time comes. No one will take you from me now I have you here."

Pen shook his head. "Now, now. No use looking for trouble, boy. The Goddess is a wise woman. She will know what is best."

He grunted and stood aside as Kalden gave him a thump on the shoulder and passed through the arch after Pen.

She went to follow, but as she did so, Faren stayed her with a gentle hand. "Remember, whatever we face, we face together."

She smiled, stepped though the arch, then reared back as the warmth of fire touched her face.

Faren's arms closed around her.

"What is that thing?" She struggled against his hold and backed up a step. A wall of flames blocked their path—at least twelve feet high. The wall of smokeless fire spread out unending into the rapidly growing night.

"The Eternal Wall." Faren spoke gently.

She shook her head. "No way! I'm not walking into that!"

Faren cast Pen a glance over the top of her head as she fought for release and forced him back another pace.

The old man spoke calmly, lowering the pyramid to sit at his feet. "It will not hurt you, lass. My people have passed through the fire for nigh on twenty-six years. Your father carried you through this fire to bring you into the twentieth century. It did not burn you then; it will not do so now. Have faith."

Kalden groaned. "You have come this far, Silverdawn. You cannot turn back. Not without one of us."

She shook her head again. Although she knew what Pen said must be the truth, yet still she feared the flames. As long as she could remember, she'd had an aversion to fire. Perhaps deep down she remembered the journey with her father and that the *wall* had taken her from her parents. "I can't. I will burn."

Faren turned, his hands on her shoulders. "Do you trust me?"

"Of course I trust you, but fire burns!"

"Do you remember nothing that Pendragon and I have told you? The flames are cold." He let her go and stepped closer to the fire until he was but a pace away. "Now I ask again, do you trust me?"

Again, she shook her head. Her mind was in turmoil, and her thoughts were incoherent. "Yes. No. I don't know!"

"Take my hand."

She hesitated, then slowly took one step, then another. She stretched till her fingertips touched his.

"I love you," he said, leaning forward, his voice strong and comforting. Then his fingers closed around hers, and he dragged her into the fire to walk the same path Mikkasah had walked almost a quarter of a century before.

Chapter Twenty-Two

As she broke from the fire, the first thing Silverdawn noticed was that she stood on a white marble platform in a strange, beautiful temple. White columns, much like those from ancient Rome, supported an immense cathedral ceiling, while lifelike marble statues guarded the three doors. Tapestries depicting heroic scenes of ancient battles, handsome men, and beautiful women hung on the walls.

A woman stood before her who could only be the Goddess Deharna.

The woman's eyes were cold black. Tiny flames seemed to dance at their centers as Silverdawn stared. The woman wore the austere robes of a temple priestess—black, red, and a single adorning white rose above her heart. The colors were representative of the Goddess—the Maiden, the Mother, and the Crone. The woman did not take her eyes from Silverdawn.

"Who is this young woman, Sir Faren? You of all people should know our rules."

"She is Silverdawn, Princess of Rastehm, and my daughter." A deep voice rumbled from the end of the hall.

Silverdawn peered past the Goddess to a large arched doorway. She knew at once the imposing figure who stood there. She had seen the king many times in her visions. And by his side stood a woman in a simple gown of gray—hair the same shade as her own. Her mother.

Tears came unbidden to her eyes, and she longed to rush down the stairs and run into their arms, but she knew she could not. She was dealing with more here than a daughter separated from parents. She was dealing with another world, another culture, and as a student of history, she knew rules applied must be adhered to.

"May I speak, my lady?" Kalden offered into the silence.

Deharna inclined her head.

"If it were not for Silverdawn, my body would still be trapped within the body of another. I had body crashed and had no memory of self."

Deharna pursed her lips. "And what Magick did this sorceress wield to free you?"

Faren took a threatening step toward the Goddess. "She is no sorceress!"

Deharna raised her hand. "Halt. I will hear Sir Kalden's words."

Kalden staggered, and Faren caught him around the waist.

"You are hurt," acknowledged the Goddess, coming toward them. She laid her hand on Kalden's shoulder; the wound closed over and healed. Then she placed both hands on the bandages covering his ribs. A faint pink light flared from her fingers. Kalden straightened, and the pain that had been etched on his pale face since he was injured faded.

Kalden bowed over the Goddess's hand and touched his lips to her knuckles. "You are most gracious, my lady."

She inclined her head. "Now you may speak."

"Silverdawn practiced no Magick, only simple logic. She drew sketches of articles familiar to me, which Faren described. Seeing those pictures freed my memory and, in turn, allowed my body to separate from the person in whom I was trapped. I would ask that you look upon the princess favorably."

Pen stepped forward and laid the pyramid at Deharna's feet. "I would also speak on behalf of the princess."

Deharna stared into the old man's wizened face, then down at the pyramid. "It would seem to be a day of returns. You, too, my old friend. You, too, defy me?"

"Not defy, my Goddess. Only plead forgiveness from those I have wronged. I will stay, but for a short time only. First, though, I shall speak for the princess."

Deharna nodded. "I sense a story here."

"To my knowledge, Silverdawn wields no Magick. For many years she has been haunted by visions of our world and the people in it, but I believe she no longer holds even this unstable power." Pen glanced at Silverdawn.

She shook her head. "Not since meeting you and Faren."

"Yet she fought alongside us to defeat Iraj. She kept the key safe all of these years, and she healed the pyramid."

Deharna remained silent, and her eyes narrowed as she cast her gaze from one member of the party to the other, as if trying to read their faces. "I shall keep all of your words in mind," she said. "I will give this matter some thought. Iraj of Istani is dead, you say?"

"Aye, my lady. The body he inhabited had been afflicted by some sort of wasting disease, which finally took its toll, allowing us to take the victory and gain the pyramid."

"Thank goodness for that. You have all done well. But…" She paused. "It seems there is another tale here, my old friend. Come, Mikkasah, Aurelia. I imagine this is something you should hear."

As the Goddess spoke, the king and queen made their way toward the dais. They climbed the steps, Mikkasah taking the queen's arm to ease her progress as she lifted her gown out of the way.

****

Reaching the platform, Mikkasah gave Aurelia her freedom, and the queen gazed upon her daughter's face, but she looked also at the young man standing at Silverdawn's side. Something tugged at her heart, recognition born within every mother. But she dismissed it for the moment. She brought Silverdawn into her arms and kissed both her cheeks, then after a long embrace, set her aside but still kept hold of her hand.

"Who…who is this?" she asked quietly, clutching at her husband's arm on the other side of her and turning back to Kalden.

The king frowned. "Why, my dear, this is Sir Kalden, a Knight of Palladia. Have you not met before?"

She shook her head. "No. I am very certain we have not."

Kalden stepped forward, knelt before the queen, and bowed his head, his fair hair falling forward around his face.

Aurelia released Silverdawn's hand and reached out hesitantly to touch his shoulder. A slight tremor ran through her body. "Raise your head, young man."

The blond knight peered into her face, and Aurelia

froze. For several long heartbeats she took in the strong, square jaw, the familiar beak of a nose, and slashing dark brows. Her voice shook as she spoke. "Rise. You will not kneel before me. You are no ordinary knight. You are my son. A prince of Rastehm."

Kalden sprang to his feet, his green eyes meeting those of the queen, then the king. "Son? You are mistaken. This cannot be." He turned a hapless glance on Faren, a look of consternation written across his lean chiseled face.

Faren shook his head and raised his hands. "I know nothing of this."

"You are wrong, dearest. You must be." Mikkasah took Aurelia's shoulders and turned her toward him. "It is the shock of seeing your daughter. Come. I will take you and Silverdawn back to the castle."

Even as he spoke, he turned and gave Kalden a penetrating look. Was he seeing the same things Aurelia saw? The similarities between their daughter and the young man who had been in his service for nigh on nine years. The resemblance was uncanny. But so, too, was the strong jaw and slashing brows that had marked the males of the king's family for generations.

He shook his head. "No. Kalden is a brilliant young man. One of my best knights, but how could my son be under my nose all these years and I not know? Impossible." He reached out and encircled his wife's shoulders and forced her to turn away. "My lady, we have no son. Our son died at birth. This man is Kalden of Malaan, stepbrother to Faren. He—"

"Enough!" Deharna raised a hand to still his words. "The wizard must tell his tale before more is said. But first, as you suggested, Mikkasah, we will adjourn to the castle."

With a flourish and without further ado, she drew her cape around her slim shoulders and led the way down the steps and out of the temple.

Five people stepped into Mikkasah's ornate study. A fire roared in the grate to dispel the chill induced by the stone walls, narrow, high windows, and tall cathedral ceiling. Ultramarine rugs covered the polished floorboards. Aurelia sank beside the king's feet and peeked surreptitiously around the room, wondering what this discussion would mean to them all.

Pen settled back into a deep cushioned chair by the fire and began to speak in a gentle tone. "There was a woman heavy with child. There was a prophecy that spoke of twins, and there was a court magician about to be banished."

Silence filled the chamber as he stared into the faces of those seated around him, for all knew the participants of the story, and each eyed the other speculatively.

"I knew I would not be present at the birth, so I entrusted what must be done to the old midwife Merrine," Pen went on.

Aurelia frowned as the years filtered away. She lay drawn and exhausted in a sumptuous four-poster bed, surrounded by golden satin curtains. But the magnificence of her surroundings had done little to lessen the pain of the impending birth of her children or the dreadful rending of her heart when informed of her son's death.

"I remember," she said hesitantly in a low voice. "My intended midwife was taken ill, and you sent me Merrine to take her place. She departed the day after the babies were born."

Pen nodded absently. "Yes, I paid her handsomely to disappear. So there would be none to tell the tale of what had really occurred that night."

"Proceed," Deharna ordered quietly, sitting primly in her chair across from the wizard.

"The prophecy stated that '*On the first day of September, of the king's year 598 of the Second Dawning, twins would be born to a queen of Rastehm. A boy and a girl. One would be born to the Magick; one would not. The firstborn, the girl, would have powers.*'

"I told the midwife she must find a stillborn babe to trade for the female child. At the time, I had noted the woman's lack of hearing and realized she was not exceptionally bright. But I had no time to find another, and I was certain she had the details right. I even made her repeat her orders.

"I had thought by taking the child who held the Magick and leaving the babe who did not with the queen, Your Majesty would retain both her children. I had intended for the midwife to come back a year later and secretly inform the king of the stolen child's whereabouts. It seems she did not return. She either died, forgot, or some evil befell her.

"The girl was to be taken and given to a rich merchant in Malaan whose wife had become barren. I did not know it was Faren's father, and I had no idea of Kalden's identity until I saw Silverdawn and Kalden together.

"The boy was taken instead, and the girl child left with her parents to be discovered and banished. I found out what had occurred when Silverdawn's foster father accidentally stumbled upon my shop. I knew who he was as soon as he entered."

Pen eased his ancient bones from his chair and crossed the room. Shakily, he knelt and took the queen's hands in his own. "I hope Your Majesty can forgive me for all of her years of grief."

For a moment the queen remained silent, conflicting emotions filling her, then she smiled sadly and gave Pen's old, weathered hands a gentle squeeze. "Rise, Archimedes, you are forgiven. Your only sin was in trying to save both my children."

Pen climbed stiffly to his feet as the queen bid. "Yes, Your Majesty, that was my intention, but in doing so they were both lost to you, and you have grieved for many years." He turned to the king. "Sire, I demand that you punish me."

The king gave a gentle smile and shook his head. "No, my friend. As the queen said, your only sin was in endeavoring to help. You should not be held accountable for a daft midwife. But I would have a little more proof than your word that this young man is my son." The king placed his large hand on Pen's frail shoulder. "Have you that proof?"

"I do, sire. There was a birthmark mentioned in the prophecy; '*The boy with the crimson dragon shall rule mightily.*'

"The birthmark was shaped roughly in the image of a deep-red dragon. I saw such a birthmark on your daughter last eve when she lifted her tunic to remove the key from where it was hidden. I believe her twin would have its like. Kalden, if you would be so kind?"

Kalden, who had been standing quietly by the fire throughout Pen's tale, dragged his tunic over his head. On the back of his right hip, as if etched in blood-red pigment, was the image of a dragon's head.

Faren nodded. "I could have told you without him removing his shirt. The mark has been with him all of his life."

"It was the reason I chose the dragon as the insignia on my shield and sword. It has always fascinated me," Kalden commented solemnly.

Mikkasah stepped forward and took Kalden into his arms. "It is good to have you home, boy." He released the knight and patted him on the shoulder, and Kalden grinned.

"It is good to be home, Your Majesty, but it may take a bit of getting used to. It is a big promotion, knight to prince." He chuckled.

Tears came to Aurelia's eyes, and she joined them. "We will do all in our power to make it easy for you. Will we not, my dear?" She bestowed a watery smile on Mikkasah, and he took her hand and brought it to his lips. Then she held out her arms to her daughter. "It has been many years, but we are a family again at last, and never shall we be parted."

****

As she crossed the room, Silverdawn smiled at Kalden standing with her parents. It was not hard for her to believe he was her brother. It would explain the feeling of fondness and the strange connection between them from their very first encounter. She'd once read that twins shared an invisible bond. Could this have been what caused her many visions of Rastehm? The indiscernible link to her brother?

She was crying and laughing at the same time as she reached her family to hug each member in turn. When she reached up to touch her lips to Kalden's cheek, she whispered, "So this is why the bond between us was so strong. We even share birthmarks."

He grinned, hefting her into the air and twirling her around. "Aye, little sister, I suppose it is."

She squealed in delight and begged for release, and he lowered her to the floor. "Forget the 'little.' I believe Pen said *I* was first born."

"Yes, but I am the taller."

Aurelia put her arm around both her children and looked into Mikkasah's eyes. "No one will ever take my children from me again." Her tone held an edge.

"You have my promise."

Deharna nodded at the proceedings and moved to stand next to Pen, her back to the fire. A gentle smile softened the harsh beauty of her face. "It seems you have wrought me a problem of some import, Archimedes." She looked at the man beside her. "I know you have never forgiven me for banishing you. Is this your revenge?"

"Revenge, Goddess?" The wizard raised a shaggy brow. "On no account. I understood your motives perfectly and know you did what you thought best for your people and this world."

"I could not risk another Iraj."

Pen looked away from her glittering ebony eyes. "I know that," he said gently, "but perhaps the time has come for change."

****

Faren studied Deharna in fascination. He had never witnessed the Goddess so agitated.

She ran a hand through her dark hair, released a harsh sigh, then turned to stare into the fire. "Sometimes it is hard even for a goddess to know the rightness of a situation. For some time now, I have felt a restlessness among my people—and in myself. For am I not the heart of my people?" she murmured, almost to herself. "I wonder now, was there wisdom in my decision? Have I been fair to all? When I made the judgment for Magick to be banished, I thought I did it for all mankind. But did I? Or did I do it out of pride and conceit? Did I want no sorcerer stronger than me?" The Goddess swung around and scanned the faces of the people surrounding her. "It might be that you are right, old friend," she said to Pen. She stepped to the center of the room, raised her hand, and all conversation ceased.

"From this day forth, I decree that each person born to the Magick shall be judged individually. Each child shall be allowed to grow to maturity and develop his or her powers. It is not right for me to banish that which the Gods of Creation have gifted. Unless of course that gift is used unwisely." Deharna lifted a dark brow. "What think you, Faren Malaan, First Knight to the Goddess and King? For I have felt in you a growing disquiet."

Faren remained silent for a moment, thinking that—had this new judgment been made two years before—a war would not have been fought, thousands not died, and Mikkasah's friend King Nordal would still be alive. But he lowered his head. "You have made a wise and just decision, my Goddess."

Deharna smiled amiably. "Then it shall be as I say."

At her words, Faren strode across the room, encircled Silverdawn's waist, and faced the Goddess. "So where does this leave the princess? Is she to stay?"

Deharna smiled and inclined her head. "I can afford to be magnanimous, for today heralds a day of new beginnings. That question shall be left to the lady herself."

Faren watched conflicting emotions cross Silverdawn's face as she glanced at the hopeful faces surrounding her. Her parents, who had waited many years for her return and given up so much. Kalden, who was not only her friend but also her brother. Pen, a man of great wisdom, who through her hoped to right an age-old wrong. And him—well, he hoped by now she would know what she meant to him.

"Before you say anything, perhaps I could suggest one thing," added the Goddess, perhaps reading the dilemma in her eyes or even her mind. Who knew of what she was capable.

"You have proven yourself a worthy warrior. Perhaps it is time I took a woman into the knighthood."

"You mean, do what Faren does? Travel through different periods of history?" She glanced hopefully at Faren, and he nodded and smiled.

"Perhaps even travel together," offered Deharna, "as a man and wife are wont to do. With Mikkasah's blessing, of course. Give the matter some thought. We will speak again at summer solstice." She bestowed a knowing smile on all of those present, brought her ebony cloak around her with a flourish, and literally vanished.

"Where…"

Faren bent and touched his lips to Silverdawn's hair and laughed softly. "You will get used to that if you stay." He hesitated, then turned her into his arms. "So what is your decision?"

She smiled, and her eyes were filled with all he wished to see.

"What else can I say? I have the man I love, my parents, and a new brother, as well as the best of both worlds and many more." She reached up and touched her lips to his in a quick, gentle kiss. "Of course I will stay. Did you ever doubt it?"

At his daughter's words, Mikkasah folded Aurelia into his arms and brought his lips down over his queen's in a kiss that held all the pent-up passion of twenty-three years.

Kalden surveyed the embracing couples, laughed, and gave Pen a hearty thump on the back. " 'Tis time we retired, wizard. Something tells me we are not required here. And I know just where to get a good ale and a willing woman."

Pen laughed. "I do not know about the woman, lad, but the ale sounds mighty fine to me."

Epilogue

Besancon, France
Present Day

As gray storm clouds gathered in the heavens and light rain began to fall, Archimedes Pendragon trudged his way to the top of a small hill. He laid a posy of red and white roses on a single grave beneath a giant oak overlooking a lush valley and an exquisite waterfall.

Todd had smuggled out of the museum the two skulls that Emile had discovered. Although it was never proven, Pen believed the woman to be Silverdawn, and he was certain the man had been Faren. There was no record of what battle they died in, and perhaps that was best. Death should never be expected.

He turned and picked his way down the hill's grassy slope, dodging the large standing stones still scattered about the ground—not half as many now that Iraj had departed the world, taking with him his conjuring. What a stir it had caused on the world news when Iraj's stones were discovered missing.

So many things had changed in so short a time. Peter Waymer's wasted body had been discovered in his office the day after the battle for the pyramid. The autopsy read that he died from complications arising from his cancer. The funeral had been a private affair, with only Serena and a few colleagues from the museum in attendance.

Serena had since married Todd, and they were expecting their first child.

Not many people came through the Eternal Wall these days, due to Deharna's new judgment, and neither this world, nor any other, would ever have to fear Iraj of Istani again.

Six months had passed since Pen last saw Faren and Silverdawn, but he believed them to be happy traveling through history. Mikkasah had given their marriage his blessing.

Pen had his own suspicions that the king had approved the marriage so quickly because he felt more than a touch guilty. Faren had been expected to inherit the throne, due to lack of an heir, but now Kalden would one day become king.

A gentle breeze caressed the old wizard's face, and he smiled. He was looking forward to seeing Faren and Silverdawn at winter solstice. But this time he would take Silverdawn her cat. The tiny ball of fluff had grown to be a giant and was driving him to distraction. Fortunately, the cat had already been at Pen's home, because the night they traveled to Rastehm, Silverdawn's apartment building had burned to the ground. The newspapers had commented that Silverdawn's remains were never found.

A coincidence perhaps? Pen wondered.

The Goddess had her ways…

A word about the author…

Julie A. D'Arcy lives in North East Victoria Australia with her two spoiled Oriental cats, Molly May and Lythriel Jade. She grew up reading the likes of *Lord of the Rings*, *Once and Future King*, and every fairy tale she could get her hands on. Later on falling in love with the works of David Gemmell, Terry Brooks, Johanna Lindsey, Rosemary Rodgers, and Barbara Cartland.

Her love of both the Fantasy and the Romance genres prompted her to try her hand at writing her own novel, and she began writing her first novel in 1995.

Her first release, *Time of the Wolf*, was published in 1999 and went on to win the 1999 Dorothy Parker RIO Award for Women's Fantasy Fiction. She was also runner-up in the Australian RWA Ruby Award. Julie is delighted to say The Wild Rose Press re-released *Time of the Wolf* again in 2019. It went on to garner 5-star reviews from all reviewers who read it and won the Crowned Heart Award from *InD'tail Magazine*.

~*~

More of Julie's novels with The Wild Rose Press:

The Cross of Tarlis: The Awakening and *The Cross of Tarlis: The Reckoning*. Both received 5-Star Awards.

Whispers Of Yesterday—Historical Romance, Ghost Paranormal, published 2024. 5-Star rating

Eternal Vow, published 2024. 5-Star rating

~*~

Julie loves traveling and has visited the UK, Thailand, and many European countries and hopes to one day visit the US.

https://www.juliedarcyauthor.com

Thank you for purchasing
this publication of The Wild Rose Press, Inc.

For questions or more information
contact us at
info@thewildrosepress.com.

The Wild Rose Press, Inc.
www.thewildrosepress.com